D1086969

OCEANS
The Anthology

First Edition

Formatting by Daniel Arthur Smith

Cover Design by Ben Adams

Edited by Jessica West

All other text Copyright © 2017 Daniel Arthur Smith.

Cover Design by Ben Adams

Formatting by Daniel Arthur Smith

Edited by Jessica West

ISBN-13: 978-1946777416
ISBN-10: 1946777412

First Edition

Story Synopses

~*~

"Bug Eater" (Nathan M. Beauchamp) When the boats that sustain the tribe don't return from their most recent raid, Angi must take a terrible risk to try and protect her people from starvation. But will anyone listen to someone with the nickname "Bug Eater" in the first place?

"Tide Sweeping" (P.K. Tyler) Dust and sand have devoured the Earth, leaving behind only pockets of salt water protected by Sweepers who serve the Tide.

"The Titan's Daughter" (Daniel Arthur Smith) A mysterious longing haunts a man.

"Dancing in the Midnight Ocean" (Caroline M. Yoachim) At depths below the midnight line, there is no sunlight from the surface. The genetically-modified humans who dwell in that darkness shine with the light of their own bioluminescence and build pipelines to power the brightwater cities. The lure of the cities threatens to pull two lovers apart, and forces them to question what it means to be human.

"Siren Song of the Mississippi Queen" (Hank Garner) Will is a commercial fisherman who has made his living from the Gulf of Mexico, like his father before him. Gabby, his sister, hears voices she believes are from the queen of an ancient civilization off the Mississippi coast. When she goes missing, Will has to decide if the legends his mother passed down to him and his sister are real, or a figment of his sister's imagination.

"The Hunt for the *Vigilant*" (Alex Shvartsman) Magic is real — and it's programmable. Eldritch gods exist but can be held at bay by consuming coffee and playing YouTube videos of warding chants. And now the whole world knows this.

An eccentric billionaire sees this as a business opportunity. He recruits the man responsible for revealing the existence of magic to the public for a mission to the bottom of the South Pacific that is more dangerous than either of them realize.

"Aquagenic" (Will Swardstrom) Allergic to water, Cora is a mystery. Four months ago she was found on a beach in Oregon, covered in a rash with no memory of her life. The memory never recovers, leaving Cora with no family and no life.

Struggling to make sense of everything, Cora befriends Dana, a nurse at her residential facility. Together, the two work to figure out how her memory and water allergy connect and who—or what—Cora actually is.

"New Year's Eve" (Joshua Ingle) The life story of a renowned oceanographer, told backward from the brink of her death in the 2070s to her childhood in the 1990s, as she probes the memories from her life full of hardship and failure for an answer to the question: Was it all worth it?

"Turtle: An A.L.I.V.E. Story" (R.D. Brady) A short breather from the mysterious R.I.S.E. base should be a relief. But for former D.E.A.D. agent Norah Tidwell, her break opens her eyes to the damage humanity is inflicting upon this planet, and offers a clue to the terrifying reason the base was created.

"Girt by Sea" (S. Elliot Brandis) During an outbreak that wiped out most of humanity, a fleet of eleven ships sought refuge on the ocean. Generations later, they returned to resettle on land.

"Full Circle: A CHRONOS Story" (Rysa Walker) A strange glowing circle buried in her great-great grandmother's garden transports a young historian to the site of an underwater crypt. Will Madi escape from the Cyrists or is she in too deep?

"Dispatches from the Cradle: The Hermit—Forty-Eight Hours in the Sea of Massachusetts" (Ken Liu) Venus is settled, and the technology exists for the Grand Task—the terraforming of both Earth and Mars—to bring Earth back. But some as inhabitants like the planet as is.

~*~

Contents

~*~

Bug Eater	1
Tide Sweeping	15
The Titan's Daughter	37
Dancing in the Midnight Ocean	47
Siren Song of the Mississippi Queen	69
The Hunt for the *Vigilant*	87
Aquagenic	115
New Year's Eve	143
Turtle: An A.L.I.V.E. Story	173
Girt by Sea	197
Full Circle: A CHRONOS Story	227
Dispatches from the Cradle: The Hermit—	
Forty-Eight Hours in the Sea of Massachusetts	257
A Note to Readers	277

Bug Eater
Nathan M. Beauchamp

~*~

I TROD BAREFOOT OVER the wave-wet sand, leaving a trail of shallow footprints that led back to the rusting *Sea Queen*. A large gap torn in her starboard hull exposed her middle decks to the dead sea a quarter-mile away. Children played on her top deck, scurrying from one place where shadows fell to another, their calloused feet at risk of burning where sunlight struck steel, their shouts and laughter lost in the roll of the surf.

Grandfather's white-pearl cataracts tracked my approach from where he sat, protected by a makeshift umbrella. How must I appear to him? A shadow against the blazing sun, a blur of umber, a mirage-person.

"Angi," he said when I drew close. "Come. Sit."

Grandfather always called me by the name my mother gave me, not my other name, the one everyone else used when they thought I couldn't hear them. *Bug Eater*. Or sometimes *Snake Eater* if one of the women was feeling especially cruel.

I crouched beside him and the rough bark of his hand closed over my calloused one. "What do you see, Angi?"

Salt wind pushed dried seaweed across black and white

pebbles. Was the tremble I felt in his fingers or mine? *Mine.* Though he would never guess the true reason. I didn't regret my choice.

"The empty sea," I replied.

The boats had not returned. Three nights had passed since their departure. We both knew what it meant for us. For our tribe. Our best men lost. No harvest, no meat drying over smoking racks, no provisions for when the sun scorched so hot it started fires and we retreated into the caves for relief.

"Good that you do not have a child," Grandfather said.

I shuddered at the mention of my greatest shame, greater than eating bugs or the women's innuendo of eating 'snakes.' I almost wrenched my hand from his. But unlike the others, he meant me no unkindness. He spoke the truth: better to starve alone.

The boats had not returned from the dead sea, and unless the tribe acted, we would follow our men into the torment of death. Grandfather pushed to his feet. Shielding blind eyes with one bony hand, he peered out over the sea, to the horizon line where the fat sun bloomed against darkening water.

"It is good," Grandfather said, finality in his voice—a pronouncement, long considered, delivered now like a judgement spoken at a gathering.

"Good?"

His milky eyes slid toward me, thin lips tight against nubby yellow teeth. "It had to end. Now, something better may come."

"Something better *will* come," I agreed. "Something we make."

His bald head slumped toward a concave chest. So old. The oldest of all of us. "You know what will happen. Grandmother has the ear of the women. All of them but you, at least." His sightless gaze searched for mine. "She'll cast lots tonight, Angi."

The sand seemed to shift beneath me, sucked away by some unseen current. "So soon?" I'd hoped for another month of work, to have a fully edible generation of beetles before

Grandmother acted.

Grandfather gestured at the sea as if its mere existence explained everything. I'd heard his stories of fish and seals and crabs washing up dead by the millions. The putrefaction of corpses. The deaths of cities, countries, the world itself, expunged by radioactive tidal waves.

"You still have time," Grandfather said.

He was extending an offer, a chance at escape. We both knew I would draw the worst possible lot. A childless woman. A misfit who spent hours in the lowest deck of the *Sea Queen*, breeding successive generations of water beetles. Eating a few of each new crop and then falling ill, wracked with sickness. But each time the sickness left sooner than the last. Giving me hope, keeping me at my self-chosen task. Selecting the next generation based on how ill I became, treating my symptoms with the tar-black moss I collected in the caves…

Bug Eater.

The children laughed when I lay with my knees tucked against my chest, stomach churning like the storms that sometimes buffeted the *Sea Queen*. The women sent delegations to try and convince me to stop. They put the matter before the gathering, and somehow Grandfather always convinced Grandmother not to intervene.

Snake Eater.

I could not bear children, and because of it, no man would take me as a wife. I might have become a whore, but what man would fuck a bug eater? But the women still talked. Once a desperate man descended the rusted stairs into the gloom of the lower decks in search of an easy target. Not so easy, not in my domain, not with the thick, stench-filled air, the pools of algae, the water beetles hissing.

I bred a great number of generations of beetles soon after the man's disappearance.

"Angi, you know what they'll do if you stay here."

"If they would only listen to me!" My single, all-consuming thought, continual prayer, never-ending frustration. "If they would help with the work, we wouldn't have to send our men out to sea. We wouldn't have to cast lots."

Grandfather shook his head, as weary of my arguments as I had become. No one would listen. Nothing would change aboard the *Sea Queen* or in the caves. The tribe had found *a way* to survive after the oceans died, and they would cling to it no matter how well I pled my case.

"You should leave before nightfall," Grandfather said.

He didn't have to explain.

The casting of lots.

I could imagine the jokes, the laughter. The one thousand, two-hundred and eighty-one generations of beetles I had carefully bred and sought to turn into the first sustainable food source in our tribe's history would perish. If I left, I couldn't take them with me. And I was so close—the last twenty generations of beetles had caused only minor stomach cramps and runny, foul-smelling shits. But shit meant I'd digested at least part of them, and my arms and neck looked a bit fuller in the cracked glass lining the *Sea Queen's* moldering ballroom.

"I'm staying."

Grandfather gave a single, slow shake of his head as if to say, *You are the most stubborn, unreasonable person I have ever come across.*

"Just make sure the lots are fair. Don't let Grandmother cheat."

A dry laugh. "You do realize I'm blind?"

"Almost blind. And you see with more than just your eyes."

"I can't promise you anything."

"No one ever has."

I left him beneath his umbrella and raced back to the *Sea Queen*. Night would come in a handful of hours. I needed to be ready.

~*~

Grandmother hadn't called for a formal gathering since the men departed in their boats. Each day they failed to return, the rumors and murmurs that coursed through the decks grew more frantic, more laced with fear. The men raided the offshore platforms two or three times per cold season. They left armed with their rifles and shotguns and pistols, extra rounds in bandoleers around their chests and waists. It seemed the world had run out of everything but guns and bullets to fire from them.

Nobody knew how many lived on the offshore platforms, or how many platforms there were. The men raided them, and while there were always casualties, the boats returned laden with the harvest, with plunder. Machines that lit up and played videos or songs and which invariably stopped working days later. Minor miracles which delighted the children and kept them occupied while the women did their work, preserving the harvest; meat roasting on spits for the celebration feast.

The rest of the harvest cut thin and suspended over the smoking pits to cure for the hot months spent in the caves.

Some of the meat from those taken from the offshore platforms, some from the men killed in the raid. All of it prepared in a way to hide its origin, to mask the abomination of eating human flesh.

Bug Eater.

Better bugs than humans.

Which was why I weighed no more than eighty pounds despite my above-average height. Why I resembled a skeleton as much as a flesh-and-blood human. Let them cast their lots. If mine fell, they would get little sustenance from me.

~*~

Children lining the *Sea Queen*'s upper deck beat the guard rails with sticks in rhythm with the dull thump of the drums signaling a formal gathering. Stars pricked the sky, a crescent moon rising over the ocean waves. Night had brought an oppressive humidity that bound the decaying cruise liner in a thick, invisible cocoon. Grandmother and Grandfather stood in front of the signal fire, neither looking at the other. The last of our tribe emerged from below decks and squatted as far from the fire as their ability to hear Grandmother and Grandfather would allow.

I sat close, letting the fire scorch. I needed good light to watch Grandmother cast the lots, and good light for what I had planned. The few men who had remained to protect the tribe stalked at the dark edges of the gathering, weapons in hand. They would follow Grandmother's command once she cast the lots.

Grandmother was not so as old as Grandfather. She wore a sun-bleached white tank top and floral skirt. Unlike Grandfather, she did not refuse the benefits of her position, and had gotten fat since the last Grandmother died. Stretch marks ringed her lower thighs and zigged from the corners of her armpits. A maroon cap with a large "A" on the front covered her silver hair. Its bill cast a shadow over her eyes so I could not see her watching me but only feel it, the hair on my arms standing on edge.

"You all know why I called for a gathering," Grandmother said when the drums and children had fallen to silence. "The men have not returned, and the fates have made it clear that they have been lost to us."

The words clung to the tribe, worse than the humidity. The sound of muffled tears came from one of the young mothers, clutching a naked baby boy to her chest. Our tribe had lost over thirty men, cutting our numbers almost in half. Fathers and husbands, gone.

"We must cast lots."

A collective wail from the assembled tribe.

Grandmother raised a hand to silence them. "All males are excluded. Mothers with children under the age of four are excluded. Everyone else must choose a lot."

The men with their weapons circled the gathering, watching for anyone seeking escape. The small package I'd brought from below decks bit into my spine, held in place by the belt I'd cinched around my non-existent hips. I leapt up, eager to be first in line. Suspicion lowered Grandmother's brows.

"Come forward," Grandmother called, voice melodious. "If you refuse to choose a lot, I will choose one for you." *Of course you will.* The lots always seemed to fall the way Grandmother would like regardless of who chose the lot, though I hadn't cared much about those outcomes. Tribal politics, who received what quarters, who would marry who—none of those things mattered to me.

Whimpers and tears from behind me. The smell of piss.

"Clarry," Grandmother said, addressing a trembling girl holding a handmade doll against her chest, "get in line." The girl tried to stand, but her legs wouldn't support her. One of the armed men yanked her to her feet and drug her to the line.

"How many?" someone called out.

"Six," Grandmother said.

"Six!"

Even Grandfather looked surprised.

Grandmother counted out shark teeth—six black teeth and nineteen white ones. "Let the fates decide," Grandmother said, shaking the tooth basket above her head. "Angi, you're first." Grandmother gave it several more shakes, reinforcing the random fairness of the process.

"Grandmother," I said, "will you select a lot yourself?"

"Of course," Grandmother said. "The fates may choose any of us."

"That is true," I agreed. "Yet they never seem to fall against you, do they?"

Grandmother's eyes hardened. "If you have something to say, come out and say it."

Grandfather straightened himself, the ceremonial sidearm on his waist glinting in the firelight.

"I do have something to say." I faced those standing in line, waiting to learn their fate. The rest of the tribe watched with fascination and horror as the armed men circled the fire. "We don't need to cast lots."

"Oh?" Grandmother said, a note of mock humor in her voice. "Would you like us to eat your bugs?"

I took the package from behind my back—a small, opaque canister with a screw-off lid.

Grandmother motioned for one of the guards. Before he could reach me, I unscrewed the lid and removed what I had brought. The screen of the small device glowed.

"Where did you get that?" asked Grandmother.

The guard dispatched by Grandmother stood silent beside me, eyes locked on the screen. It displayed verdant green fields from an aerial view, spider-like watering mechanisms working their way over food crops.

"Before the washing, our people grew more food than a thousand tribes could eat in a year. Machines and chemicals helped make the work easy."

The guard gripped my wrist, wrenched away the screen, and handed it to Grandmother.

Grandmother held it up for all to see. "This world doesn't exist. The washing destroyed it. We cannot survive on dreams of what was lost. Instead, we will rely on the strength, resilience, and *sacrifice* of the tribe."

"We could help to bring it back," I said, raising my voice over the crackle of the flames. "Like the ones on the platforms above the submerged city. Instead of hunting them, instead of eating ourselves, we could help restore the oceans, help restore the land. I've worked for years to create a food source for our tribe. One woman, doing science in the bowels of the *Sea Queen*. And given time, I will succeed. Imagine what we could do if we worked together?"

"*Bug Eater*," Grandmother spat. "Stop wasting our time and draw your lot."

"We've all drawn our lots," I said. "We've drawn them again and again. We send our men to attack the platforms, to kill those working to save this world from the effects of the washing. Is killing one another better than eating bugs?"

Something hard smashed into the small of my back and I fell to my knees. Head whirling, the basket appeared in front of my face, it's black opening beckoning for me to reach inside and choose my fate.

"They will help us if we let them—they will give us seeds and show us how to grow them. They will help us—"

Another blow, this time to the back of my head.

"Choose!" Grandmother shouted.

"Choose!" the tribe echoed.

Choose.

I'd made my choice the moment I first powered up the device I'd stolen from one of the men the last time they'd raided the platforms.

The device did far more than display images. First, a short lesson on how to restore its power using the sun. Next, lessons in numbers, lessons in letters, in writing, in reading. Some of the women in the tribe knew the basics of these things, but after months of study, I had surpassed them all. I'd learned how to read the library of information on the device, and studied its contents as I grew additional generations of beetles. I'd learned to ask the device questions and receive answers. And one day, the device had spoken my name.

"Choose or you will be given a black tooth," Grandmother said.

Unsteady, head still whirling, I pushed to my feet. "Grandfather, will you choose for me?" It was my right to ask—some preferred not to choose their own lot.

"Yes, daughter," Grandfather said.

If there were such a thing as fate, I would answer mine soon enough.

Grandfather reached into the basket. Grandmother's eyes tracked his movements as he removed a closed fist. Opened his hand.

A white shark tooth.

"What?" Grandmother said, shock spreading across her heavy face.

Grandfather showed the tooth to the tribe. "The fates have spoken."

"It's not…" Grandmother spluttered.

"It's not what?" I asked.

"You cheated!"

"I did not choose my lot," I said. "Are you accusing Grandfather of cheating?"

Grandmother's face darkened with rage. She rotated the basket, turning it back and forth until all the shark teeth fell into her cupped hand. She counted them out—six black teeth, and eighteen white ones.

"Take Grandfather away," Grandmother said to the guard who had shoved me to the ground. But Grandfather had his sidearm out, barrel pointed at Grandmother's temple. His milk-white cataracts didn't waver. Neither did the sidearm.

"Open the basket," Grandfather commanded.

"What do you mean, 'open it,'" Grandmother protested. "It can't be opened."

"It can. Angi, open it."

I reached for the basket. Grandmother pulled it against her chest with both hands.

"Give it to her or so help me I will kill you where you stand," Grandfather said.

Grandmother released the basket. I took it, studying its construction, the way the weaving overlapped. I twisted it in my hands, feeling the weaving shift. Then in an instant, I felt the truth of the thing. The basket came apart into two sections, divided by a section of netting. Turned one way, and a hand would find one set of teeth. Turned another, another set…

"The lots are fixed," Grandfather said. "Grandmother has betrayed the tribe."

Guards and women and children crowded forward, eager to examine the basket.

Grandmother's jowls worked, fear turning her eyes glassy.

"Give her a black tooth," shouted a woman—not *any* woman, but the next to oldest, the Grandmother-in-Waiting.

"No," I said. "No more lots."

No one listened. Bodies rushed forward, hands grabbing for Grandmother.

The sharp report of Grandfather's pistol, the acrid smell of gunpowder.

Screaming and blood. Someone fell into the fire and rolled out again, hair aflame. Grandmother slashed out with a knife, cutting a guard's arm. He screamed and she groped for his sidearm. Another crack and she fell back, a gaping hole in her forehead.

More sweating bodies shoved forward, others fled. Everywhere, pandemonium and chaos. I plucked the device from where it lay in a pool of Grandmother's blood and slipped away, down the stairs, into the lower decks. I had changed nothing. The tribe would have Grandmother-in-Waiting in place and Grandmother's flayed corpse over a smoke pit before morning.

In the near total darkness of the lowest deck, I wiped blood from the surface of the device. It came to life, screen casting blue shadows over the breeding pools where water beetles skittered over brackish water.

"They wouldn't listen," I spoke into the device. "I tried my best."

"Understood. We'll send a boat for you. Can you be ready by morning?"

"Yes—I have the most recent generation packed and ready."

"Good. You did the right thing, though I would have preferred getting you out of there sooner. You're lucky those animals didn't kill you."

"I had to try one last time," I said. "I thought I could convince them, but I couldn't."

Footsteps from behind me. Grandfather moving forward with the confidence of someone accustomed to living without sight. "Angi? Who are you talking to?" His voice told me he didn't need my answer to confirm what he already knew. He leveled his pistol at my chest. Whooping and screams echoed down the stairwell, the sound of reveling, of the tribe preparing to put a new Grandmother in place.

"Who are you talking to?" he asked again.

I held up the device. "You know."

"What did you do, Angi?" Anguish in his voice.

"It had to end," I said, repeating his words from the beach back to him.

"All our men…sent to their deaths…"

"Now, something better may come," I said. *Though not for you. Not for the tribe.* I would leave them, and teach the platform people how to better protect themselves from attack. They had promised me a place, and the opportunity to continue my work.

"Let me go, Grandfather. Let me go and share my beetles with those able to appreciate them."

The gun wavered, held steady, waivered.

"Grandfather?"

But Grandfather didn't answer.

~*~

A Word from Nathan M. Beauchamp

This story's title gives away a bit of the plot, though it hides its most important secret until the final page. I wanted to put the larger realities of this post-apocalyptic world front and center and let the less-obvious details coalesce into something more sinister in the final third of the story. Bleak worlds often demand bleak characters. Angi—Bug Eater—is my attempt to present someone both bleak but aspirational, someone willing to make sacrifices to achieve her aims. How necessary some of those sacrifices may ultimately have been is up to the reader to discern.

About the Author

Nathan serves as acquisitions editor for Centrifuge Press, an independent publisher of speculative fiction. He co-authored the award-winning YA science fiction series **Universe Eventual,** including the novels **Chimera, Helios, Ceres, and Ascension**. His short fiction has appeared in numerous anthologies and fiction magazines. Nathan holds an MFA in creative writing from Western State Colorado University and lives in Denver with his wife and two young sons.

For more information visit njtanger.com.

~*~

Tide Sweeping
P.K. Tyler

~*~

JASJA STOOD AT THE TEMPLE gates, staring across the vast nothingness of the Arctic desert. The high cloudless sky glowed with boundless hues of red and purple as the sunset rippled through the scorching heat. Skimming the horizon, the hazy line of a small caravan swept up sand and dirt into the still air, leaving a billowing trail behind it for miles.

They'll be here soon, then. By the middle of the next day at least. Enough time for another sweep.

As the last remnant of the sun fell, the palate above shifted to a faint band of tangerine and gold that gently drifted up into the coming blackness.

Jasja watched for a few more minutes, enjoying the last of the day's warmth radiating up from the sand before the night cooled the world to temperatures near freezing. When the chill pulled at her bare feet, she closed the large wooden doors made of the last trees old enough to hew for planks. All five of the temples had featured wooden doors.

Individual homes no longer used wood but stone and brick. Such wastefulness in a world where trees were a limited resource would not be tolerated. But for the temples, wood represented one of the four holy elements and the presence of massive oak doors with metal hinges and knockers impressed upon all who entered that this space was to be honored as no other.

Now, even the doors of the four other temples had been ransacked for their precious resources. They hadn't welcomed worshipers for decades, and eventually, the people could no longer resist the temptation of real wood. All of this had happened long after Holy access to the Sea had been revoked.

And so Jasja kept watch over the last Ocean on earth.

Jasja descended the winding stairs of the wide main room, the temperature becoming even and comfortable against her skin. Down here, below surface level, she breathed in the cool, fresh air. She missed it during her daily vigil, her open welcome to any who made the journey to worship. Fewer came each year, and she knew that soon they would stop altogether, but still, she would open the doors and wait—a beacon leading those who sought respite to the water.

She climbed down to the lowest level. A door behind the stairs led to her private rooms, storage for holy relics, and makeshift accommodations for other Sweepers from the days when there were more than one. In the main space, she tilted her head back, looking up through the thick glass ceiling of the temple out to the distant glow of twinkling stars.

She removed her golden robe and hung it at the bottom of the stairs so that when she awoke the next day to take her place standing in the doorway, glittering in the bright sun, all would see her shine. It was sewn together from past Sweepers' robes and new strips of fabric donated from Pacificer pilgrims where they wove real gold into wheat strands, ensuring its presence, no matter how small, remained. Other pilgrims from the now arid lower regions brought fabrics for clothing and flags, rare stones for repair, and other tributes unique to their homes. But mostly, they came for the chance to submerge in the last salinized reservoir leading to the lost Ocean.

The room was a perfect circle, mimicking the shape of Oceans of old. The limestone floor sloped down from the edge to the deepest point where it flattened out to a thick glass floor. Perfectly circular holes had been drilled into the floor, letting the fresh cool water of the Ocean filter in, continually refreshing the reservoir. The depth of the pool no longer changed over the course of the month. Tides were a thing of the past as well. But even still, pilgrims traveled for days, sometimes months, to dip their toes in the last Ocean.

Jasja slipped into the water and reveled in the change from the heaviness of gravity to the buoyancy of the ocean water. Her sunburnt skin soaked in the moisture. Her upbringing had taught her that using the Ocean for her own comfort was selfish, but as the throbbing in her shoulders stopped she couldn't resist a sigh of relief. She cupped water in her hands and poured it over her red tinged face, it drew out the pain. Pilgrims called it an Ocean miracle when they dipped their toes in for the first time and all their aches drifted away with the sting of the salt water touching blistered feet. The water pulled them in, replenishing their bodies and soothing their souls. The holiness of the Ocean was undeniable, and Jasja's job was to care for it, not to take it for granted.

She dove down and swam toward the glass pane at the bottom and grabbed at one of the holes with strong fingers. Her fingertips slipped through, curling around the thick floor to enter the unknown Sea below. The sand came away easily. It had accumulated in the openings during the day from the settling of the sandy air above and the encroachment of the underground debris, threatening to cut her temple off from the water as it had the other four.

She moved from hole to hole, sweeping them clean with quick, efficient movements. Her breath held longer than the others before her. Each generation born to the water was able to remain submerged longer and longer. A quick breath at the surface before diving down again, and again, and again until each circulation hole was clean. But tonight, she could see the sand drifting in the water, resettling at the openings, threatening to close them off again. Even the edge of the floor had sand pressed against it from below, narrowing the pool ever so slowly. Jasja could not reach those edges from the holes drilled in the glass floor.

Jasja floated on the surface of the pool on her back, letting her front side dry in the open air while slowly kicking her legs in the sea water. If the Ocean itself conspired to cut them off, it must be time for another sweep. The briny scent filled the open space above her as she stared up at the stars through the glass ceiling and thought, trying to convince herself she could wait, that there was time. But time was the enemy of the Ocean, and if the sands came too fast, humanity may drop from one Ocean to none.

Jasja drifted to the edge and stood, letting the salt water dry on her skin. For those visiting for the first time, the smell struck them before anything else, before the taste of salt in the air, before the moisture upon their skin. But Jasja was accustomed to it and the dry dust of the world above was what struck her as alien. She was a creature of the Sea.

With deliberate movements, she walked around the pool, extinguishing the lights spaced evenly throughout the room until only the flame at the bottom of the stairs burned bright. Fire was known to be a trickster, hypnotizing as it danced on the water. Only Sweepers were permitted to be alone with the Flame and the Ocean, its seduction known to drive even the strongest of minds insane. More than one Sweeper had drowned while tending the Flame, ensnared by its dance, but it must be lit first and extinguished last. The Gods must meet at the beginning and end of each day. Otherwise the next may not come.

She snuffed the flame and allowed a drop of water to fall from her finger into the chalice with a silent prayer. In her small room, Jasja ate her evening meal from the food given to her by the villagers and tributes brought by the few pilgrims who travelled this far. There would be time to sweep tomorrow night, the caravan was still at least a day away.

In the morning, Jasja woke up, sheets tangled around her and a head full of pressure clogging her ears. She ate millet with dried berries a pilgrim from Western Atlantica had brought as a tribute in the hopes of gaining an hour alone in the Ocean with his barren wife. Had the water worked its miracles? There were plenty of stories of such things happening. Jasja didn't know for sure, but still she stayed, and she swept.

After eating and straightening her small living space, Jasja returned to the main room where the pool awaited her. She struck a match and blessed the water with the morning fire first and then lit the rest of the Holy room. The holes in the pool floor wouldn't need to be cleared again but the edges—she waded into the water to look.

Sand had encroached farther in on the floor during the night.

Jasja ran a foot along the glass, no grain or piles of silt touched her skin.

The invasion was from below.

Last night the sand had covered less than an inch of the outer perimeter. Now it pressed up against the glass, hiding almost a foot of the Ocean below. The sands had moved quickly. Faster than before. Much faster than the last time. She'd swept only a few days ago, the need to do it again at all was unusual, but for so much to accumulate so quickly…

The sound of footsteps overhead drew her attention. Frosten had arrived from the nearby village to do the daily maintenance of the temple. He swept the roof, keeping the view clear from the pool, and maintained the building. Sometimes, when there were no visitors, he would sit with Jasja at the temple doors and tell her about the village she had never been to, the kind of life she would never have. He was her only friend, and had become so much more. After sunset, she would often invite him in, to dip his toes in the pool or to relieve her loneliness. There would be no time for that tonight, though.

She shook thoughts of a normal life from her mind and loosely braided her hair as she walked back to her rooms. Farther in, past the storage area and the extra rooms, where the building wrapped back around, Jasja came to the door of the passage room. No one but the Sweepers knew what was contained inside.

After slipping out of her sleeping clothes, she opened the door to the small space with nothing but a light and a ladder heading down into the cold. Each rung stung the bottom of her feet as the metal bit with a cold burn. She climbed to the bottom, to a door closed and locked with a circular hatch. The floor was damp and moldy. Slime slipped between her toes.

She turned the hatch lock and opened the door, stepping inside a round metal room. When the door clicked shut behind her, she turned to a second door and cranked it once to open holes in the walls and ceiling that allowed the frigid water of the deep sea to fill the space. She shivered and held herself still to try and conserve what energy she could. If she ran out of air too soon or allowed the cold to paralyze her, there were no others to rescue her, and no apprentice to take her place.

When the water reached her hips, Jasja unlocked the second door of the chamber, the one that led straight out into the Ocean. On the other side of this metal hatch was the wild open Sea buried deep below the earth, an unexplored expanse that no one but Jasja knew how to enter.

The door opened and water rushed in, filling the rest of the chamber and lifting Jasja off her feet until she was suspended in the salty liquid. She swam through the door and began quickly, scraping the sand from the edge of the glass, pushing it back and sending it to drift out to another shore.

This was how all the temples died. The sand came faster and faster until one day, there was no more access to the Ocean's bounty. Until one day, even the Sweeper couldn't push aside the encroachment fast enough.

Jasja held her breath and worked her way around the perimeter of the large pool. The glass was infused into hard stone, but the sand loved to creep in and make itself at home. Handfuls of sand and seaweed and other debris had settled up against the glass. It took time, time she didn't have much of, to scrape it all away. Her hair came undone and swayed in the water like an echo of her movements. Fish darted between her kicking legs, and a snail crawled upside down along the newly uncovered glass. She took a moment to let it slip onto her finger. The small creature's antennae seemed to sniff the water, trying to understand the woman who felt more at home here than above ground, but who could not hold her breath forever.

Time slowed as she worked and her abnormal lung capacity held out until she had almost finished scraping the last of the sand away. She had so little left to do. She wanted to finish and return to the air only once, to not have to go through the pressure chamber to catch her breath and then return again for so little. So she pushed on, willing her exhale to slowly sustain her. She let the movement of the Ocean carry her along, instead of wasting energy swimming, but soon spots dotted her vision and her lungs burned to take a breath.

Not quite yet.

Jasja heard the voice of her mentor, of the Sweeper who had trained her. But the blackness of the Ocean deepened, and she couldn't see anything but the door to the pressure chamber. She hadn't finished, sand remained pressed against the bottom of the glass. At the bottom, but above her. And farther up, Frosten swept the sand away from another glass pane. Up or down? Floating in the Ocean, it all became the same. Voices of her ancestors, Sweepers of generations, carried her in the darkness and unfamiliar hands surrounded her.

Her eyes drifted shut, and without meaning to, she took in a deep breath.

When Jasja opened her eyes, she lay in a pool of water within the pressure chamber, the release door to the temple ladder open and filling the space with air. Her hair hung down around her face, pulling up in tight curls as it dried. She coughed but felt no water in her lungs. She must have swum back and let herself in without finishing the sweeping. Her heart sank. She'd have to return before the caravan arrived, but first, she needed to open the Temple doors.

The stairs were no kinder to her tender feet on the climb up, but the warmth of the temple air helped unfurl her anxiety. Back in her room, she drank rainwater from the tank and nibbled on some bread from the local villagers. They fed her and cared for her. Was it a burden or an honor? As the last temple, she imagined many didn't see any reason to bother, and yet, even those who doubted made their way to her and the Ocean eventually.

In the main room, Jasja looked down into the pool. The sand had not filled the access holes, and she had done a good job cleaning the edges. She searched the perimeter, walking down into the water, but couldn't find the section she had not been able to sweep. The entire pool was clean and clear and no sand danced in the water. Had she finished her job before coming back inside? It wasn't possible. She hadn't had the air.

"Jasja?" Frosten's deep voice called from high above her. He had opened the temple door without permission. If she chose, she could have him strung up outside the temple entrance for breaking the sanctity of the Ocean. Anger filled her at his audacity, but the quiver in his voice spoke of something urgent.

"I'll be there in a moment." She climbed out of the pool and slipped on her golden robe, the material absorbing the water from her flesh. The stairs seemed to take twice as long as usual to climb, but she wouldn't rush, she wouldn't run. She was a Sweeper and she moved with the Tide, not at the whim of any other force.

Frosten stood just inside the door, his hands buried deep in his pockets, his head hung low.

"You've entered the temple."

"The caravan approaches and you weren't here. I…I worried they would arrive before you emerged."

"And what concern is that of yours?"

Frosten turned his head to the side, his blond hair falling out of the tie holding it back from his face. "Only that I know you would be disappointed to not be in position."

His concern soothed her temper. "You should not enter without my permission."

"I know, Jasja."

"Not again, Frost, even if I am late and you are concerned."

He dared glance up at her, his sun-reddened cheeks dimpled as he smiled at the nickname.

"You have no more rights here than any other."

"I know, Jasja." His smile grew.

"Stop smiling at me like that." Her own smile grew, revealing white teeth against brown skin.

"There is no wrong kind of smile that I know of." Frosten winked then tilted his head toward the plume of sand and dust making its way toward them. "They are making good time. I imagine they have diesel or clockworks driving them instead of mules."

"Would that they should. They've undertaken a long trip."

"From all five regions. I can't imagine such a thing. It's good the Offering only happens every twenty years. It may take them that long to return home."

"They aren't that close yet. They'll retrieve Ndjeke from the village before coming to the temple. So, even as close as they are, there was no reason for you to worry about my presence."

"Your robe glows brighter than you think, pulling all eyes in your direction from the village and well beyond." Frosten's eyes dipped down to her lips.

Jasja fought the blush creeping up her chest, threatening to cover her face and force her eyes to turn away. But she was no village schoolgirl. She'd grown up in the temple and had no time for the flirtations of a man. But still, his attention burned her cheeks.

"If the world were arranged more fairly, I'd kiss you now," Frosten whispered.

"If the world were arranged fairly, I wouldn't be here tending the last Ocean on earth."

"Just my luck, a desert full of women and I have to love the one who moves with the tides."

Jasja's eyes darted to Frosten's, but he didn't meet hers. Instead, he pulled on the edge of his long tunic and let his white-blond hair fall over his eyes.

"I should finish with the roof and sweep the entrance path, so everything is set when they arrive."

Jasja nodded, staring after his back while he climbed the sandstone steps winding around the temple, leading to the glass ceiling.

In the temple doorway, Jasja watched the caravan of delegates approach the village for their final attendee and let Frosten's words swim around inside her chest. He had to love the one woman…love…. A forbidden word for her. All she had was the Ocean. All she would ever have was the Ocean and the companionship of the next Sweeper who she would train to take over when she died, just as she had done when her own mentor had sunk beneath the wild sea while sweeping. They, too, would know only her until she joined the tide. Then their charge would arrive with the next Offering. One after the next, never knowing love or having children or life beyond the walls of the temple. Because more than this would be a distraction, and she tended the last of the earth's Oceans. Distractions couldn't be indulged.

But still, she wished Frosten had risked himself and kissed her.

An hour later, the caravan turned from the village and aimed its approach directly toward the temple. The doors were wide open, and the dry heat filled the air with waves of distorted vision.

Jasja stood in the center, golden robe cascading down off her strong shoulders and draping over the stone floor. The walkway was swept and clean. Frosten had left without a word. He knew as well as she did that she'd have less time for him after the Offering, and tonight, she had to wear her official mantle as Sweeper.

The carts pulled into view—dust, sand, and villagers all seemed to be chasing the line of vehicles. The roar of diesel growled loudly as they approached. Unlike what she'd expected, this was not a row of many cars but one massive car, pulling behind it a line of smaller vehicles on wheels with cloth coverings to protect the inhabitants from the sun.

Five carts followed the main vehicle.

Five Oceans.

Five Offerings.

The caravan pulled right up to the end of the walkway and a large man with hair so dark it seemed to absorb the light around it climbed from the main car. His tall frame and broad build gave him a grand appearance, but when he reached back and donned the robe of the Orator his features took on mythic proportion.

Garbed in hues of blue, the Orator's robe was as patched and run down as Jasja's own. But for the first time, she could understand what she must look like to the villagers and occasional pilgrims who journeyed to the temple. He pulled on the robe, and the tattered edges and mismatched colors disappeared. Before her, he transformed into a god.

"Sweeper, we come bringing Offerings and tributes." His voice rose up to her like a thundercloud.

"Orator, first allow me to welcome you to the Arctic Ocean, a place of tranquility and peace. I would have you rest in the shadow of my temple and join me in celebration tonight." She followed the script as it was written in the old books, speaking the same words her mentor had spoken at the last Offering twenty years ago.

"We thank you for your generosity and accept your hospitality. Tonight, we shall feast!"

Villagers began to arrive, trickling into the crowd as travelers climbed out of the caravan. The scene now had an audience, and the Orator stood tall, clearly relishing in his role. This was the last stop of a long journey and he had prepared a long time for this.

"You must unpack and rest from your travels, the five regions are distant from here and from each other," Jasja called down to him from her position in the temple doorway, the whole thing strangely comical as they shouted pleasantries scribed generations ago.

"Yes, we are travel weary and hungry, but first please allow me to present our Offerings to the Tide."

From each cart, a massively pregnant woman emerged with the help of attendants who doted on them and made sure they could climb down easily. One by one they came forward to stand beside the Orator.

"I present an Offering of life from each of the 5 regions, one from each of the five Oceans, so that the Tide may never sweep us away."

A young woman with long hair twisted in braids around her head stepped forward. Her stomach rolled as she walked, her hips already spread wide, ready for birth. "This is Yadira of the Pacifica."

The next woman stepped forward, with skin almost as dark as the orator's hair. "This is Soura of the Indica."

Another. "Alinor of the Atlantica."

Another. "Koorine of the Antarctica."

And finally, "Ndjeke of the Arctica."

The five women beamed, hands on their swollen bellies, ready to burst with life and honor.

The scene made Jasja tear up. It was nerves. Pride. The significance of the occasion. She told herself that over and over, despite the sinking blackness in her stomach.

Jasja raised her hands, and the crowd now forming at the base of her usually solitary temple took a break simultaneously, pulling the oxygen out of the space and leaving her light-headed. "I welcome you. I accept the honor you have offered to the Tide. But today, let us dance."

She descended from the temple and greeted each of the women as the travelers and villagers unpacked and began digging fire pits for the night's festivities. The sands around the temple would blow over whatever mess they made in a day or two, so the crowd spread out, not worrying about maintaining the pristine landscape. Tents in all colors were erected around her and Jasja's eyes were drawn to the dark burgundy of Indica's fabrics.

"Are you from Indica?" Soura, the woman from that region, asked.

"I don't know what region my mother was from. I am of the Ocean."

"Of course." The woman bowed her head and stepped

back a pace.

After speaking with them a moment, the small group turned quiet and awkward. The women, girls really, spoke to Ndjeke, excited to meet the last of their group. None would meet Jasja's eyes, though some would steal glances at her after talking, as if worried of her judgment. She wanted to put them at ease. To join in with the giggling and swap stories the way the villagers and travelers did. Working side by side, together toward a goal.

But she was not one of them.

She could not hold their hands and giggle over the feeling of Frosten's lips against hers, or the tightness in her chest that had bloomed since he said he loved her. That is what he'd said. She was sure that was his meaning. She longed for a friend to talk to, but these girls would never be that.

She left without a word, leaving them to their chatting in peace.

"They are in awe of you," the Orator said, now dressed in the dark pants and tan tunic of the desert people.

"I am in awe of them, Orator."

He laughed, full and deep. "My name is Zhdan, no need to call me Orator."

"My name is Jasja."

"It is doubly lovely to meet a Sweeper with such a lovely name and smile." He bowed and took her hand, kissing her fingers lightly.

Jasja glanced around them. No one touched her, other than her mentor and Frosten. No one had the courage. Would Frosten, had they met now instead of as two children sneaking out into the desert to explore? Would he have stolen that first forbidden kiss if he met her after she'd donned her golden robe?

They walked through the crowd together, stopping to watch as the pilgrims erected the tent from Atlantica, tall and colored orange like the sun. The smells of meat cooking wafted through the air and soon the villagers played fast-paced and festive music, songs familiar to Jasja but as foreign to her guests as theirs were to her.

"Would you dance?" Zhdan asked.

"That I could."

"I might be able to teach you."

"You are from Arctica?"

"No, but dancing comes from inside, not from your region." He smiled, and dark hair framed his broad face, narrowing the world down to black eyes intent on her answer.

She blushed and shook her head. "It would not be proper. The celebration is for the Offerings, not for me. I would only distract from their revelry."

"Perhaps they would be relieved to see you are not, in fact, a god waiting to bring down judgment."

"Perhaps it would only make them question their dedication." Jasja swept away from him, her golden robe dragging in the sand and leaving no trace of her foot steps behind.

She climbed the temple stairs as the sun rose to its highest point, beating down on the day and heating up the air.

At the top, she turned back and looked at the festivities. Would this be the last offering? Certainly the only one she'd ever see. Would her Ocean last that long?

Inside the main doors, the only light came from the clear glass above. As her eyes adjusted, she saw someone standing against the wall, waiting for her.

"Frosten?"

"The Orator likes you quite a bit, I think."

She shrugged, the flattery of his attention having worn off. "He's just a man."

Frosten stepped closer. "So am I."

"And I cannot have a man. You know that," she breathed.

"But I'm here, nonetheless, and you have yet to tell me to go."

"You shouldn't have come into the temple. I told you earlier. And now with people outside, someone will see you leave."

"Then don't make me."

His hand reached for her and she couldn't pull away, couldn't resist when he pulled her against him and brought his lips to hers. The familiar feel of his touch, the warmth and safety of his arms, wrapped her up and broke her resolve.

"There's nothing for you here," she whispered into the air as his lips traveled down her neck. "I can't be your wife or your woman. I can't give you anything and you deserve more."

"I wish to be nowhere else."

Later, as they lay together on her small bed in the back room of the temple, he whispered to her dreams of making a pilgrimage of his own, to see the other peoples of the world, the never-ending desert of their earth. He wanted to climb the tall mountains of the Appalachian where rumors said people still lived, despite there never having been a temple to sustain them.

"People are spreading out, moving away from their villages and regions. With no Oceans, there's nothing to keep them there."

"Is that what you would do, leave the Ocean behind?" she asked.

"Not so long as you are linked to the Tide."

"You should make plans of your own, not be reliant on me. I will be tied here until I'm taken by the Sea. There's no future in this. I keep telling you."

"Yet I keep hoping. I may be the only man who wishes to see the last Ocean covered in sand and buried like the ancient cities, but I would lose all that others pray for if it meant a life with you."

A tear came to Jasja's eye, salty like the Ocean itself.

"One day you will resent me for the life you aren't living."

"It's my life to decide how to live, and I choose to spend it swimming forever after you."

Late in the night, the thunderous music woke them. It shook the temple walls, vibrating through Jasja's bones. It was almost time for the Offering. She had been right to let the people celebrate without her, but, looking at Frosten, sadness filled her. She would never give life like the women who had come here. She would never truly know love and, somehow, she had to convince him to leave her. But the thought dragged her down like weighted boots in the underwater expanse.

Frosten followed her into the main room and watched as she dove in and cleared the floor so the water could wash through, clean and fresh. It wasn't forbidden for him to be there, but it felt like a sin. She checked the edges, and the sand had encroached again, so quickly. It blocked the holes nearest the edge but there was no time to sweep the Tide away, and that was something Frosten could never know about.

"You should leave now," she said, emerging from the water, her hair springing back into its natural curls.

"Watching you swim, it's better than a dance or a feast. It's a miracle. You were made for the water."

"I was born of it."

"Could you ever leave?"

It was the closest he'd ever come of asking her to choose.

"The Offerings will be ready. I must go."

He nodded, looking into her eyes for an answer she couldn't give. "I'll slip out now then."

Alone, Jasja pulled her hair back and clipped it tight before painting her neck and hands with the gold powder saved for ceremonies. She donned her golden robe and climbed the winding stairs, letting each step take her further from her thoughts and questions and bringing her nearer to her Holy role.

She swung the temple doors wide, and firelight lit the sands.

Immediately the crowd fell silent, only the crackling of the fires could be heard. The smell of roasting meat filled her mind and reminded her she hadn't eaten since morning. All the better for what came next, but the rumbling in her stomach was uncomfortable.

She raised her hands up, a visage of gold flickering in the firelight.

"One Ocean once ruled this world, flowing over and under all life. It spanned from horizon to horizon, separating the people and engulfing entire lands. Separated by name alone into Five, they flowed one into the next, impossible to distinguish between them as Water unified the earth, the Tides brought life to the Pacifica to the Arctica and on and on in a never-ending wave."

She paused, and all eyes stayed locked on her as she lowered her arms, the golden robe clinging to her body.

"One Ocean became five as the sand devoured the earth. Heat dried up the rivers and lakes and the Oceans alone survived with the salt of life flowing in the waters. But still, the sands came, burying city and town until deserts spanned from coast to coast. The Oceans retreated, avoiding the evils man had brought on this dead sand. No life could grow within it, no water be retained. The land itself became dry and barren, forcing our people to capture the rainfall and grow food above ground to survive. And then Atlantica touched Pacifica. And then all the Oceans were swallowed by the sand."

"Not all the Oceans!" someone from the village cried out. They knew the story, it had been told by each generation to the next, but still, the magic in the air and the crackle of the fire brought out their excitement like children in the rain.

"Not all the Oceans. Because our ancestors were wise, and they built vast walled villages to protect what remained. The Oceans grew so small they could live within one humble temple." She gestured behind her.

"And it is our duty, a duty passed down through the Offerings, to tend our beloved Ocean and Sweep the Tide."

"Step forward!" the Orator cried, again wearing his blue robe.

"Yadira, Soura, Alinor, Koorine, and Ndjeke. You are the beloved mothers of the Ocean. You bring life to what is an otherwise barren world. Do you make your offering with open hearts?"

"We do." The women said in unison as they'd been instructed. They held hands and looked up at Jasja as if she were a god descended from heaven.

"Come, the water will bring its blessing."

The women exchanged looks and, for a moment, Jasja wondered if one of them might change her mind. Run. What would happen if they did? No instructions had been left from the Sweepers of the past for that. It was not done.

Her fears washed away as they climbed the stairs together, the Orator following behind. His job now was as witness, as scribe, as herald of the Ocean's choice.

The people cheered and the music began again. They would celebrate deep into the night until the final word was announced.

Jasja led the girls down the spiral stairs, her robe trailing behind her ensuring they remain a distance from her lead. The descent was silent.

At the water's edge, Jasja slipped off her robe and snuffed all the lights except for the holy flame. It would witness and guide the Offering, bathing the mothers in its burning light, purifying them. She strode naked into the ocean. Her gold tinged hands and neck maintained their color, the water slipping off like beads. The water swirled around her, the movement of her body creating ripples. It distorted her view of the glass floor, making it appear as if the moving water was really the flowing hair of Sweepers past come to witness their newest descendant.

"Atlantica, come."

Alinor removed her clothing and slipped into the water, sighing as the buoyancy of the salt water relieved the weight of her pregnancy from her bones.

One by one Jasja called the Offerings into the water until they circled her. Fully immersed, they looked like goddesses, perfect creations of the Mother Earth and her sister Ocean. The sacred fire danced upon the rippling Ocean's surface, kissing each young mother's face with its light.

She waded to the edge and took a cup prepared by the Orator. Within it, he had mixed drops of scorpion venom with crushed Belladonna and Burdock Root. Ginger gave the liquid its spicy flavor and Black Cohosh its color. The poison of the Pennyroyal herb and Cassava plant ensured the women would enter a paralytic state. One by one, the Offerings drank.

No pain appeared on their faces as the women laid themselves down around Jasja in a five-pointed star. The slope from the edge gave them each a natural bed to lie upon, their feet submerged, their heads above the surface. The water swirled with pink as the herbs did their work and the women silently labored.

Koorine moaned and Jasja dripped more of the concoction into her mouth from her fingers, soothing her until her closed eyes lay still.

As the pool changed from blue to pink to red, Jasja handed the Orator the cup and took from him the ceremonial knife. He offered no friendly smile of encouragement or flirtatious twinkle of the eye now. The truth of the Offering, the secret the two of them alone shared, loomed.

Jasja approached each woman and, with a swift hand, inserted the curved blade between their legs and pushed against the resistant flesh until she felt the rush of blood enter the water. She turned her wrist, pulling it hard up and over the woman's stomach, revealing the miracle within. With her hands, she spread the opening and sliced the cord connecting child to motheras final breaths escaped the Offerings, bringing the child within free.

Five babes, fully submerged in water, birthed directly into the Ocean by the hand of the Sweeper. They were from no region, no land, no mother. All five moved. The first fear abated, they were alive.

Jasja handed the knife, dripping with pink salt water, back to the Orator before returning to the center of the circle. There she stood. And waited. The babes drifted in the water, instincts guiding them from the safety of the womb. She stood in a red sea as the next Sweeper sought their destiny. One by one the babies struggled, moving with the quickly swirling water pushing them along with the strength of the Tide until even Jasja no longer knew which had come from what Offering's body.

One swam while another sank.

One drifted while another opened its mouth and drank in the Sea.

One reached out, grabbing as if seeking what came next.

Jasja made out the figures of young offerings and past Sweepers beneath the glass floor, the red tint tricking her eyes into seeing swaying hair and outreached hands.

The Orator stood and watched with stoic determination, not looking away from the scene before him. It would be his duty to tell the story of the new Sweeper to those who waited outside.

When the first child touched her, Jasja picked the baby up and cradled him in her arms. He gurgled, clearing his lungs of the waters of birth and Sea, intermingled now in the child's soul. No others made their way to her.

The Ocean roared and the feeling of the glass floor slipped from beneath Jasja's feet. Without the barrier, the Tide burst forth, waves which had been held at bay with no release rushed over her and swept the water into a frenzy. She held her newly born son close and let the wild Sea wash over them. Red water splashed as waves rose and broke over the Offerings, drawing them into the depths. The water carried the Offerings and their offspring below the surface as waves broke up and over the edge, soaking the Orator and whipping through the sudden wind pulling the water to heights it shouldn't reach.

Submerged arms cradled the uninitiated children sinking down into the depths, holding them close and cooing words Jasja could not hear.

A wild torrent of waves surrounded Jasja and her new successor, the only child she would ever bear. Within the storm her mentor appeared, long brown hair hanging down past her shoulders and skin stained red with the blood of the next generation. *You will do right. You have always done right. Soak in the water and I will be here when your time comes to hold you as you hold your new charge. Teach him well.*

The water crashed over them again and she was gone. The Tide had demanded its due and, satiated, it calmed into a still blue pool with a glass floor.

Jasja carried her son from the pool and painted his body with the same gold that still remained on her hands and neck, then followed the Orator back up the stairs to present the world with the Sweeper who would keep the Ocean safe once she was gone, joined with her brothers and sisters in the depths below.

~*~

About the Author

P.K. Tyler is the USA Today and Wall Street Journal Best-Selling author of Speculative Fiction and other Genre Bending novels. Primarily known for her Science Fiction and Meta-Fantasy work, she's also published works as Pavarti K. Tyler and had projects under that name appear on the USA TODAY Bestseller's List.

"Tyler is essentially the indie scene's Margaret Atwood; she incorporates sci-fi elements into her novels, which deal with topics such as spirituality, gender, sexuality and power dynamics." — IndieReader

Pav attended Smith College and graduated with a degree in Theatre. She lived in New York, where she worked as a Dramaturge, Assistant Director and Production Manager on productions both on and off-Broadway. Later, Pavarti went to work in the finance industry for several international law firms. Now located in Baltimore Maryland, she lives with her husband, two daughters and two terrible dogs.

For more information visit pktyler.com.

~*~

The Titan's Daughter
Daniel Arthur Smith

~*~

WHEN WE FIRST SET SAIL, her face was a constant glow, no matter the time or the weather. At least, that's how I remember her. She was never a bikini girl. Her penchant was for wearing flower-print sundresses and nothing beneath, particularly the thin-strapped kind that rested lightly on her shoulders, the thin fabric kind she could wriggle out of with a twist and a shake. Her hair was longer then, too. Countless times I watched her humming to herself as she tied it back, never able to restrain those wild wisps that fell to her cheek and across the soft nape of her neck.

I was younger, too. But in those late-night dreams, I am absent and she alone lounges on deck, on that teak chaise that long since broke beyond repair.

Her breathing changes when I stir. She rolls in the bunk. A signal to me to let the ruminations pass—but then, they are ruminations and, being such, are as the waves that endlessly and indifferently roll in from the sea and return—an ever-consuming reminder that there are things perpetual I cannot change. The waves roll in, the waves roll out—they roll in again. Mine eyes mist.

She, of course, disregards such things altogether. Looks to the calm of the sea. Or so she attests.

The calmness of the sea is relentless.

I abandon the cabin for the deck, my nightly sojourn. I lie to myself that the salt tang of our darkened harbor will rejuvenate me, but my mind continues to race and the burden of malaise weighs heavier from lack of sleep. There was a time when I didn't need the rest, when my wit was most inventive and keen in the late hours. I could crew all shifts without wavering, without my mind wandering to replay a year lost.

Though the harbor is dark, the heavens are alive with the light. An emerald aurorae flames from the horizon, the brilliant lapping swaths obscure all but a cluster of constellations—the Dolphin, the Eagle, the Archer—my late-night companions. The helm chair is firm against my back. The musty wool covering is wet with the warm midnight dew, but I don't mind. I uncork my elixir—the bottle of fruit brandy stowed in the console. The syrupy fire drips down my throat, drawing a quiver up my spine. I instinctively straighten to stave off the eruption. It's good to sit straight and the vantage from the helm allows distraction. I search back to a time when the stars were shining just for me, when they guided my way, and I raise my hand against them, index finger up, thumb extended out, and frame the brightest. The gesture is familiar, a map to...

From the silence, the melody of her song seeps into my thoughts and drives me to hum the honey sweet notes—*Di da dutt-dutt di-da*. Memories fall away. I sip more.

~*~

At some point in the early morning, she has covered me and my eyes flutter a crack when the warmth of the blanket rouses me. The sunrise is as many I've collected. Fuchsia, violet, and blue. There is a voice with hers behind me. A man. "Forever," he says, a dream as we two are alone. The wind caresses my cheek, so I nuzzle deep into the blanket. Sleep has not finished with me.

~*~

I wake to a gentle touch on my shoulder. We share a smile. We share a kiss. We are a pair. The lines of our flesh, baked, tightened, and bronzed. She remains far more fit than I. The light in her eyes has shifted from youth but her effervescent glow has not dimmed—her beauty still burns bright.

With grace, she gathers the fresh water from the mesh catches. Her wrist floats and flits as she pulls then spills each cup into her pail. She makes the morning look easy. My hips and muscles warm slowly, my stride is a waddle. But a few stretches put heat where it need be.

The masthead telltales indicate a good west wind. From the stern, I let loose the thin line to launch our kite. The wide white wings need merely a mild breeze to fill them as they lift the turbine in its cradle high into the pink of the morning sky. The blades spin, charging the power cells hidden in the hull.

"The weather is with us today," she says.

"I believe it is," I reply.

"Then today will be the day," she says.

Calculating her meaning, I say, "Could be."

The years have taught me that the hint of satisfaction she offers before going below is for my sake, not hers.

Will this be the day?

On the console, left for me to find, a leather-clad journal that I have not seen since…*since when?* The tanned cover is soft, worn tender from the salt air, yet the yellowed pages are stiff, brittle between my fingers, so fragile that I fear if they're bent while turning they will crumble. Still, I cautiously leaf through, and with each page comes a flood of imagery. Colored shadows with little form, and the phantom sensation of…sand.

I remember sand caked onto my cheek, the sensation so vivid that, with a lick of my tongue, I clear my lips and raise my hand to wipe away the damp grit. But there is nothing. An urge prompts me to flip to the back of the small book.

There I find the words *Seven Years,* written in my own hand followed by an earnest inscription, bonding me to her.

I taste the saline that isn't there. My chest, my lungs ache. The viridian waters engulf me.

I was drowning.

From the cabin, she sings.

Di da dutt-dutt di-da.

The whistle of the kettle draws me below to the promise of steeping tea.

"You found your journal," she says as she pours my cup. "Read it. Today will be the day."

I smile as she settles to her loom, but her meaning is still unclear.

Today will be the day.

She's already fallen into her melody, the rhythms of which appear to propel her golden shuttle—a fluttering aspen leaf, drawing the woof backward and forward through the warp.

Mine eyes lock on the glint of the shuttle and my ears on her song.

She notices. She winks. Then, with a slight facial contortion, she directs me toward the leather book.

The binding is loose, so I place the book flat to the table rather than risk destruction by my hand. The journal is a log and a diary. The pages to the front detail an inventory, the quantities of food and water aboard each of twelve ships. The next pages lists names I should know but cannot place. In the margins beside the names are notes of morale and constitution, and, spread randomly amongst those, deliberations of my love for her. The following entries aren't dated, but they are recognizably a record of events, each paired with a flicker of memory. With the reading of a name comes a reflection of a face. An image of a landmark, to the sketch of a place. Undoubtedly the words belong to me, but the story isn't mine. *Or is it?*

"What is this?" I ask.

Her humming is faint, in tune with the shooting of her shuttle.

Again, I ask.

Not pulling away or missing the push of a pedal. She says, "Read it."

And I do. But the events portrayed are fantastical, of great storms that hurled the ships across the sea to foreign waters and skies. Fresh water and food exhausted, the men took to an island to refill their stores. There they discovered a people whose sole sustenance is the bloom of a shrub that steals the passion from men and leaves them with no other care than flower consumption. On the next island they encountered a giant, a one-eyed shepherd, who trapped many of the men in a cavern and fed on them one by one. *My men. They were my men, my ships, my small fleet.* A large ember-tipped lance fills my mind as I read of blinding the creature, an act the entry reads as having been performed by *nobody*.

Nobody.

Another tale speaks of a race of giants who launched rocks from high coastal cliffs, destroying all but one of the twelve ships. They then plucked the crews of those wrecks from the waters and devoured them.

Before me broken timbers bob in the foam of a scarlet surf.

"This can't be real," I say.

"What's that?" she asks.

"What I'm reading. How could this be? It's impossible."

"Is it?" she asks, yet she shows no doubt.

"It says that a witch turned half of my men into pigs after feeding them cheese and wine."

"Think on it," she says. "Do you see them?"

A ridiculous question. Yet the witch stands before me, a beautiful dark-eyed creature, and beside her, the men.

"Yes," I say. "As clear as day. But I still cannot map the faces of these men to the names written on the page."

"Continue then. When I'm finished with the cloth, it will be time."

I gaze at the cloth in the loom, the thread shimmering as golden as her shuttle. She is near finished already.

"Continue," she goads.

On the next page, I read of being bound to the mast of my ship, and though I see no tether taut around my hands, my wrists are constricted. And...the song...a different one from hers.

"Breathe," she says, and I realize that I've stopped,

overcome by a void, a silence. She must sense it because her hum escalates...*Di da dutt-dutt da-da*...and I sigh, and breathe.

Her eyes fix on the open journal.

The next entry details a six-headed beast which poisons my nostrils with acrid stench.

The following pages return to the mundane, the endless gathering of fresh water, the slaughtering of cattle for the food stores, and then...

The remaining pages are blank.

"It's unfinished," I say.

"Is it?" she asks.

"There is no more. No more written anyway." I shirk away the journal. "What happened to the men?"

"You know," she says. "Think on it. Think on the day I found you."

The day I found you.

I'm drawn to the glimmer of her racing golden shuttle. Again, I taste the sea. I'm swallowed by waters, then sand.

"I was washed to the beach," I say.

"And before that?"

"Before that, I was drowning."

"Yes. But how did you get there?"

"Where?"

"The sea. How did you fall into the sea?"

"Lightning," I say. "White surf, waves towering the mast." I look to the ceiling. My eyes wince closed to avoid the bombastic blast of the fierce white squall. The rushing wall of water crushes down, timbers shatter, and men who are as brother to me are lifted and tossed and consumed by the angry sea.

"A shipwreck," I mutter.

"A shipwreck," she repeats.

"And I'm the—"

"The sole survivor."

A decade of memories return. With them come the names of the ships, of the men, of the—

"The woman in the journal," I say. "It isn't you. There is

another I love."

"Yes."

"I must return to her."

"And you will," she says, silencing her loom. "I've finished my cloth, and the west wind has brought a ship."

"There have been no ships here in…" *How long? Years? Ever?*

"Go above deck. You'll see, a ship is coming."

The cabin floor sinks beneath me as I rise, and my knees wobble from my weight as I climb up top.

The wide wing kite and its windmill burden float above me. The west wind is still strong. I place my hand above my brow to shield the sun and inspect the horizon. There, as she described it, the tip of an angled sail rises from the edge of the sea.

I return below. "How did you know?" I ask.

"I received a message while you slept."

"A message?" *The voice.* "What was it?"

"I was reminded that your destiny is not to live with me forever."

Forever. It wasn't a dream.

"It's peculiar," I say. "I remember now. The voyage. My wife. But how long I've been here with you is cloudy, unclear. An eternity, yet no time at all."

She hums her melody. *Di da dutt-dutt di-da.* She comes to me. As we kiss, she lets her dress fall from her. She is young again, as am I.

Singing softly, she leads me by the hand to the forepeak, then onto the V-berth that is her bed. As we touch, my mind empties of all but our soft, sweet, salty kisses.

When we have finished, it's not a pout that she gives me. No. It's something far more complicated, and when she has soaked me in and can drink of me no further, she hands me the result of her earlier labor, a gold linen cloth, then kisses me once more.

"With this I let you go," she says.

With this I let you go. Jaw agape, I appeal for clarity.

"The cloak is thin," she says, wrapping my neck. "But it will warm you when the air is cool, cool you when the air is warm, and will remind you of the love we've made."

My heart is pulled across the sea to the woman that I love, and it's anchored here—with her. I don't have the words, but I don't need them. Her face is saddened but the sparkle in her eye assures me that we are the same.

"The sloop draws near," she says. We kiss.

With this I let you go. These are the words she spoke.

My gaze stays fixed across the crystal-clear ocean, until the white wings of the kite finally dip below the horizon. Her song rides the wind, is still with me. My heart is clean.

~*~

A Word from Daniel Arthur Smith

I've long been fascinated with the fate of Odysseus and his adventures in the Homeric epics of the *Iliad* and the *Odyssey*. As a boy, I didn't know they were Homeric. I watched Kirk Douglas on the Saturday afternoon and didn't really distinguish his Ulysses from Sinbad the sailor, Perseus, or Jason and the Argonauts. I suppose it was Alan Dean Foster's novelization of **Clash of the Titans** that truly piqued my interest in the Epic Cycles and began a pursuit of the mythological, first by taking in all matter of media on the subject—books, movies, comics—as a teen tends to do, and then later at the university level where I studies the insights of Joseph Campbell and the interpretive writings of James Joyce and Nikos Kazantzakis among others. The power of these tales, for me, is not only their longevity and adaptability, but the evolution of the metaphor throughout one's life. I didn't pay much attention to Calypso when I was young. A Cyclops far outweighed the adult dilemmas associated with a nymph. I'm now viewing through a different lens, and the metaphor of mid-life analysis and self-redemption have become as relatable as the monsters one must face, as the Sirens or the Cyclops.

About the Author

Daniel Arthur Smith is a USA Today and Wall Street Journal Best-Selling author. His titles include **Spectral Shift, Hugh Howey Lives, The Cathari Treasure, The Somali Deception**, and a few other novels and short stories. He also curates the phenomenal short fiction series **Tales from the Canyons of the Damned**.

He was raised in Michigan and graduated from Western Michigan University where he studied philosophy, with focus on cognitive science, meta-physics, and comparative religion. He began his career as a bartender, barista, poetry house proprietor, teacher, and then became a technologist and futurist for the Fortune 100 across the Americas and Europe.

Daniel has traveled to over 300 cities in 22 countries, residing in Los Angeles, Kalamazoo, Prague, Crete, and now writes in Manhattan where he lives with his wife and young sons.

For more information, visit danielarthursmith.com

~*~

Dancing in the
Midnight Ocean
Caroline M. Yoachim

~*~

I WAS ONE OF MAYBE FIFTY FISHFOLK working deeper than the midnight line, assembling a massive pipe that stretched from the brightwater city down to the hydrothermal vents. Mariana had sweet-talked the supervisor into giving us a job applying epoxy, which meant plenty of time for conversation in the pauses between bursts of work.

"The heated water from the vents will generate so much power," I said, "and none of it for us."

"If we had electricity down deep, I'd put strings of lights all along the edges of our habitation cubes, like they used to do surface-side for Christmastime. Then old Ten-gill Bill could do his sewing again, even though his fingers have lost their glow." Mariana leaned her head on my shoulder, and we looked up into the black, watching for the next segment of pipe.

"Wouldn't that be lovely, Cora?"

"We could have a lot of things if the city-dwellers shared their resources. Medical centers, better schools, food that doesn't taste like sulfur from the vents." I didn't say that none of it was likely to happen. City-dwellers were a greedy bunch of air-breathers.

A transport team brought a piece of pipe the size of a baby orca to be fitted and fastened. I turned to protect my eyes from the bright flashes of the electric arc welding rods. Mariana shielded my face with her hands to further block the blinding light. She hated to see me hurting. We listened to the steady burble of the air bubbles that formed a barrier between the welders and the electric current of their rods.

When the welders finished, Mariana and I spread an even layer of adhesive goo on the joint between the pipe segments. Our friend Ellie trailed behind us and applied a fiberglass wrap designed to slow corrosion. We worked by the dim light of our own bioluminescence, tiny glowing points of blue against an otherwise absolute darkness.

The deep rumble of the day-end horn sounded, time to turn in our tools and return to the mid-spiral checkpoint and get paid. I followed Mariana's shadowy outline up into the twilight water, admiring her strong efficient kicks. She'd pulled out a copy of an ancient novel—one of those space opera/fairy-tale mashups that were popular a couple years before the Submersion. She held the book in one hand, and she pointed the bioluminescent fingertips of her other hand at the recycled-plastic pages so that she could see the words. Her ability to read and swim at the same time was a feat of coordination that I found baffling, and impressive, and endearing.

She noticed me watching and flashed me a smile that sent my gills all aflutter. We'd ascended well into twilight, and the giant Plexiglas-and-steel sphere of the soon-to-be city's habitation dome loomed above us. The city-dwellers had built that part themselves, working in pressurized bubbles, staying forever in the air. This city was only for them, not for us, but their comfort was built on our labor.

"We build their cities and they treat us like we're not even human."

"Maybe they're right." Mariana marked her place in the

book with the laminated photograph of her mother that she carried with her everywhere—a serious-looking city-dweller named Yvonne, with dark hair and glasses, dressed in a lab coat. Mariana tucked the book into a carrying pocket on the back of her suit. We joined the line of fishfolk waiting to be paid for our day's work on the power pipeline. There was a commotion up front, and then someone I didn't recognize swam by, fuming. "…not a woman or a virgin. Mermaid my ass."

Only city-dwellers called us mermaids, an untrue name for most of us in varying degrees. Mariana was oblivious to the commotion. Her eyes were fixed on the dome, scanning as though she was searching for something. "Wouldn't it be amazing to live in a city, breathe the air, wear the clothes. Think of it, Cora, we could go dancing in ball gowns with twirling skirts and fancy shoes…" Her voice trailed off, the reality seeping in. "I'm too fat for their dresses, and my webbed feet won't fit in their shoes," she ended sadly.

"You're getting all the wrong ideas from those books of yours," I told her, reaching up to caress the smooth skin at the top of her head, the light of my fingers shining blue circles onto her scalp, the glow fainter here in the twilight water than it had been in the deeps. "Standards of beauty are…arbitrary. Irrelevant. You and I are made for the ocean. We can dance down here, just as we are."

We got to the front of the line. Instead of our usual foreman, a city-dweller wearing a full exoskeleton handed Mariana the packet that held the physical portion of the day's payment: food supplements and vitamins. I found city-dwellers awkward and unpleasant to look at—gaunt and hairy, their movements stiff and jerky. They weren't adapted to an underwater life, not as we were, but Mariana couldn't see any of that. She was first-gen fishfolk, a rare thing these days. All the other fishfolk I knew were descended from a single genetically-altered generation, five gens back, but Mariana's parents sold her into labor—presumably because they needed the credits, though Mariana tried to convince herself they did it to give her a better life.

I claimed my food packet and held out my card. The city-dweller added the day's credits. Up close, I could see the long red hair inside her helmet and the pale freckles dotted across her white cheeks. Or maybe his cheeks, or their cheeks. With the exoskeleton suit it was hard to tell.

As soon as we were clear of the line, Mariana gushed, "Wasn't she lovely, Cora? Like a princess in a fairy tale."

I frowned. "And I don't look anything like a lovely princess."

"Oh, I'm sorry." She chewed her lip. "I didn't mean to make you jealous. She's probably wretched and spoiled, not beautiful on the inside, like you."

"Probably." I rarely gave my body much thought, and Mariana—she couldn't see that she was gorgeous, well-adapted to the deeps, strong and sleek. It stung that she found a city-dweller nicer to look at than me, insides be damned. I wished I could make her see how twisted her standards were, how beautiful she really was. How beautiful I was.

"I'm sorry," she repeated, at a loss for things to say.

She refused to lie, even to save my feelings. I could tell that she wanted to reassure me about my looks and make me feel better, but she couldn't. I shrugged it off. A lie wouldn't help either of us. We swam through the twilight in silence, back down into the midnight depths, down to the sea floor where the ocean was warm from the hydrothermal vents. We stayed clear of the jets of superheated water and headed for an outcropping of rock that was covered with giant tube worms.

Verve and Ellie were there, heads close together. Verve had stayed in the deeps, too sick to work today, and it was always hard for him to be parted from Ellie. Normally the four of us ate together after work, but they clearly needed privacy. Mariana and I kept swimming. Our friends would find us when they were ready. Probably best for us to have some time to ourselves, anyway. I was still sulking from Mariana's comment about the damn city-dweller, and angry with myself for feeling bad about it, and just generally prickly.

Hunting by the quiet clicking of claws and the light of her fingertips, Mariana deftly plucked a white crab from between the tube worms. She handed it to me. I resisted the urge to make her kill her own crabs, that would be petty. It wasn't her fault that she'd internalized a bunch of bullshit from the so-called family that bioengineered her for the deeps. I snapped the crab in half, killing it quickly, and waited for the legs to stop twitching.

She caught another crab, this one for me. I traded her the dead crab for the live one. We made a good team. In so many things we had complimentary abilities. She was quicker, more coordinated, a better hunter...but very squeamish. Before we'd met, she'd mostly eaten tube worms, which were disgusting, and food supplements from the cities, which were scarce.

Mariana was sleeker now, with lovely curves, but she saw herself as fat and therefore ugly. Fat like me. Ugly like me. I forced my thoughts away from appearances. Our lives fit together, it didn't matter what Mariana thought of my body. We sucked the meat from our crabs and let the shells drift down.

I couldn't tell if she found the silence peaceful or awkward. Maybe for her it was the comfortable silence where her mind wandered through a world from one of her books. Whatever was in her head, she didn't seem inclined to bring up our discussion from earlier, but it was eating at me a little. I didn't like to let things fester. "I—"

"Concert tomorrow night?"

So much of my focus had been on Mariana I hadn't noticed that Verve and Ellie had joined us. Ellie held Verve's hand, and I noticed that her fingertips were slightly brighter than his. I wondered if the difference had always been there, or if it was from Verve being sick. "How are you feeling?"

Verve smiled, but there was no sparkle in his eyes. "A little tired. I'll be fine by tomorrow, I hope. Something I ate, or maybe a vitamin deficiency. Ellie made me take all the vitamins from her pack today."

"I'll be fine without them!" Ellie insisted.

"Who's playing tomorrow?" Mariana asked before they could start arguing over vitamins.

"Hvalsang," Verve said, his eyes finally lighting up. "Gregor is in rehab, and my brother—Tako—is filling in for them on the hydraulophone tomorrow night. He has a crush on the rotacorda player, so he's beyond excited about it."

"And he got us a bunch of booze tickets," Ellie added.

"Sold!" I said, but Mariana looked oddly disappointed. Verve and Ellie swam off without noticing. "What's wrong?"

"I heard there was a concert at the base of the city tomorrow night, and for a moment I thought that maybe—"

"You wanted to hear the city-dweller music."

"I'm sure this will be good, too. I didn't mean to be disappointed," she said. "This way we'll hear music from the instruments of the performers, not something piped into the water by speakers."

She put her glowing fingertips against the side of my face. "I know you don't understand my fascination with city-dwellers. It doesn't make sense for me to love them…but I love you, too."

Not I love you, but I love you, too. What a difference one small word could make. No, this was my bitterness twisting her words. I was quick to read meaning where none was intended, and despite her fascination with the city-dwellers, Mariana was a wonderful partner. I brushed her cheek with my fingertips. "And I love you."

~*~

The concert was at Buoy 17, about a hundred meters into the twilight. There was very little current here, and it was a good place for music because of the sound channel—the sweet spot where the temperature and depth gradients were optimal for sound propagation. The buoy was several meters across, part of a chain of research buoys from some Pre-Submersion science experiment that was likely never finished. A bunch of bands had teamed up a few years back to build a makeshift stage on top.

Mariana and I held hands and followed Verve and Ellie. We

were early enough to claim a good spot—close enough to the stage to see the band and underneath the area where the hawkers hung out so we'd have no trouble claiming our booze tickets. Several dozen fishfolk milled around above and below us, some close to the stage and others lingering farther back. In an open ocean concert, there was no way to charge everyone who listened. The sound simply traveled too far. The credits came mostly from hawkers—the assorted vendors who sold food and booze and split their profits with the band.

Verve swam off with our tickets.

"I made you something," Mariana told me. She reached into the pouch of her suit and pulled out a tiny whale carved from a piece of shell. I had no idea when she'd found the time to make it.

Ellie leaned in and nodded her approval. "It's lovely."

"Thank you, it's beautiful." There was a blowhole at the top of the whale so I could wear it as a necklace. "I wish I had something for you. I didn't know we were doing gifts tonight—"

"I was saving it for later, but the name of the band is Hvalsang, and it's a whale!" Mariana explained, excited. "Plus I'm terrible at surprises because I'm not good at keeping things a secret, so I thought it would be best to give it to you sooner rather than later."

"Thank you." I rubbed my finger along the smooth edge of the whale's back. I had a coil of floss in one of my pockets, and I carefully cut off a piece long enough to tie around my neck. I threaded the whale onto the floss, and Mariana tied a knot in the back to hold the necklace in place.

"Nice whale." Verve came back with four tubes of booze and a mesh bag of oysters.

"We only had tickets for the booze," Ellie chastised him, "and those must have cost a fortune."

"Can't have alcohol on an empty stomach!" Verve responded cheerfully. He started handing around oysters.

Ellie didn't argue it further. She got out her knife and slid the blade into the oyster, popping it open before passing the knife to me. I had my own blade, but mine was thicker, not as good for oysters. "Thanks."

We slurped down a couple rounds of oysters, all happy to be eating something that didn't taste like sulfur from the vents. Mariana was delighted by the oysters because they'd been farmed in a city somewhere. I didn't ruin her moment by telling her these oysters were cast-offs that some foolish city-dweller had harvested in the middle of the mating cycle, nearly flavorless compared to oysters in season. The cities only gave us cast-offs because to them we were cast-offs, too. It irked me that I still found the oysters delicious. The only reason I even knew they were lacking was that Pa had worked food processing on the underside of Nueva Angeles for a couple years when I was a kid, back before they stopped hiring fishfolk for that kind of work.

Verve passed me two tubes of booze, and I passed one to Mariana. They were bigger than usual, doubles instead of singles. I took a long draw, pulling seawater through the filter to mix with the near-pure alcohol that slow-released from inside the tube.

Mariana tasted hers and made a face.

"Sorry," Verve said, grinning. "They didn't have the sweetened ones."

"It's more like smoking than like drinking," Mariana said, shifting the focus of the conversation away from herself. "In the cities, they sip their booze out of cups, pre-mixed, which is nothing like this. But they sometimes wrap plants in paper and light them on fire and suck the air through...Well, they used to do that on the surface. I don't know if they do it in the cities. Maybe I'll send a message to Ocean City and ask."

Ellie put her hand on Mariana's shoulder. "Your parents haven't answered in a long time, maybe you should stop trying."

Mariana took a long pull on her tube of booze. "They're just busy. I'm sure they'll write back when they have time. Someday they'll have time for me." Her voice got quieter. "Someday they'll want me."

I put my arm around Mariana, and she tucked her head against my chest.

The band started warming up, and I listened to Tako on the hydraulophone. His glowing fingers danced over the instrument. It sounded fine, but he played with less flair than Gregor, who I'd dated for a while, back in my musician phase. Gregor had a fiery temper and a serious alcohol problem, but damn if he wasn't good with his hands. We all had our strengths and weaknesses, I guess. I glanced down at Mariana, who was still sucking down her booze, trying to drink away the pain of shitty parents.

"They're not worth it, love." I told her, running my fingertips gently down her arm. "They changed who you were before you were ever born, and sold you down into the deeps without even thinking to ask you. They're the ones who aren't human."

She nodded silently, her head on my chest.

"Round two?" Verve asked. He collected our empty booze tubes without waiting for an answer. He swam up to where the hawkers congregated and traded in the empties for fulls, paying with another round of tickets. He got back just as the band started to play.

True to their name, the band's songs were reminiscent of whale songs, eerie and haunting. I drank my booze and held Mariana close and let my mind drift in the music. Dark shadows passed high above us, blocking the light for a moment. City-dweller submarines or whales—at this distance it was impossible to tell.

The water vibrated at a frequency too low for me to hear. It was a silent rumble that seemed to come from the wrong direction. I took another pull of booze and realized that the music had shifted mid-song—the band was playing call and answer with a pod of whales somewhere behind us, less than a kilometer away if I could feel the low notes.

Another shadow passed above us, this one closer, and Mariana reached her arm out as though to touch it. "Here pretty whale, come sell your children into a better life. See what riches we have? With the credits you make, you can buy ball gowns and beautiful shoes!"

She laughed, attracting glares from the concertgoers around us. Mariana took the last drag of her tube of booze, and made a sweeping gesture with both arms, accidentally releasing the tube and setting it adrift. Ellie quickly caught it and handed it to Verve. "If we don't have four tubes to turn in at the end of the evening our free booze will cost us a whale's weight in oysters."

"I'm a whale with a million oysters clamped in a line along my tail," Mariana said. Suddenly she pulled away from me, her eyes bright. "There is a fairytale about that. A mermaid with oysters clamped to her tail. A sea witch makes her human so she can live on the surface and win the heart of a prince."

"So you want a prince now?" I asked her, teasing. For all her fixation on city-dwellers, Mariana had been consistent in one thing—she wasn't interested in men. "Besides, love, I know for a fact that you are no longer a maid."

One of the fishfolk from the group behind us swam up. "Keep it down a little? We can barely hear the music over your drunk friend here."

"Sorry. We'll try to be quieter," Ellie said.

The whales moved on, and Hvalsang went back to their usual set. Mariana started shouting for the whales to come back. The crowd around us was getting angrier.

"I'll take her home. Tell Tako he was great on the hydraulophone." My second tube was nearly full but I quickly sucked down the booze and handed the empty tube to Verve.

"You want us to come with you?" Ellie asked.

"Nah, we'll be fine, you stay and listen to the rest of the concert." I took Mariana's hand and we wove down through the crowd, into the darkness below. She sang quietly as we swam, her voice eerie and haunting, like a whale song in a minor key.

My spine prickled. What if there were predators out there, swimming in the dark? I pulled Mariana faster, but we were going the wrong way. I changed course, and we darted in a different direction.

"You're even drunker than me." Mariana pulled on my arm until I stopped my frantic swimming.

"It's your fault! I rushed my second tube to take you home." I hated disappointing her. I hated that I couldn't swim straight. The ocean was spinning. I was doing everything wrong. I loved Mariana, but I would never be what she really wanted. "You don't like how I look, you don't like me being drunk, maybe you just don't like me at all! Go find some city-dweller, maybe they can take you home."

"Cora…"

I was so dizzy. My insides churned like a school of bait fish swimming in the too-bright water near the surface. Mariana didn't want me, she wanted a pretty city-dweller, to live a better life than what I could give her down here in the dark. My churning-fish insides swirled faster, tighter—a ball of bait fish under attack by dolphins. Panicked fish, darting every which way, searching for an escape.

I swam down, deep into the darkness. I needed to escape Mariana's rejection. A light flashed in front of me, so bright it was blinding. Harpoons of pain shot through my already-spinning head. I collided with something hard, and the blackness of the surrounding sea flooded in through the cracks in my mind.

~*~

I woke surrounded by yellow-white lights that made my head throb. I called out, and the echoes of my voice sounded wrong. I gave a tentative kick with one leg, and my foot hit the bottom. My eyes adjusted, revealing patches of shadow in the brightness. I gently felt the bottom with my foot, and discovered that it was flat and smooth. Not the ocean floor, but a tank. My entire right side was sore, and my arm was badly bruised but hopefully not broken. I tried to remember what had happened, but the only thing that filled my mind was me yelling at Mariana and then swimming away.

I reached up and traced the outline of the carved-whale necklace she'd made for me and remembered the way her fingers had brushed against the back of my neck as she tied it on. She'd made me a gift, and I'd gotten drunk and abandoned her. She probably hated me now, and I deserved it.

A shadowy figure approached. I was surprised to see that they weren't a city-dweller, but one of my own kind. They removed an assortment of equipment from their body and slid into my tank.

"Too bright," I told them.

"You'll get used to it," they told me. "I'm Yvonne. You collided with a research sub, and they brought you to Ocean City for medical treatment. I'm here to check your vitals. Put this in your mouth, please."

She handed me a thermometer and I dutifully placed it under my tongue. Yvonne was Mariana's mother's name, but this fishwoman looked nothing like the picture that Mariana treasured. Still, it seemed too strange to be coincidence. She pulled thermometer out of my mouth.

"I know someone whose mother's name is Yvonne."

The fishwoman flinched. "You know her? My Mariana?"

"I'm surprised you have medical tanks to treat fishfolk," I said, changing the subject. If she couldn't be bothered to answer Mariana's messages, I wasn't about to give her updates on her daughter's life. "Although I suppose if there are fishfolk city-dwellers—"

"This isn't a medical facility, it's a research center," Yvonne corrected. She paused for a moment before mumbling, "And also a vet."

Of course. Doctors were for humans, not misshapen creatures of the deep. The only fishfolk clinic I'd ever seen was on the underside of Nueva Angeles. It was massively understaffed and half the equipment wasn't designed to be used underwater, much less on gill-breathers. My dad took me there once when I was a kid, because his job got the whole family access to the clinic. I'd had some kind of gill parasite, and they gave me pills for it.

City-dwellers had nicer medical facilities for their pets than fishfolk had.

There were more books and equipment on the shelves of this one room than I'd seen my entire life down in the deeps. There were tanks of varying sizes. Most of them were empty, but across the room one tank was surrounded by city-dwellers. They were preparing to do...something...to a creature that was halfway between a dolphin and a tropical fish.

Yvonne took my blood pressure and examined my gills.

"How can you stand to live here?" I studied her body. Her posture was warped and twisted from all the time she'd spent in air. "What is so damn fantastic about this bubble that you would sell your daughter off to the deeps?"

"Petri couldn't leave. He had breathing problems. Chronic. Serious. He used a high oxygen mix in his breather tank. We were very lucky to find work for both of us here in the city, first as research subjects, developing the equipment that let us function in the air. Now I am too old for their studies, and Petri...he died a long time ago. My sister is a good person. I knew she would take good care of Mariana. She's better off in the ocean, it's what we were made for."

"Mariana's aunt died when she was very young. Your daughter grew up mostly alone, eating tube worms. She'd probably still be eating tube worms if I hadn't found her. You abandoned her and I took care of her, I love her...but her dream is to find you and live in a city. She hates herself because she doesn't look like that photo you gave her."

Yvonne fidgeted, sloshing water up against the side of the tank. "I didn't have a picture of me, and I'm so ugly she'd never want to look at it even if I did—but I thought she should have something to remember her mother by. The picture is Dr. Kanawi. Part of the research team that ran tests on me to develop that." She gestured at the pile of equipment she'd removed before entering my tank.

Yvonne looked ragged, broken. I almost felt sorry for her, but then I remembered how badly she'd hurt Mariana. How badly she was still hurting Mariana. "Why don't you answer her messages? It kills her that you never answer."

"I haven't been getting any messages. Petri had a

connection, a city-dweller friend in communications. After Petri died, the messages from Mariana stopped. At first I tried to find another way, a new connection, but the research took so much time, and I never had money for bribes. I thought by now she would have forgotten me. It has been so many years."

Her eyes were pleading for forgiveness, but I had none to offer.

After a few minutes of silence, she climbed out of my tank and reattached the assorted equipment that let her function in the air. A breathing apparatus covered her gills and mouth. It came with a backpack tank of water so heavy that she hunched over when she put it on, despite the braces she wore on her back and legs. She fastened on other things I did not know the purpose of. It was like the exosuits the city-dwellers wore to swim the depths. We were as badly suited to life here as they were to life in the ocean.

~*~

I spent two more days in the tank before I finally convinced them to release me. Mariana would be so very worried…unless she was so angry I'd abandoned her that she didn't care. I deserved anger. She deserved better. I had to find her, apologize, make it up to her somehow. I couldn't bear the thought of losing her.

Yvonne came to my tank with a handful of city-dwellers. They had a chair to wheel me to the nearest escape trunk, and Yvonne explained a complicated procedure of opening and closing hatches in sequence, flooding the chamber to equalize pressure. I didn't pay much attention. All I had to do was float in the water while the chamber filled to the right pressure, then swim away when the outer hatch opened.

Then I could find Mariana.

Yvonne put me in a harness, and the city-dwellers hoisted me out of the tank with cables. My gills cleared the surface and collapsed. I couldn't breathe. I wanted to thrash, to struggle, to fight my way back to the tank. I needed to breathe. I couldn't. I forced myself to hold still. They lowered me into a chair. I couldn't breathe. Yvonne attached a mask over my gills and mouth. My gills fluttered and my panic eased. The tank on my back was crushingly heavy, but at least I was getting oxygen again.

My skin itched in the dry air, and out of the water the pressure was wrong, directional instead of uniform, pushing me down instead of embracing me on all sides. I could barely hold myself upright, even in the chair.

"Are you okay?" Yvonne asked. Her voice sounded muffled, spoken into the water of her breather apparatus before being transmitted into the air. "It's hard the first time. I sometimes have trouble with it even now."

I shook my head, then feebly waved my arm in the direction of the door. My limbs were heavy, my body such a useless weight. I needed to be back in the water. I wouldn't be okay until I had escaped this wretched place.

It was a struggle to speak, but for Mariana I forced myself to say the words. "You should come with me."

Yvonne was not the city-dweller whose photograph Mariana held so dear, but she was the only relative Mariana had left. The old fishwoman walked next to my chair as one of the city-dwellers wheeled me out of the research lab and into a long hallway.

"I can't," Yvonne said. "I'm too old, and I've been in the city too long. Please tell Mariana that I love her. That I am so sorry. City life is hard, but things are not as bad for fishfolk as they used to be—if Mariana can get a work permit, they'll let her into the city, and we could…"

I tuned her out. These were terrible words. Words I couldn't bear to think about. Mariana had no idea what the cities were really like, but she desperately wanted to live in one. And now here was her mother, asking me to give her this message, this invitation.

We reached one of Ocean City's escape trunks, and the city-dwellers removed my breather tank and lowered me into the cool water that filled the bottom of the chamber. It wasn't as bad the second time, the moments without breathing. Awful as it was, a fishperson could get used to it, if they wanted this life badly enough. Mariana could get used to it.

She might decide to leave me for it.

That was the dread in my mind as the escape trunk filled with cold seawater.

~*~

I found Mariana with Ellie and Verve, hunting white crabs as they darted between the tube worms. Mariana turned to hand Ellie a crab she'd caught, and saw me. "Cora? Oh, I can't believe you're really here. Are you okay? You disappeared and I was so worried. How could you just disappear like that?"

She swam to me, part panicked and part relieved and probably part angry, too, because she hated not knowing what had happened and, after all, I had abandoned her. I swept her into my arms. Up close she could see the dark bruises where the sub had hit me, navy blue in the dim light of her fingertips, and she clung to my other side, trying to hold me tight but not wanting to hurt me. Ellie came over, too, and quickly assessed my injuries. She touched me gently on the shoulder. "You two have things to talk about, but I'm glad you're back."

She swam away, pulling Verve along with her.

"I got hit by a sub. They took me to Ocean City for treatment, kept me in a little tank of water inside the dome. They only just released me. I swam straight here as soon as they let me out. I'm sorry I couldn't send word."

"We looked everywhere for you," Mariana said. "No one had seen anything. No one knew anything. I had no idea what happened to you. And you were so angry when you left, I thought maybe you didn't want to be with me anymore."

"I'm so sorry." I ran my fingertips along the side of Mariana's face. "I felt like no matter what I did, I would never be enough. I'll never be a city-dweller."

"No, I'm sorry for driving you away." Mariana leaned her head against my chest. "Are you okay? Does it still hurt?"

"I'll be okay. I passed out when the sub hit me, but it's mostly just bruises. Surface wounds." It was tempting to stop there, to not tell her what I had seen in the city. Who I had seen. She'd forgive me for my drunken outburst, for running away in a panic. We could go back to our life together here in the deep.

I could keep her mother a secret, but it would weigh me down. She and I would be out of sync—like swimming at different depths even when we were together—the lie of omission always on my mind. She would believe that this life was all there was, all there could ever be, but I would know it wasn't true. We would drift apart, or perhaps she would find out about her mother's invitation some other way and be angry. Telling her was better. She would probably still leave me, but at least this way it would be her choosing something that she desperately wanted instead of leaving me for something I'd done wrong.

"I met your mother when I was in the city," I told her. "She's not like the picture—she's a fishperson like you...but she's also a city-dweller. She thought that you could probably get a work permit and live in the city, if you wanted. They have equipment that will let you breathe in the air."

Mariana's eyes flicked upward for a brief moment, her attention drawn toward the cities even though it was impossible to see anything but blackness above us. We were so deep that the only light was what we made ourselves. I could see the longing in her face. Living in the city was her dream.

A million questions came pouring out of her in quick succession, "My mother is a fishperson? Who is in my picture? How can she live in the city? What were they wearing? Did you breathe the air?"

I didn't even know where to start. I loved her, and it felt like she was already gone. "I didn't breathe the air. I was in it for a while, and it burned. There are tanks of water that fishfolk wear, like bringing a little bit of ocean everywhere you go."

"You look so sad," she said, putting her hand on my arm. "Will you really miss the ocean that much?"

"What?"

"Oh." Her face fell. "You're going to stay here. You won't come with me?"

It was an option I hadn't considered, and for a moment it eased my sadness that she wanted me with her. But only for a moment. I couldn't live in the city. In the distance, I could see the fingertip-lights of Ellie and Verve, far enough away to give us privacy, but close enough that we could find them if we needed to. Our friends were here. My life was here. I was a creature of the deep. "No. It was awful up there, Mariana. Everything about the city is wrong, and even with all the equipment they've developed, we'd never really belong there."

"I've always dreamed of this, but I thought you would come with me," Mariana said.

"Your dreams don't match the reality—the cities aren't full of ball gowns and fancy shoes. Your mother is an old fishwoman, not the city-dweller whose picture you carry around."

She got out the picture and studied it for a moment. She brought it to her lips and kissed it, and then she let it go. It drifted into the darkness. "I realized something, when I thought you'd left me. You really are beautiful. Not by city-dweller standards, because you are not a city-dweller. But your body is yours, uniquely you, and I love you. And that makes you more beautiful to me than any city-dwelling stranger."

These were words that I so desperately wanted to hear. Not that I was beautiful by someone else's arbitrary standard, but that I was good enough for her. Beautiful to her. I reached out and took her hand. "Stay here. Stay with me."

"I can't. My mother is up there. If I don't go meet her, I'll always wonder. It will eat at me."

There was nothing I could say to talk her out of this. She was right. This was something that she had to do, something she had to see for herself. All I could do was hope that once she got there, once she really saw what city life was like, she would come back to me, at least to visit if not to stay.

~*~

I held the memory of it in my mind, the moment when we said goodbye. The way our fingertips touched, and touched, and then they didn't anymore. She swam away, leaving only echoes of her voice inside my head and darkness without her brilliant bioluminescent light. Losing someone that close was like losing a sense, or a limb, or the rhythm of my heartbeat.

I picked at the pain of that moment like a scab because I liked pain better than I liked emptiness. Ellie got me transferred to a transport team because she knew that doing the work I'd done with Mariana would break me. Transporting heavy sections of pipe was strenuous enough to wear me out. Otherwise I'd never sleep. Ellie made sure I went to work, made sure I went home. She and Verve hunted crabs for me, killed them for me. The way I used to kill crabs for Mariana.

I oscillated between hope and despair. It had been a week. She'd gotten into Ocean City. Found her mother. Not knowing more than that filled me with dread. I had been miserable in the city, but perhaps she loved it, despite the harshness of the air. Maybe she would be content to live her life there, without me, mingling with city-dwellers and getting to know her mother.

Mindlessly I followed Ellie up into the twilight when our shift was finished. We had made the right choice, both of us. Some things were not meant to be. Sometimes love was not enough. I couldn't ask her to give up her dreams for me, and I wouldn't live in air, not even for her. Our lives had only fit together when she thought she had no other options.

"Cora."

Her voice was the sweetest sound. I turned, and she was there. "Mariana."

"I missed you."

"I missed you, too." I held my voice steady, tried to stay calm. "Are you coming back, or is this only a visit?"

"Neither. Or maybe both? They have research studies that need samples of life near the vents, and studies of living in pressure and darkness." She slid aside the collar of her suit. "I've got all kinds of sensors, and I'll report back to Ocean City every few days."

It was not how I had pictured things. I'd imagined losing her, and I'd tried to squash the hope that I would someday have her back forever. It seemed like such a difficult thing, to bridge both worlds, to have her dream but also stay with me. I couldn't live like that, forever torn between two places. But Mariana had always been better at juggling things—she could even read and swim at the same time. If anyone could find balance in that kind of life, it was Mariana.

"Do you like it, living in the city?" I asked, worried that she would change her mind and disappear into the air, never to return.

"I'm happy to get to know my mother, but it isn't quite what I imagined," she admitted. "Still, someday I will buy us ball gowns, and the fabric will flow so gracefully in the currents, swirling around us as we dance."

"I would love that," I told her. "We will be so beautiful, dancing in the midnight ocean."

"Yes," she said. "We will."

~*~

A Word from Caroline M. Yoachim

I knew as soon as I got the invitation to participate in this anthology that I wanted to write a story that took place (at least partly) below the midnight line—at depths so deep that there is no sunlight from the surface. There are some pretty cool documentaries on creatures that live in the darkest parts of the ocean, and I am fascinated by the ecosystem that surrounds the hydrothermal vents down on the ocean floor.

I often write stories by combining several elements together, kind of like putting together puzzle pieces. I find that picking several unrelated things and combining them can yield interesting results. Something that has been on my mind lately is standards of beauty—how they have changed over time, what they are based on, etc. Mermaids in fiction are often depicted in ways that are not particularly functional for life underwater, so I thought I would play around with the appearance of my underwater humans, and use that as a way to explore what it means to be beautiful.

From that starting point, I searched around for other elements to incorporate into the story. One thing I stumbled onto was a cool band called Aquasonic, that does concerts underwater (with each musician in a separate tank). I listened to several of their songs on YouTube while writing this story, and that was the inspiration for the underwater concert scene. Also for the concert scene I had to figure out how alcohol consumption might work for people who were genetically modified with gills and lived submerged in salt water.

So those are a few of the elements that came together in this story. It was a fun one to write!

About the Author

Caroline M. Yoachim is the author of over sixty published short stories, appearing in **Asimov's, Fantasy & Science Fiction, Analog,** and **Lightspeed,** among other places. Her work has been reprinted in Year's Best anthologies and translated into Chinese, Spanish, and Czech. In 2011, her novelette **Stone Wall Truth** was a Nebula finalist. Caroline's debut short story collection, **Seven Wonders of a Once and Future World & Other Stories** showcases a wide-ranging selection of dark and beautiful stories.

For more about Caroline, visit carolineyoachim.com

~*~

Siren Song of the Mississippi Queen

Hank Garner

~*~

I

WILL STEPPED OFF THE BOAT and stretched his tired muscles. The evening sunset painted the water with an orange glow. He unlocked his truck and pulled his cell phone from the console. Fifteen missed calls. Not a record, but a lot for a Monday.

He scrolled through the missed calls, made a note of the ones he needed to follow up on, and clicked the one at the top of the list. Gabby called no fewer than five times a day, normally, but this must be a special day—she'd called eight times.

Ugh, no way in hell was he going to call her right now. But he could spare a moment to text her.

I'll call in a few. Everything okay?

He dropped the phone into his pocket and cranked the truck, rolling down the windows to allow the stifling Mississippi Gulf Coast heat and humidity to escape while the air conditioner got up to speed. The phone vibrated before he could even put the truck in gear. With a sigh, he retrieved the device and checked the caller ID—as if he didn't know it was his sister.

"Well that didn't take long," he mumbled under his breath.

"Hello, Gabby. How are you?"

"Will! Why didn't you answer earlier?" she spewed.

"I was out on the boat. Same as every day. Working. Is. Everything. Okay?"

He could hear her pacing, bumping into the chair in the dining room like she always did. Her breathing was erratic, though. Something might really be wrong this time.

She sucked in sharply and blurted, "Will, they're talking again."

He fidgeted with the air conditioner vent, willing it to blow colder. "Gabby, honey, have you taken your pills today?"

Eddie James—the new guy with two last names, the butt of every joke—walked by. Will rolled his window up, sending him a glare that dared him to say something if he'd overheard what Will had said.

Eddie rushed past without even a second glance in Will's direction, disappearing into his own vehicle.

"Will, I don't like the pills. They make me feel funny. They make it feel like I have cotton in my head. I don't like it at all."

Will sighed. "I know you don't like them, but you have to take them. It's important."

The phone went quiet for a moment. He pictured her sitting on the stool next to the old rotary phone mounted in the kitchen between the pictures of Jesus and their mother.

"Listen, Gabby, look at the picture of Mama."

"I'm already looking at it."

"Mama would want you to take your medicine. Remember all the times she took you to the doctor and helped you when things got bad?"

"Yes. But I didn't like the pills then and I still don't like them now."

Will rubbed his temples. "I'll be over in a little bit. I just got off the boat and I have to take a shower first. Give me just a little bit and I'll bring you supper. How's that?"

"You're the best brother in the world."

"Well, I don't know about that. Why don't you turn on the TV and watch something until I can get there, okay?"

"Okay. I'm going to try to not listen to the lady until you get here."

"The lady?"

"You know, the lady from the water."

"Right," he sighed. "I'll be right over."

II

Will drove west on Highway 90 from the marina and onto the Biloxi Bay Bridge. Traffic was moving along at a nice clip if not full speed. The boats of tourists were coming in from a day of deep sea fishing and dolphin watching. The larger ferry making the last return trip from Ship Island for the day was overflowing with sunburned and exhausted looking day-excursioners.

The air conditioner was finally blasting cold air and he was thankful for the small things right now, and thankful he wasn't sporting one of those sunburns so prevalent on the boats for hire. He had worked as a commercial fisherman and shrimper long enough that he didn't make rookie mistakes like that. *"Never leave home without your hat and for god's sake cover up before you get burnt,"* still rang in his ears even twenty years after his father drilled it into his head.

Will drove slowly into the old residential neighborhood, watching for the ever-present kids that might dart out on a bicycle at any moment. A couple of streets off of the beach fronted highway and it was a different world from what the tourists would see. The row of old houses had gone through many renovations through the years, mostly out of necessity after one of the notorious gulf hurricanes, his notwithstanding. He parked and hustled inside to get a quick shower and change of clothes.

As he headed out the door, he picked up the bottle of pills he kept on the shelf of the little china cabinet in his dining room. The backup bottle for when Gabby got carried away and dumped her pills. Will had an understanding with the pharmacist since he had become her de facto guardian after their mother passed away.

On his way, he debated what to get for supper. Ralph's was the best dive bar, hole in the wall around, but his hands already smelled like raw shrimp and probably would for days, so he opted for burgers from a drive through instead of seafood.

He arrived at the house he grew up in, now occupied by Gabby alone, to find the curtains drawn and all the lights off. He slipped his key into the lock and turned it, but it only opened about four inches and the chain caught. Crap.

"Gabby, it's Will. Let me in," he called out.

No answer. He leaned closer, trying to see through the crack in the door. It was dark inside except for the soft glow of Wheel of Fortune on the television in the corner. He concentrated to try to make out any sound, but all he got was Pat Sajak.

Will walked along the front of the house to get a peek through the corner of the windows. Nothing. He checked the door at the carport that led to the laundry room, but it had been blocked by boxes of their mother's Harlequin Romances years earlier.

Cursing under his breath, he made his way around to the back of the house. The sliding glass door was slightly ajar. Sliding it all the way open, he called out for his sister again but got no answer. The house was dark and the fading daylight wasn't helping. He switched on the light and let his eyes adjust. No sign of her anywhere.

Despite the cool breeze of the central unit, beads of sweat formed on his brow.

Will walked through the dining room and looked around the corner into the living room. Everything seemed normal. The kitchen was as it should be so he walked down the hall, switching on lights as he went. The bathroom door was open. The contents of the medicine cabinet were scattered all over the floor.

I'M COMING HOME was scrawled on the bathroom mirror in tooth paste. His heart sank.

He pulled his cell from his pocket and dialed 911.

"911, what's your emergency?"

"I need to report a missing person. She's not well and I believe she is in danger."

"Do you have any idea where she might be?"

"Yes, ma'am. She's probably on her way to the gulf."

III

Amy Holland sat on the beach of the barrier island in the Mississippi Sound known as Ship Island. Fort Massachusetts, a relic of the War of 1812—now merely a tourist attraction for over one hundred years—sat behind her as a dark sentry, guarding the lonely strip of land from invaders.

The marine archaeologist was nervous about the upcoming expedition that had so far been fraught with strange coincidences that threatened to derail the project on a weekly basis, or so it seemed. She had lost crew members to accidents and injury: one to a mysterious mosquito borne illness and the latest to a freak car accident. She sat alone, weighing the implications of moving forward and the even greater fallout from calling it quits and packing it in.

Her grandmother had told her the stories that came from the legends of the island city that once sat in the Gulf of Mexico just off the Mississippi coast. The legends referred to a place that the Biloxi, Pascagoula, and the Moctobi tribes called their original homeland. For generations, they would paddle out in their canoes and trade furs and animal skins for jewels and trinkets. More importantly, they maintained their connection with the "original people." According to the stories, the people who lived on this island city had maintained a culture with advanced technology and wisdom concerning every subject known to man, but it was all eventually lost. It was as if they were from another time and place. One day after a horrific storm, the tribal leaders paddled out to the island and couldn't find it. It had simply vanished. All that remained of the civilization were the stories.

Amy had known since she was six years old that she would make it her life's mission to locate this lost city, if it existed at all. She collected stories that had been passed down for generations from the native ancestors and had amassed the largest collection of circumstantial evidence for the location very few people believed had ever been real. Now she sat there on the beach thinking about the next few days and what they might bring. She hoped she would be vindicated, and finally taken seriously. If not, she would need to find a new line of work since she had expended every bit of good will and political clout within her professional community. There was room for a crackpot or two if they could provide results every now and then. So far, she had struck out every time, but at least she was going down swinging.

Her latest benefactor was footing a hefty bill for this outing and she was grateful. But being the money man for a number of late night cable conspiracy shows, if this expedition turned up nothing, her name would no longer attract even the fringe 'researchers.'

Standing up, she dusted off the seat of her pants. She waded out to the boat tethered just off shore and climbed in. Careful to go slowly so as not to create a wake and disturb the beach line, she motored around the island, then headed back toward Biloxi Bay.

IV

Will turned the corner onto Beauvoir Road and saw the flashing blue lights in front of one of the many cookie-cutter ranch style houses. He pulled his truck over and jumped out. Gabby sat on the curb, waving her arms at the officer sitting next to her. The female officer was attempting to console her when Gabby caught sight of her brother.

"Will! What are you doing here?"

Will rushed over and asked the officer, "Is she okay?"

The officer stood up, her face relaxing, and said, "We found her after receiving a call that someone was climbing a fence in their back yard. She was apparently attempting to make her way to the beach by going through yards so that she would go unnoticed. We talked with several people that saw her and it doesn't look like anything was harmed, other than just spooking several home owners."

He looked at her badge. "Officer Delaney, is it? I'm her brother. She is schizophrenic and if she doesn't take her medication properly she has these episodes. I called 911 because I went to check on her and found that she was missing." He pulled the pill bottle from his pocket and handed it to the officer.

"If it's okay, I'll take her home, get her meds in her, and make sure she's safe."

Officer Delaney read the label and handed it back to him. "Nobody here wants to file a complaint. No damage was done, but I need you to make sure this doesn't happen again. She could have been hurt by someone thinking she was a burglar, and I couldn't blame them."

"I completely understand. Thank you." He shook the officer's hand and her face eased into a smile when she saw how concerned Will was for his sister. Officer Delaney backed away and let Will sit down next to his sister.

She spoke into her shoulder microphone as she entered her patrol car and switched off the flashing lights.

Will gave her a wave as the patrol car slowly pulled away. He wrapped an arm around Gabby.

"Gabs, what's going on? I went to the house looking for you and you weren't there. I saw the note on the mirror. What gives?"

Gabby looked up at her older brother and even though he knew she was having a manic moment, he thought her eyes were clearer than he had seen in months. "Will, the lady is talking to me again."

She was holding a little stuffed dolphin plush toy. He gently took it from her hand and held her hand in his. "Oh, Gabby. I'm sorry. You haven't been taking your medicine, have you?"

"Don't be sorry. It's not a bad thing. I don't know why you

can't see. Mama didn't see either. She wants me to come to them. I have to go to them, Will."

Will's heart ached for his sister. *Why did it have to be this way? Why couldn't she just be normal?*

"And I told you, the pills make me feel bad. If they make me feel bad, why should I take them?"

"Gabby, we've been through this before. The voices aren't real. It's just your mind playing tricks on you. Dirty tricks. The medicine will help."

He unscrewed the cap and fished for a pill to give her. Gabby's hand flew up and slapped the bottle away. The light pink pills scattered all along the street.

"The voice is real! The queen says I have to come!"

V

Will opened the door to their little bungalow and guided his sister into the living room and into her favorite chair. He made sure she had the ever-present stuffed dolphin, then walked into the kitchen and emptied his pockets onto the counter and tried to sort out the pills he had managed to recover from the street. He cursed under his breath and made a vow he knew he'd never keep. No matter how frustrated she made him, she was his sister and the only family he had.

He dusted off one of the pills and inspected it under the light. "What do you want to drink?" he called out after taking a glass from the cabinet.

Gabby didn't reply. She was mad at him. Wasn't the first time, and probably wouldn't be the last.

He filled the glass with water from the sink.

"Here you go," Will said, handing her the glass then the pill. She made a dramatic show of swigging the water then popping her medicine into her mouth. She guzzled the rest of the water then opened her mouth like a three-year-old, showing him it was empty. "Satisfied now?" she spat out.

"Thank you, Gabs," he said, taking her glass. He took it to the sink and washed it, then put it away in the drainer.

Will flopped down on the couch and propped his feet on

the coffee table that separated them, picking up the remote control. "You watching this?"

"Nope, watch whatever you want."

He flipped the channels before landing on the station that played reruns of old black and white comedies from the sixties. Andy Griffith was mediating a squabble between a shop owner and a jaywalker in his easy going, down home manner. Will glanced at his sister who had her eyes glued to the TV and barely moved.

"You okay, Gabby?"

"Mmmm Hmmmm," she mumbled, never taking her eyes off of the glowing box.

"Want to talk about it?"

"Nope."

"Have you been feeling bad lately?"

"Said I don't want to talk about it."

He watched her, looking for any sign of what could have set off the latest episode. Normally, she'd be calming down by now. At least enough to speak to him. He decided not to press the issue. If she was settling down and watching TV, he would take that as a good sign. Her meds would kick in soon enough and she'd happily doze off.

After a few minutes, he reached over to the coffee table and picked up the photo album and flipped it open. The pages were yellowing around the edges, but the photos themselves were holding up regardless. The book was always on the table. Will used to come over and help her straighten things up, and he would always put the album on the shelf in the dining room, but no more than ten minutes later Gabby would take the album down and put it right back on the table.

The pictures of his parents with Gabby and him brought back a flood of memories. Most of the images were at the beach, or on the boat that they spent so much time on when they were kids. His dad taught him to be a fisherman, and Will never thought of doing anything but following his father's footsteps. "The salt water seeps into your blood," his father had told him, "and you can't never shake it." He was right.

Their mother loved the water, and the beach by extension. She would walk with Gabby, hand in hand, and tell her the stories that her mother and grandmother told her. The legends of the people who would become the Gulf Coast Native Americans, and how their little island city vanished after a strong storm. The stories of those people and their queen became her stories. Gabby loved the tales, and in her mind, they were as true as anything she had learned in school.

The problems began when Gabby became a teenager and started hearing voices, then she ran away. Time after time they would find her at the beach, sometimes in the water. It was a miracle she hadn't drowned.

The doctors told her mother that the chemical imbalance was making Gabby believe the fairy tales were real. They encouraged her mother to find things to root her in reality instead. So, she stopped telling Gabby the stories and started giving her the medication. She took her to the aquarium and encouraged her to study marine life. Real marine life. During their first visit, their mom gave Gabby the dolphin. The dolphin, patched and sewn together, had not left Gabby's side in the twenty years since. Even as the medicine changed her, the dolphin was a reminder of the things she was not supposed to talk about.

Will couldn't bear the pictures any longer. The slow parade from happiness and joy to the medicated, hollow eyed stare of her late teens broke his heart. He placed it back on the table and looked over to her. Gabby's eyes were closed and her chest rose and fell with the slow pace of her breathing. Will decided to just stay where he was for the night. He plumped up the pillow and stretched out.

VI

Will woke with a crick in his neck and rubbed it as he sat up and tried to get his bearings. It took a minute to realize he was on the couch in his childhood home. The photo album still lay open in front of him, but his sister wasn't in the recliner where she was when he'd fallen asleep. He jumped up and made his way to the bathroom, but she wasn't there, either.

The sliding door was open a few inches, just like when he found it earlier. "Dammit!" She hadn't actually taken the pills. Will cursed himself. He should have known better; it wasn't the first time she'd fooled him.

He found his cell phone and punched in 911 again, explaining that his sister had once more gone missing. The operator told him to try to look for her at her usual haunts while she got a patrol car dispatched. He looked at the kitchen clock when she asked him how long she'd been missing. It was five thirty a.m. and he figured he'd dozed off at around eleven. As far as he knew, she had a six-hour head start. He sprinted for his truck.

He eased down the familiar streets, looking into backyards along the way, but found no sign of her. He made his way to Highway 90 and scanned every stretch of beach he thought she could have gone to. The sun was peeking over the horizon to the east, making thin fingers of gold and orange across the gently cresting waves. He drove west as far as Gulfport, then turned back around before finally parking by the Biloxi Bay.

He flagged down a patrol car and told the officer his story. The office radioed in but there was no sign of Gabby. The officer assured him that they would find her, they always did. Will thanked him and walked down to the beach.

He had walked this beach many times with his mother, the free-spirited wanderer of the family. His father was the pragmatic type—the ocean was business, no matter how enchanting it seemed to others. Will still remembered the stories of the ancient people on the island, the Mississippi Queen and her people, and how his mother lit up when she told them. He loved the stories, but they meant something completely different to his sister.

When the sun had risen enough, he called Frank and let him know he wouldn't be going out on the boat today, family emergency. It wasn't long before two patrol cars joined him and for the entirety of the day, they combed the beach and surrounding areas.

He checked the marinas and tourist beach spots all day, asking if anyone had seen a woman fitting his sister's description. No one had. He walked the pier at a marina on the back side of Biloxi Bay and saw a boat readying to leave. A young woman with an arm load of charts caught his attention.

"Ma'am, I'm sorry to bother you, but have you seen this woman?" He showed her a picture of Gabby on his phone.

"No, sorry. I've been so caught up in getting out that I really haven't paid any attention to anything."

"Are you sure? Would you take one more look?"

"Sure, but I really don't think I've seen her. Who is she?"

"My baby sister," he said scanning the water as he held the phone out for her to look at one more time. "I'm afraid she's done it this time."

Amy looked quizzically at him. "Done what this time?"

"She isn't well. She takes medication for her illness, and when she doesn't take it properly she hears voices. She's not crazy," he explained, "she's just not well. I don't want you to get the wrong idea."

"I can tell you are very protective of her, and I don't think she's crazy. We all have something to deal with. I'm sorry about your sister." She handed him the phone back. "Why don't you give me your number and when I go out, if I see anything I can call you."

"I'd really appreciate that," he said.

She pulled out her phone and typed in the number he gave her. "What's your name?" she asked.

"Will."

"Where there's a Will, there's a way." She grimaced immediately, probably regretting the corny joke.

Will gave her a half smile. "If you see any sign of her, please let me know."

"Of course. I'd better get going. I hope you find her."

"Thanks. Where are you headed to?" he asked.

"Out past Ship Island. I'm an archaeologist and we're looking for a lost island. Nobody's ever seen it, but there are a bunch of old legends. We're going to try to put it to rest once and for all."

The blood drained from Will's face. "My sister believes the legends, too. She thinks the Queen calls to her."

Amy nodded. "The legends are powerful. I'm sorry about your sister. If we see anything, I promise to call you."

Will watched as Amy climbed into the boat and prepared to leave with the rest of her crew. He wondered if the crew would actually find anything out there. He kind of hoped they would so that at least his sister's delusions wouldn't be completely unfounded. He waved as their boat eased out of its slip and motored toward open sea.

When the boat faded out of sight, he walked back to the beach and sat in the sand. The tide was low. The sand dissolved under him as the water washed back out to sea. He called the police dispatch number and asked the lieutenant in charge if there had been any sighting of his sister yet. Nothing so far. He thanked her and hung up. He tossed the phone onto the sand to his side and stared out at the water.

The water had been his life, and literally his livelihood, but remained a mystery. Life began there, in a practical sense. *Maybe the legends were mere metaphor about us crawling out of the water and becoming who we are. Or maybe the mysteries are much bigger than that.*

VII

Six days passed with no sign of Gabby. Will had exhausted every contact, and searched every place he could imagine that she might have remotely thought about. In his heart, he would not believe that she was gone, but his head had already been filled with doubt. The police had stopped calling with updates. "We'll let you know if anything comes up," was the last thing he heard, and that was three days ago. He had to go back to work—life carried on—while praying that some lead about his sister's whereabouts would pop up.

It was the peak of shrimp season and Frank was happy to have him back on board. He spent the day in a mental fog as he scanned the horizon for any sign of his sister. The water was choppy and as the bow of the boat rose and fell, he swore he could hear his sister's voice in the roar and spray. He convinced himself that his mind was playing tricks on him.

As they trolled back to shore that evening, his head ached and he felt like he would be sick to his stomach. He couldn't bear the thought of going to bed one more sleepless night knowing his sister was still missing and that there was absolutely nothing he could do about it.

When Biloxi Bay was in sight, he gathered his belongings, ready to get away from the boat and the mindless chatter of his mates. Before he reached his truck, a voice calling his name caught his attention. He looked up to see a smiling, friendly face.

"Amy."

"Hi Will. I'm sorry to hear about your sister. You're in my prayers. I'm sure she'll be found soon."

Will nodded and gave her a sad smile. "Thanks. I'm holding out hope."

"You should. I believe there's always hope." She smiled.

"So how did your expedition go?" Will said.

"You'll never believe it, but the ground penetrating radar picked up on an anomaly on the fourth day out. We went in the next day and started taking samples, then the following day we sent divers down. I don't know what it will prove, but we've found something. Something really is out there, Will."

Will's eyes widened. "Wow, that's great, Amy. Congratulations. What did you find?"

"Some pottery at first. Not sure what period, but old and oddly preserved. Also, some jewelry, possibly royal. We have experts that are about to check it out. We brought several boxes of samples. My hope is that this evidence is enough to get the community talking, and ultimately to lend credibility to my search so that I can perform a full excavation."

Will chuckled to himself. "My mom told those stories to Gabby and me, and I believed they were just tall tales and legends. It's really amazing that it just might be true."

"Right, or at least there might have been a civilization that these stories were based on," she countered.

"Right. I mean, I don't expect you to find evidence that it was some alien race that seeded life from this advanced civilization in the Gulf of Mexico, but it would be cool if some of it was true."

Amy gave him a quizzical look. "Did you say your sister's name was Gabby?"

"Yeah. Gabby LaCroix."

"That's so odd. Stay here." She ran back to her boat and scurried aboard. Soon, she emerged from below deck with something in her hand.

"We found this mixed in with the first container of samples the divers brought up. It was buried twenty feet below the ocean floor. I have no idea how to explain it being there."

She reached out and handed him a dirty and waterlogged stuffed dolphin. The tag on the tail had Gabby L. written in magic marker.

~*~

The siren song of the Mississippi Queen
Has called a many a soul to the deepest sea
Upon the waves they do sail
To a place beyond this mortal veil
Where the lucky few are chosen by hand
To dance upon the golden strand
The siren song of the Mississippi Queen
Calls to us, her song to heed

~*~

A Word from Hank Garner

I love legends of lost civilizations and the thought that there might be things out there that we just can't explain. When Daniel invited me to tackle Oceans as a topic, I started thinking about ways I could tie the sunken city legends with some of the Native American traditions of the area where I live.

I came up with the character of Gabby after thinking of a relative of mine. He was a great-uncle, and a veteran of WWII. He would hear voices and hated the medication the doctors gave him. As a little kid I would talk to him and I couldn't help but wonder if he knew things I didn't, and if he might be the one that was right all along.

I hope you like this story, and I hope it encourages you to look closer and the ones around us that are "strange". Maybe they know something the rest of us don't.

About the Author

Hank Garner is the author of **Bloom, Mulligan, The Witching Hour, Seventh Son of a Seventh Son, Writer's Block**, and has contributed to several anthologies. He also hosts a weekly podcast called Author Stories where he interviews successful authors each week about writing and the creative process.

Hank's days are filled with interviewing the bestselling authors of today for **The Author Stories Podcast** and writing stories about life. Hank lives in Mississippi with his wife of over twenty years and five children.

Find the podcast at hankgarner.com

~*~

The Hunt for the *Vigilant*

Alex Shvartsman

~*~

AFTER WHAT I'D DONE, the last thing I expected was for them to release me. It's not every day someone reveals to the world that magic is real and then publishes the source code online, allowing anyone with a passing knowledge of Java to program spells and incantations. And sure, I did it to save the world, but a surprisingly large percentage of people found that excuse insufficient.

My face was plastered all over cable news while the talking heads argued whether I was a hero or a traitor, and the traitor faction was winning. Terms like "notorious" and "infamous" were thrown around whenever the media mentioned the name Kyle Palermo. Or so the guards told me. Ever since turning myself in I was kept locked up, though not officially incarcerated, as I awaited a "disciplinary hearing." They were very careful to point out that I hadn't been arrested, even if the locked doors and presence of armed guards told a different tale.

There was no TV, internet, or even newspapers in the not-prison where they kept me. I complained and was given a dog-eared paperback of *Crime and Punishment*. Someone among the guards must've thought themselves clever. Reading Dostoyevsky was better than staring blankly at a gray concrete wall, but only by a small margin.

One day the guards unlocked the door and led me outside. Whatever hearing took place — and I'm certain there were many meetings — the higher-ups made the improbable decision to let me go. I squinted at the sun, which I had not seen in my windowless cell for several weeks.

As this was an unanticipated turn of events, I had no idea what to do next. I wandered the streets of Boston for a few blocks until I saw a pub, which reminded me that I hadn't had any alcohol during my involuntary staycation.

The pub was grungy and dimly lit in a way that reminded me of my cell. But instead of a boring 19th century Russian novel, rows of bottles beckoned me from behind the bar with their colorful labels.

There were a few groups of patrons but plenty of empty stools as it was mid-afternoon. I sat at the bar and ordered scotch on the rocks.

"It's you, innit?"

A tall, broad-shouldered man hovered over me. He stank of sweat and liquor.

"Pardon?"

"You're the guy on TV. The one who leaked cassified information." *Cassified* is how he pronounced it. The big guy studied my profile. "Yeah, yeah," he said. Then he grabbed two fistfuls of my shirt and yanked me upward.

This must've been some sort of record for getting into a bar fight, outside of old Western movies. I didn't even have my drink yet. The bartender stopped what he was doing and watched us, but he wasn't rushing to my aid.

The drunk pulled me toward him until his face was uncomfortably close to mine. I leaned a few inches back and my nose thanked me for it.

"If I had a gun with two bullets and was locked in the room with you, Snowden, and Assange," he told me, "I'd shoot you twice."

I struggled in his grip and tried to come up with a witty response. Or any response. Something about how my actions helped stop the eldritch forces from breaking through the human defenses and devastating our world. But the part of my brain responsible for generating snarky comebacks was refusing to kick in under the circumstances.

"Unhand him, you inebriated cretin," someone spoke in an accented voice from behind me. He sounded like a BBC news anchor.

My assailant and I both turned to discover a thin man with long, straw-blond hair. He was dressed in tan pants, plain cotton shirt unbuttoned by several more buttons than his scrawny middle-aged frame could reasonably justify, and flip flops. Another man, who wore a tailored suit and was nearly twice as large as the Brit in both height and shoulder width, stood behind him.

"Mind your business, Fabio," said the drunk. "Or I'll punch you in your limey teeth."

The Brit assumed a boxing stance, each of his fists maybe half the size of the drunk's. "If it's a fight you want, you dim-witted Neanderthal, jolly well then," he said. "I'll have you know I was quite the pugilist in my day."

The drunk spent several seconds trying to decide which of us presented a more appealing target. "We ain't done," he said as he shoved me aside and stepped toward the Brit.

Without preamble, the drunk swung at the smaller man's head. The Brit ducked, stepped forward, and jabbed twice at the drunk's chin. Over the next several seconds the Brit dodged around his larger opponent and landed a flurry of punches, but the drunk seemed to shrug them off with the practiced indifference of a veteran bar brawler.

The Brit stepped back and eyed his opponent. "We haven't the time for this," he murmured. Then, louder, he said, "Hit him, Gerald."

The man in the suit moved with the fluid speed of a Hollywood action star. Before the drunk could react, he closed the distance between them, made a fist, and punched him in the temple. The drunk slid onto the floor and was still. Gerald retreated to the spot he had originally occupied, his calm face displaying no emotion.

The Brit examined his vanquished opponent with a satisfied smirk, as though it was he and not his bodyguard who had just defeated this man. He straightened his shirt and rubbed his bruised knuckles. Then he turned toward me. "Mr. Palermo, permit me to introduce myself. I'm Sir Bertram Gresley of Drakelow, and I wish to present you with a mutually beneficial opportunity." The drunk moaned on the floor. "Shall we adjourn to discuss it in friendlier climes?"

~*~

The limo crawled down congested Boston streets. Sir Gresley poured amber liquid from a decanter into two glasses and offered one to me. "Grand Marnier Cuvee 1880. This is better than any swill they may have served at that pub."

I accepted the glass and took a sip. The cognac was heavenly. We enjoyed our spirits in silence for a few moments while my nerves calmed. I had so many questions. I started with something simple. "How did you find me?"

"We were waiting at the front entrance alongside the paparazzi and the gawkers," he said. "It was a veritable hullabaloo. When you didn't emerge at the designated time, I deduced that they must've sent you out the back door."

"There were reporters waiting for me?"

He nodded. "Quite so. You're somewhat of a celebrity at the moment, having captured the imaginations and the attention of the masses. Like Kim Kardashian or O. J. Simpson."

I frowned deeply as I didn't consider these to be the most flattering comparisons.

He went on. "When we discovered the alternate point of egress, I labored to put myself in your shoes. Where would a man go to celebrate his newfound freedom? So I had Gerald google the nearest watering hole."

I glanced at the bodyguard, who remained impassive at the mention of his name. He hadn't spoken a word in the bar, nor when he climbed into the back of the limo with us.

"Okay," I said. "So you found me. What now?"

Gresley poured himself more cognac. "I'd like to offer you a job."

I gaped at him. I figured my track record of whistleblowing at my last two jobs made me unemployable. Then again, I hadn't been officially laid off by the Coffee Corps. "I have a job," I said.

"Your star is not exactly at its zenith with the U.S. government or any of its secret branches, including the Coffee Corps," said Gresley. "Furthermore, there's an excellent chance the Corps will not exist as such for much longer. Ever since your revelation it's been chaos, with the media serving up details of conspiracies and horrors suppressed by the world governments for decades." He took another sip. "There have been coups and civil unrest all over the world. Many of your congressmen and senators have either resigned or made such clowns of themselves on the telly, there's practically no chance they'll stand for re-election. They learned quite quickly that the survival strategy is to disavow all knowledge of the arcane and act indignant. So they're pulling funding and rolling the functions of outfits like the Coffee Corps into the official government bureaucracy." He saluted me with the glass. "So you see, even if you remain on the Coffee Corps payroll, you might soon be reporting to some paper pushing wanker at the U.S. Department of Obfuscation."

"If people are now aware of the threats we're facing, wouldn't they want us to have the resources and support we need to stop them?"

"You'd think that," said Gresley. "In reality, the sort of blokes who go into politics will always put their careers ahead of the public good. That's the bad news. The good news is, the private sector is ramping up the push to merge magic and technology, with its top visionaries—yours truly included—

leading the way. Jeff Bezos is working on adapting the Java Espresso code you released to run the Amazon cloud servers more efficiently. Elon Musk is investigating the means of magically generating clean energy. Steve Jobs is incorporating personal wards into the iPhone OS system. Sergey Brin—"

"Wait, isn't Steve Jobs dead?"

"That's what Big Silicon Valley wants you to think."

As much as I wanted to follow this line of inquiry, I had to focus on what was important. "Okay," I said. "So what's your angle? And how do you fit in with such august company? No offense, but I've never heard of you before."

"Nor should you have. While some of my peers focus on building brands, I rake in the pounds by keeping things simple." Gresley smiled at my confusion. "I make generic products," he said. "Vast factories around the world churning out off-brand everything, from charging cables to headache medicine. Someone else can be the innovator, sinking billions into R&D or into TV commercials for their brand. My people can reverse engineer whatever it is for pence on the pound and sell it to the consumer a few months later for half the price." He drew himself taller. "Sir Bertram Gresley, the giant of generic wares."

Sounded more like the king of crap to me. Like most folks, I've purchased enough cheap generic widgets online to know that they're often plagued by shoddy workmanship and subpar parts.

"Enchanted items are the next big trend in consumer goods," said Gresley. "Who wouldn't spend a few dollars on a cross that can truly bless their home, or on a warding charm that really wards? Your understanding of both magic and technology makes you uniquely qualified to oversee the establishment of mass production for such trinkets."

I pictured a plethora of shoddy magical artifacts flooding Amazon. "That's not really what I see myself doing with my life," I said.

"It's not glamorous, but we'll both make a fortune. Spend a couple of years to get this going and you'll be wealthy enough to pursue whatever hobbies you fancy."

It wasn't the hobbies and leisure that occupied my mind. If what Gresley told me was true, I was seriously concerned about the Coffee Corps and about humanity losing its struggle against the Deep Ones, the Outer Ones, and any number of other unearthly factions; not through weakness, but through apathy and poor choices. I told him so.

"The best way you can help humanity right now is by working with someone like me." He flashed me a smile. "Preferably me." He rested his palm on my shoulder. "Look here old chap, why don't you sign on for a single mission? See how we do things, travel in style, and try on all the gadgets, eh? It'll take under a week. I'll pay you well for your time and if you don't want to join the winning team after all that, we'll part as friends. What say you?"

I thought about it. He was making a lot of sense. I'd need funds regardless of what I decided to do next, and signing on for a few days with Gresley would give me something to do while I caught up on the world news and hopefully keep me away from both reporters and 'fans' like the drunk I encountered at the bar.

"Deal," I said.

"Splendid." Gresley tapped on the divider and privacy glass slid away to reveal the driver. "Take us to the airport," ordered Gresley.

"Where are we headed?" I asked.

A twinkle in his eye, Lord Gresley answered the question with a question. "Fancy a tropical holiday?"

~*~

A private jet flew Gresley, Gerald, and me to the South Pacific. Traveling with a billionaire sure beat stewing in coach; his staff plied us with good food and even better booze, there were private cabins with soft beds and hot showers, and best of all, there was access to the internet.

I excused myself as soon as it was polite to do so and logged onto the web. Everything I read confirmed Gresley's summary of events. If anything, things were worse than he said, and getting worse yet.

The world was in chaos and shock, its population looking for ways to cope with their new reality and taking out their frustrations on the politicians who dared hide the truth from them for so long. It was open season on the entrenched with presidents being impeached, dictators overthrown, and congressmen resigning faster than a reporter could say "sex tape." Every day special elections and no confidence votes were being called as constituents couldn't wait to get rid of their incumbents in misguided hope that the next batch of bureaucrats to occupy those seats would be any better.

Churches and various organized religions experienced an unprecedented renaissance. Existence of magic was proof enough for most people to rediscover some sort of faith, even as a smaller number abandoned their religions, angry over their spiritual leaders participating in the conspiracy of silence.

Elected crooks around the world were in full survival mode and there wasn't anything they wouldn't do to try and remain in power. They feigned outrage in front of the cameras, claiming they too were kept in the dark about magic and always blaming the next guy. They practically trampled over each other to propose bills and vote to cut funding, disband, or reassign any and all clandestine programs that dealt with the supernatural. None cared that their actions might allow the Outer Ones to breach our defenses, or cause a zombie apocalypse, so long as some junior senator or MP got to keep their office for a couple more years.

When I shared my thoughts with Gresley, he shrugged. "Whoever said politicians are just like diapers and must be changed often and for the same reason didn't take into consideration that, unlike diapers, politicians are supremely good at resisting change."

I pressed him for the details of our mission but he smiled cryptically and demurred. "All in good time," he said. "Enjoy a hot meal and a good night's rest." After weeks of eating prison food, it was difficult to disagree.

~*~

Our plane landed in Totegegie, which is a part of the Gambier Islands in French Polynesia. The runway was barely long enough for a jet our size and I was quietly thankful to realize this only after having disembarked. A blast of humid heat assaulted me as soon as the plane doors opened. The strip took up more than half of the length of the island and its width was barely greater than that of a two-lane highway. The airport was the only building on this patch of asphalt and sand. A ferry connected it to a village on a nearby island that was large enough for a traveler to actually stretch their legs.

When our small group boarded the ferry, it didn't sail toward the landmass. Instead, it headed out into the open ocean. By the time Totegegie was barely a dot on the horizon, the water ahead of us swelled. Something large was rising from beneath the waves.

I looked to Gresley who appeared unconcerned. He was seemingly amused at my confusion.

A submarine surfaced.

"Woah," I said as I watched the metal behemoth rise. "That's huge."

"It's actually rather humble as Russian military submarines go," said Gresley, his voice oozing smug satisfaction. "Kilo class, seventy meters long."

I stared at the vessel agape as the port or door or whatever the submarine people called the entrance at the top of the ship opened. The sailors extended a wooden plank to connect the two vessels, and Gerald handed the ferry captain a thick roll of bills.

Inside the submarine felt small and claustrophobic despite my first impressions. We made our way down narrow halls, with the crew opening and closing airtight doors for us. Cyrillic characters marked the entrances and some of the walls, and we passed several spots where hammer and sickle logos were painted onto the walls.

"Bought it on the cheap in the early nineties, when the Soviet Union was collapsing," said Gresley. "Times of uncertainty and change often result in great business opportunities."

"So you own a nuclear submarine," I said. "Are you sure you aren't a Bond villain?"

"It's diesel-electric, not nuclear," said Gresley.

We made it to the bridge, or whatever one might call a command center on a submarine. It had loads of sensors and some rudimentary displays that made me think of *Tron*, but also modern computers retrofitted and wired into the electronics inside the walls. According to what I could see on the monitors, the submarine submerged as soon as we took our seats. The submarine's course overlaid the map.

"Don't you think it's time you filled me in on this mission?" I asked. "I know we're headed toward R'lyeh. What I don't know is, why?"

"There are certain areas on the planet where the natural wards are at their weakest and the walls between dimensions are thin," said Gresley. "These are the prime gateways through which the eldritch creatures enter our realm. These are the places people such as yourself are called upon to guard. The best methodology is always the same—a patchwork of shrines and pentagrams and stone circles that focus Earth magic, worn like the padlocks upon the dilapidated chain gates.

"In New England, it's relatively simple to hide the pentagrams underneath a network of coffee shops. In the Bermuda triangle, the logistics are a bit more involved but there are enough islands in the area where such installations can be placed, away from the prying gazes of tourists."

I knew all this, but I let him talk, hoping his lecture might provide an insight into the man himself.

"Our weakest point is here, in the Pacific, hundreds of miles away from land. No people to chant the mantras, nowhere to place the wards. This is where the Deep Ones gained a foothold into our world, where they've been hiding for centuries, hatching schemes and spreading their influence and their madness.

"Even if they weren't well equipped to handle the threat, the ancient Pacific Islanders did everything they could to combat it. Polynesian canoes braved the enormous distances, navigating by the stars, and ferried Maori sorcerers and Samoan shamans to the troubled waters above the area that became known as R'lyeh.

"They built rafts upon which they placed totems and shrines. Magic practitioners from a hundred human cultures worked together to keep our eldritch enemy at bay. But these rafts were fragile things, susceptible to attack from below as much as the natural storms. Time and again, the people of the Pacific would rebuild, incorporating the knowledge of both seafaring and magic they gained from the travelers from the Occident as well as the early European explorers to visit the area. This loose confederation of warriors, sailors, and sorcerers become known as the Kaitiaki, a Maori word for 'guardian.'

"By the early 1800s, the Kaitiaki fleet began using submarines, wondrous machines that melded magic and science. They were durable and could ride out the worst of the storms underneath the waves, and they were maneuverable and stealthy to avoid being destroyed by the Deep Ones."

I nodded as though all of this was old news to me. I didn't know about the Kaitiaki, though it was reasonable to suspect some organizations similar to the Coffee Corps guarded the Bermuda triangle and the South Pacific against eldritch incursions. There were many things I hadn't had time or occasion to learn during my brief stint at the Coffee Corps. If Gresley and his ilk thought me an expert on all matters supernatural rather than just a competent programmer, it wasn't within my best interest to correct them.

"Let me guess," I said, "whatever the source of their current funding and support, they're experiencing upheaval like the rest of the world?"

"Precisely that," said Gresley. "Whatever preternatural threats may exist, humanity remains its own worst enemy."

"What do you propose to do about it? Are you hoping to take charge of the Kaitiaki? To provide them with their funding? To buy yourself a discount submarine as their fleet collapses, like you did with the Soviets?"

"The Kaitiaki has been fighting the Deep Ones for longer than any other humans on Earth. Their magic is wild and different, a medley of so many different rites and incantations that they built upon for millennia. A magic they keep secret even from their allies." Gresley looked up from his own screen and his eyes were alight with greed. "I want to know everything they know, and, thanks to you, I have that opportunity."

"Thanks to *me*? How's that?"

"There are lads out there who consider what you've done an act of heroism," said Gresley. "An act some of them have been persuaded to replicate."

"They want to release their magic to the world?"

"They're willing to share it with you, my famous friend," said Gresley. "To utilize at your discretion in battling the Deep Ones. They feel the Kaitiaki moratorium on sharing such data with their allies is selfish and dangerous to the prospects of the human race, you see."

"So these dissidents decided to seek me out?"

Gresley steepled his fingers. "They rebuffed my initial overtures, but I managed to sway them by promising you were going to be onboard for this. Figuratively and literally."

Thoughts swirled in my mind as I tried to sort out how I felt about this. I realized Gresley was an opportunist and already had the impression there was a streak of a con artist to him. Was he really what he appeared to be—a budget knockoff of Richard Branson—or were there hidden depths to the man? Why did he pursue this magic knowledge instead of waiting for someone else to develop mass-produced magical artifacts and then replicating those designs like he did with everything else? And did he initially lie to whoever he was negotiating with about my involvement, or did he know I'd be released in time for him to execute his plan? Did he have a hand in my abrupt release, and, if so, how much influence and power did he wield?

Trapped in a small confined space with Gresley's loyalists deep under the Pacific, I wasn't in the best position to challenge him on any of this, but I didn't regret coming along because remaining a part of his plan put me in the position to uncover some answers.

"Well then," I said, "let's go learn their secrets."

~*~

As our submarine sailed to the rendezvous point, I prepared for the hand-off. I was surprised to find that, even deep underwater, we had working internet.

"How's this possible?" I asked Gresley. "Water dissipates radio waves. A phone is supposed to lose its cellular connection even a few inches under water."

Gresley lounged in his chair, his face stuck in his phone. "Magic," he said. " Indubitably," he added, noting my surprise. "We use magic to keep the high frequency radio waves focused and protect them from being broken apart by saltwater. Thanks to this melding of the technological and the arcane, our satellite reception at the tail end of the Pacific is as good as if we were docked in the port of London." He glanced up at me. "This is precisely the sort of commercial applications we'll be racing to bring to market."

I nodded and proceeded to work. Thanks to the internet connection, I was able to log in to my virtual terminal and avail myself of various routines coded in Java Espresso. It kept me busy until Gerald cleared his throat and pointed at one of the displays. This was as close to speech as I'd heard from him to date.

"Ah," Gresley said. "I present to you the *Vigilant*."

On the screen, I saw what could only be a Kaitiaki vessel.

"If you only knew all the efforts it took to separate this impressive specimen from its pack and get it temporarily placed in this spot," Gresley said proudly. "I say, it would have made quite a Tom Clancy novel. 'The Hunt for the *Vigilant*' has quite a ring to it."

I didn't reply, instead studying the *Vigilant* as it grew larger on the view screen. It looked more like a UFO than a traditional submarine. It was a floating hemisphere with a base over one hundred meters in diameter. The base disc was about five meters thick and contained dozens of evenly-spaced openings through which rotors were visible. A much larger turbine was attached at the bottom of the disc. Its rotor rotated steadily as it held the vessel afloat.

Atop the disc rested an opaque, geometrically perfect hemisphere which appeared to be made of some sort of energy rather than metal. There were no portholes or airlocks; presumably they simply dropped the forcefield whenever the disc rose to the surface.

I couldn't see inside the ship, but I knew I'd find a pentagram or some local arcane equivalent at the center of the disc, possibly enhanced by the glyphs and incantations from dozens of cultures etched onto the disc's surface. Similar setup to what we used in New England. I imagined dozens of these majestic vessels floating over the R'lyeh region of the Pacific, the Kaitiaki fleet holding its silent centuries-old vigil to prevent the Deep Ones from spreading across our world. And here we were, preparing to steal their secrets like burglars in the night.

"The Kaitiaki ships don't have the sort of communications capability we do," said Gresley. "We have to get within a kilometer and use a magically-enhanced version of Bluetooth to reach our contact inside."

I eyed the hemisphere wearily. "Won't they see us coming?"

"Our friend is running interference on their equipment," said Gresley. "We should be okay unless one of their crew feels a sudden urge to look out the window."

I squinted at him.

"The sphere is opaque on the outside but transparent from the inside," explained Gresley.

Before I could respond, a series of beeps emanated from Gresley's console. "I do believe there's our friend now," he said as he clicked Accept on the video call.

"Hello?" said the male voice. "You're here!"

"Of course we are, Jeremy. As promised," said Gresley. "There's someone I'd like you to meet." He added me to the video conference call.

The feed appeared on my screen. I saw a bookish young

man who looked barely out of his teens staring nervously at his webcam. His hair was cut short and slicked back. A hint of a mustache resided on his lip. His eyes grew wide as he took in the new image that popped up on his own screen.

"Mr. Palermo! It's an honor to meet you, sir. What you did…" the kid stammered a bit. "It's an inspiration to us all!" He spoke with an Australian accent.

"Hello, Jeremy," I said. "It's nice to meet you as well."

"The Americans, they should've given you a medal instead of a court-martial," said Jeremy. "You're a hero, and I'm very glad to see that you're safe."

It wasn't a court-martial and I didn't feel especially safe, but it didn't seem like a good time to say so. I smiled instead. "Thank you."

"The information, if you please?" asked Gresley. He looked like a cat watching his human refill his bowl, barely restraining himself from lunging at the food.

"Of course," said Jeremy. "I'll initiate the transfer now." He typed some commands on his keyboard and a file transfer window opened. It looked like a huge amount of data.

"I'm certain you'll put the knowledge to good use protecting our planet, Mr. Palermo," he said. "You're the only one my friends and I would trust with this."

I nodded at him and struggled to keep the smile plastered on my face. What would young Jeremy say if he knew the data he was transferring was destined to further enrich a peculiar billionaire? Kid, never meet your heroes. They're bound to disappoint you.

"We've been thinking," Jeremy said. "The information I'm sending is useful, but so much of our magic is tied into the ship itself. I think we can do better, for the sake of the human race." He straightened in his chair. "My friends are going to depose the captain and take over the *Vigilant*."

"Wait, what?" I said. "That sounds dangerous…How many of the crew are with you?" Out of the corner of my eye I saw Gresley practically salivating at the idea of adding a Kaitiaki vessel to his submarine collection.

"There are five of us," said Jeremy. "It's enough, though. My friends are going to take over the bridge and lock themselves in before the others know what's happening. I've disabled communications to the rest of the fleet, and the crew won't be able to do anything about it until we surface at the time and place of our choosing." He beamed a proud smile at me.

"Have you thought this through?" I asked. "This was supposed to be a quiet, stealthy mission. We aren't prepared for this and I'm not sure this is such a great—"

Gresley cut me off. "I can get a ship with reinforcements to meet you within a day. Perhaps sooner."

"It has already begun," said Jeremy. "I gave the signal as soon as we established communications with your sub."

He was so eager, so proud. Is this what the young Russian Bolsheviks looked like as they stormed the Winter Palace in 1917, or the Iranian youth deposing the Shah in 1979? History teaches that revolution—or mutiny—often doesn't produce the hoped-for results, but that's never stopped the next generation of rebels from trying.

"It's happening now," said Jeremy. He patched in another screen, providing us with the live feed of the *Vigilant*'s bridge.

Four men in their twenties and thirties entered the bridge. They moved like a wolf pack, carrying long knives. As the bridge crew turned toward the commotion, one of them hit the nearest officer on the back of the head with the hilt of his knife. The man slumped in his chair.

Five officers stood on a bridge the size of an average living room. The captain shouted orders we couldn't hear—the bridge feed offered no sound—and the remaining officers drew knives similar to what the mutineers were holding. It seemed either there were no projectile weapons on the *Vigilant* or no one dared use them on the bridge.

It was four against four as the captain and his staff—older men and a woman in her forties—engaged their young opponents. It was a brutal close-quarters fight, blades clashing and punches being thrown. Another officer fell as his assailant's knife found its way past his guard and into his side under the ribs. The woman dodged the blade and jabbed her attacker in the solar plexus. As he doubled over, she sliced her blade across his throat.

It was the most brutal fight I'd ever witnessed, and I'd seen battle sorcerers take on shoggoths.

The captain, a portly bearded man a head taller than anyone else in the room, rushed the mutineers without a weapon, but his oversized fists proved as deadly as their blades. He punched an adversary, shoved at another, and when one managed to jab a knife at his belly, the blade glanced off without ever touching the man's uniform. What looked like a personal forceshield glimmered briefly where the tip of the blade failed to connect.

The fight was over in well under a minute, with two mutineers dead and two others moaning on the ground. The officer who suffered a knife wound was alive and ministered to by one of his peers who suffered a shallow cut, as did the woman. The captain appeared unharmed. I wondered if the mutineers knew about his personal forceshield or were foolhardy enough to attempt their rebellion despite it.

"Oh, God," Jeremy whispered. Faced with the demise of his co-conspirators, he grew pale. "You should go," he told us. "It won't be long until they discover you." Alarms blared on the *Vigilant*, clearly audible through Jeremy's microphone.

"We must complete the transfer," said Gresley.

I glanced at the transfer bar. It hovered at around twenty percent.

"They don't know of your involvement, Jeremy," I said. "Leave the transfer running and go to your duties. Perhaps you can avoid being discovered."

"They'll know," he said grimly. "They'll make Trevor and Cixin talk. They have methods that can't be countered. Best I can do is keep the door locked to make sure you get the data."

Jeremy looked to me for approval like an eager puppy. I felt horrible; I may not have pushed him to revealing those secrets and to mutiny—though my temporary employer likely had—

but he did those things foolishly following my example. And there was nothing I could do to help him, except to offer moral support.

"You're doing the right thing," I lied. "You're a hero, too."

A smile spread on his face but was quickly gone as there was banging and shouting on the other side of the locked door.

The transfer bar approached thirty percent.

"They seem preoccupied," said Gresley. "We'll be gone before they realize we—"

An explosion shook the submarine. The old Russian vessel groaned and lurched, shaking our seats as though we were the bridge crew of the starship *Enterprise* under attack by the Klingons.

"They're firing energy weapons at us, sir," called out a woman from among Gresley's crew. "A single direct blast didn't penetrate the hull, but I'm not sure how many more it'll take to sink us."

"Get us out of here," said Gresley. His voice remained steady but he was tense as a snake preparing to lunge. "Jolly good thing they're only equipped with weapons meant to combat the eldritch threats or we'd be up to our necks in the old effluent."

The crew worked feverishly to turn the submarine around and speed away from the hemisphere. The *Vigilant* gave pursuit. It fired energy beams from some of the ports alongside the circumference of the disc. It appeared not all of them were meant for navigation after all.

"Anything you can do to throw a spanner in their works, lad?" Gresley asked Jeremy.

"I can't control the weapons systems from here," said Jeremy. He typed feverishly. "I'm sending you some wards that can partially dampen the beams."

Lines of code scrolled on my screen. At first glance, it wasn't too dissimilar to the Java Espresso programming language we used to fuse science and magic.

"Can you implement this, Kyle?" asked Gresley.

"Maybe. I need time." I tried to shut everything out and

focus on the code.

The submarine shook violently as the *Vigilant* continued to pommel it with energy blasts.

"We won't last much longer, sir," said one of the crewmen.

"Dive deeper," ordered Gresley. "Toward R'lyeh. Perhaps they'll be reluctant to follow."

"Sir?" Out of the corner of my eye I saw the hesitant look on the face of the woman who spoke earlier.

"Yes, it's where the Deep Ones live," said Gresley irritably. "It's possible death there or certain death here."

The submarine dove deeper. The *Vigilant* followed, but the dive earned us a temporary reprieve as the angle was too steep for their energy weapons.

"Don't position yourself directly underneath the *Vigilant*," cautioned Jeremy. "We have depth charges."

As if to underscore his point, the *Vigilant* dropped what looked like an upside-down air balloon, the airbag portion of it shimmering with magical energy. The submarine sped away from the object at top speed as it continued to descend. When the balloon reached our depth it exploded, the resulting wave tossing our vessel and spinning it like a plastic toy.

I hung on to the panel that held my display and keyboard with both hands, struggling not to throw up.

The sturdy old submarine righted itself and the chase continued. Something flashed at the corner of my screen and I looked away from the code to realize the data transfer was complete. There was pounding on Jeremy's door, which was bending inward as the crew of the *Vigilant* used some sort of a battering ram.

"It's done," he said as he continued to type. "I'm transferring remote control of my console to you. Perhaps you can find a way to use it to your advantage before they figure out we're communicating. Good luck!"

Before I could respond, he turned his monitor off. The webcam and his computer remained on, and we watched as he turned toward the door. Several more hits with the battering ram and the door burst open, hanging off the metal frame on a single hinge.

Several of the crew armed with the same curved knives entered the room. Jeremy raised his hands.

"I surrender," he said. "In time, you'll come to understand that I did what I did for the sake of humanity."

An officer stepped up to Jeremy. "Traitor" he hissed, the hate in his voice causing the younger man to take a small step back. Then the officer raised his knife and plunged it deep into Jeremy's heart.

~*~

Tears streaked down my cheeks as I continued to adapt the Kaitiaki code. The men who broke into Jeremy's room trashed his laptop by breaking it in half and crushing the circuitry with their boots, but it was connected to the ship's network and the connection Jeremy had opened remained active.

I could do nothing to help him and I hated being forced to watch as he threw his life away for a dubious reason. But I could still make his sacrifice count for something, to use the information and access he gave me to save our ship.

The *Vigilant* continued its single-minded pursuit. They were taking a risk approaching R'lyeh, as were we, but the risk hadn't deterred them. It was a game of cat and mouse, the two vessels jockeying for position with the larger vessel opening fire any time they found themselves at an advantageous angle. Our crew did their best to buy me time, and I wasn't going to disappoint them.

"There!" I shouted. "Our own forceshield coming online." I activated the adapted Kaitiaki code and it coated the submarine in a protective layer made of magic. To the outside observer, it would now look like it was covered in the same opaque-from-the-outside material as the *Vigilant*.

"Huzzah!" said Gresley. "Well played!"

The *Vigilant* lined up for another shot. They fired and the submarine shuddered. It wasn't nearly as bad as the previous hits, but it wasn't a love tap, either.

"They can still get us," said a crewman. "It'll just take them longer."

"Keep evading their fire," I said. "I'll dig deeper."

I worked, trying to make sense of the petabytes of data Jeremy transferred. I was certain there were things there we could use, if only I had enough time to make sense of it all. I'm not sure how much time passed. It felt like hours, but it couldn't have been more than ten minutes by the time I looked up from the screen. "I have a crazy idea. Head closer to R'lyeh."

Despite the obvious danger, the *Vigilant* did not disengage. We were deep near the ocean floor of the Pacific, as close to R'lyeh as any human had ever been, as far as I knew. I could see it on the screen below: it wasn't a city, not really. There were…things down there. Structures of non-Euclidean geometry that weren't buildings or roads, or anything a sane human mind could hope to understand.

The Kaitiaki fleet bravely stood between the Deep Ones who inhabited this realm and the rest of humanity. It was too bad they saw us as their enemy. When it came down to it, it was going to be them or us, and I was going to do everything I could to make sure it would be us. Besides, they murdered Jeremy.

"Here goes nothing," I said and I activated the scripts I'd been working on, sending commands to the computers of the *Vigilant* through the back door Jeremy left open for me. "Be ready to get us out of here, fast," I told the crew.

"When?" asked the woman.

"You'll know it."

For another minute or so, nothing changed. We kept limping away from the *Vigilant* as it steadily deteriorated our forceshield and hull with its energy weapons. It was perhaps the longest minute of my life.

Then something stirred below.

A writhing mass of appendages that looked more like eels than tentacles shot up from below the *Vigilant*. Each was nearly half as thick as our submarine. They coiled themselves around the hemisphere of the Kaitiaki vessel, and they pulled.

"Rise!" I shouted, but the crew didn't need my prompt.

They were already working at top speed to put as much distance as they could between ourselves and the horror unfolding below.

The *Vigilant* struggled in the grip of the Deep One's arms. It fired its energy beams at them and released more balloon-like depth charges. I could see the arms strain against the turbines of the vessel, like a child trying to keep an inflatable float submerged under water.

It seemed the *Vigilant* was going to escape but more arms shot out from the depths entangling the ship and pulling it slowly, inexorably, toward the ocean floor. We were almost out of visual range when the forceshield of the Vigilant cracked like an eggshell and dissipated around the eel-like arms of the monster. Debris exploded outward from the ship and rained on the alien structures below. Given the depth and pressure, I was certain the deaths of the crew would have been instantaneous—a small mercy, considering.

With the shield gone, the slithering arms wrapped around the disc, twisting and pulling apart the metal segments. It reminded me of a video I once watched of a fridge being crushed by an industrial shredder. By the time they dragged what was left of the *Vigilant* to the bottom of the ocean, only bits of the outer metal shell were still intact.

"That was...fortuitous," said Gresley.

"It wasn't luck," I said. "The Kaitiaki ships use magic to hide themselves from the Deep Ones. I figured out a way to reverse the spell, turning it into a beacon instead, calling out to the things that inhabit R'lyeh."

I felt horrible. I just helped a terrible alien creature destroy a ship full of people who dedicated their lives to protecting the rest of us from the very fate I condemned them to. But I had no choice. It was us or them.

I kept telling myself that.

"Ha!" spoke a booming voice. "An enemy of my enemy is my friend. I like it."

I turned to discover the source of the amused voice. It was Gerald. The first words I ever heard him speak, and they didn't exactly endear him to me. Nor did I think highly of his master. It was Gresley's machinations and greed that resulted in the loss of all those lives.

But it wasn't time to confront them yet. The mood on our bridge was significantly improved but we still had to escape both the Deep Ones and detection by other Kaitiaki vessels. We weren't out of the woods, and I had more work to do.

~*~

Two hours later, our wounded submarine floated on the sunbathed surface of the Pacific, well away from the waters guarded by the Kaitiaki. We waited for the ship to tow away the sub and to take us to the nearest airport.

Gresley walked over and clapped me on the shoulder. "You've done well, lad. I knew I was right to approach you! I can't wait to delve into the secrets we've learned, and to see what else we can accomplish together."

"No," I said.

"Beg pardon?"

"No, I won't be working for you."

"It's a pity," said Gresley. "I'll have to find someone else who's interested in becoming immensely rich to head the new enterprise, then. I will, of course, pay you handsomely for your efforts today."

"Before you offer that, you should know that I will not be releasing the Kaitiaki files to you," I said.

Gresley's face sobered. "Say what?"

"I've transferred them to a secure account in the cloud and deleted them off local drives," I said. "I'm the only one who can access the files."

"But...You're reneging on our deal!"

I waved him off. "You tricked Jeremy into providing these files to me under false pretenses, which ultimately cost the lives of his entire crew. Least I can do is honor his intentions and ensure the Kaitiaki secrets are used to combat the eldritch incursions rather than sold piecemeal for your personal enrichment."

Gresley sneered at me. "And how will you do that? The

Coffee Corps is in disarray, the world is in upheaval. You need me!"

"So I do," I said. "I intend to reform the Coffee Corps as an independent group, not beholden to any government or corporation. And I need you to finance it."

Gresley laughed. "Why in the world would I do that?"

"Because when I go over the Kaitiaki data, I will find bits of it that are safe enough and give them to you so you can make your profits. And I'm sure I will come across other information in the future that you will find useful and profitable as well." I looked him in the eye. "It's the best deal you're going to get. If you don't like it, I'm sure one of your billionaire pals will be more amenable. I hear Jeff Bezos loves acquiring stuff and he doesn't yet have Amazon Ghostbusters in his portfolio…"

Gresley's shoulders slumped and he chewed his lip. "A lesser man would simply have his bodyguard throw you overboard," he said.

Gresley clearly didn't like losing, but I was betting he wouldn't let his pride stand in the way of turning a profit.

"Kill me and you're back to square one. Do you think you can con another Kaitiaki crewman into slipping you their secrets?"

Gresley thought it over. "You would appear to have me over a barrel, Mr. Palermo. We'll have to iron out the details of this…arrangement you're proposing but I agree to your terms in principle."

We shook hands and I retreated to my cabin so I could get some sleep, trying not to let my body language betray my nervousness as I went. I needed the rest.

I would have to talk the other Coffee Corps members into joining me in this mad venture, and to convince the world at large who saw me only as a compulsive whistleblower, that I was someone serious about solving a problem that was bigger than all of us. Forces within and without conspired to keep humanity apart, to prevent us from uniting in our fight against the eldritch invaders. Perhaps I could change that. Perhaps I could use my newfound notoriety to herd together the ancient orders of sorcerers and monolithic government bureaucracies and gaggles of eccentric billionaires, and forge them into something that could take on this existential threat and defeat it once and for all.

Succeed or fail, I had a feeling once we got back to civilization I wasn't going to get much rest for a long time to come.

~*~

A Word from Alex Shvartsman

This story is a sequel to **The Coffee Corps**, a way-over-the-top humor urban fantasy piece which presupposes that beneath every Dunkin' Donuts in New England there's a hidden chamber which houses a pentagram. A secret government organization called The Coffee Corps uses a network of these installations to prevent the Lovecraftian elder gods from breaking through the dimensional barriers and into our world. Also, drinking coffee fortifies one's mind against the eldritch madness.

This was meant to be a standalone story, but in the course of its events the existence of The Coffee Corps, eldritch horrors, and magic itself is revealed to the general public. (I'm going to remain intentionally vague here as to how or why since you may get the chance to read the original story one day.)

Writing that scene was my **Stargate** moment.

Here's what I mean. There are lots of TV shows, movies, books, what-have-you about secret organizations that deal with alien or supernatural threats while the general population is none-the-wiser. **X-Files, Buffy, Men in Black** all fall into this category. And then there are space opera universes where we see humanity using alien tech or developing their own to reach out to the stars. **Stargate SG-1** is among the few stories that shows the transition. They begin as a secret organization but over the course of its ten-season run the existence of aliens becomes known and we watch humanity perfect the use of stargates, build a fleet, and become a space-faring society.
Likewise there are many stories in settings where magic is part of everyday life, and even more stories where magic is hidden from most people (almost every urban fantasy ever.) I thought

it would be really fun to write a series of stories that deal, in various ways, with the modern world coping with not only the sudden realization that magic is real, but also handed a how-to manual. My characters get into some of the implications in the story presented in this volume, and I look to explore more of this idea in the future—while hopefully maintaining the zany, fun feel of the original.

About the Author

Alex Shvartsman is a writer, translator and game designer from Brooklyn, NY. Over 100 of his short stories have appeared in **Nature, Galaxy's Edge, InterGalactic Medicine Show,** and many other magazines and anthologies. He won the 2014 WSFA Small Press Award for Short Fiction and was a two-time finalist for the Canopus Award for Excellence in Interstellar Fiction (2015 and 2017). He is the editor of the Unidentified Funny Objects annual anthology series of humorous SF/F. His collection, **Explaining Cthulhu to Grandma and Other Stories** and his steampunk humor novella **H. G. Wells, Secret Agent** are currently available. His website is alexshvartsman.com.

~*~

Aquagenic
Will Swardstrom

~*~

CORA SQUIRMED IN HER CHAIR. She hated these sessions with Dr. Finkle. Gazing at the clock behind the doctor's desk, she watched it tick. Another second...and another...and another...

"Cora?"

She lazily shifted her eyes from the clock to Dr. Finkle. She didn't reply, but let her eyes show her boredom with the session.

"Cora, I need to know that you're making progress here. We'd really like to be able to move on from where we've been," Dr. Finkle said, jotting a few notes on a pad as he spoke. The air in the room was stale and tasted of cheap plastic. The scratch of his pencil continued for a few more seconds until she finally spoke up.

"Move on? You'd like to move on? What the hell is that supposed to mean?" The way she said it might have indicated frustration or anger, but her face was a stone. She knew it was all meaningless. She knew what her situation was. In fact, right next to Finkle's stupid clock was the camera taping her every moment during this current session.

Finkle paused. She didn't change her face, but she chuckled inwardly. She caught him. *He* wanted to move on…get away from her craziness…but she would never move on, and he knew it.

"Well…you know, there's always a chance for improvement," the doctor said. He leaned forward and dropped his #2 pencil on the desk. Cora considered the chance he was sincere. "You may feel like we are on a treadmill here. I get it. But I firmly believe there is an epiphany close at hand. When it comes, it can break through all the walls in your mind. You are a special girl, Cora, and these sessions are the key to figuring out who you truly are."

Cora let his words sink in for a few seconds, then stood, shoved her chair backward, and said one word before walking out.

"Bullshit."

~*~

Dana Trexler privately despised Dr. Finkle. She'd only worked for the facility for three-quarters of a year, but something about him gave her the creeps. He always asked her about her boyfriend. It was such a hassle, she eventually just made one up. With that firmly in mind, she tried to spend as much time with the patients and as little time around him as possible.

At the age of thirty-six, she had long-given up on a Knight in Shining Armor to rescue her, no matter what they might look like. Dreams were no longer on the menu for Dana. The longer she worked as a nurse, the more she came to realize what a wretched world she lived in. Dreams weren't just unavailable, they were a joke, foisted upon innocent children to brainwash them into accepting society as it stood. She did what she could to alleviate just a little bit of the pain in the world, one person at a time. Most of the time her personal mission involved wiping up vomit and feces, but one does what one can.

The outlier in her world was Cora Smith. Unlike many of the other residents at Sheltering Pines, Cora wasn't a vegetable, or an addict, or some other case deemed beyond hope. She seemed…normal? Dana tried to maintain a professional distance, but it was hard to not like Cora and her usually happy personality. Usually, that is, until she walked out of Dr. Finkle's office, cursing under her breath at the facility's psychotherapist.

Dana rounded the corner, coming back from a particularly nasty bodily fluid cleanup in Room 137, and nearly bumped into Cora.

"Oh! Sorry, Cora. I didn't see you."

To Dana, it seemed as though Cora forced a smile. "No. I should be more careful, Nurse Trexler."

Dana was grateful for a coherent conversation and shook her head. "Cora, I've told you before you can call me Dana. Just don't yell it down the hallway." She paused and noticed Cora's agitation. "Are you okay?"

"Yeah…just frustrated. I've been here four months now and I feel like I'm going nowhere. Dr. Finkle…" she trailed off, staring past Dana.

Dana needed the job, so she knew she had to keep her mouth shut about Finkle. She put a hand on Cora's forearm. "Hang in there. I know you're going to have a breakthrough soon. I believe it."

Cora offered a weak smile, and continued down the hall toward her room. "I'm glad someone does. It seems like there is no one left in this world who even knows I'm alive."

Dana watched the young woman walk away. It wasn't the first time she'd heard Cora talk like that, but she couldn't help but hurt for her anyway. Hopefully, she'd have a breakthrough soon. Hopefully, she could find whatever family was out there looking for her.

~*~

Cora was glad for Nurse Trexler. After talking to Dana just for a few seconds in the hallway, the stress of Dr. Finkle's questions rolled off her back like waves in the ocean. At least, what she imagined waves would be like.

Even though she'd been found on the beach a little less than four months ago, she had little memory of it. The memory thing…kind of a buzzkill.

She'd been at Sheltering Pines Residential Facility for over three months, on the outskirts of Portland, Oregon—a little more than an hour from where she'd been found lying on Cannon Beach. Found nearly naked and unconscious, Cora was physically healthy, except for the rash covering her whole body and a few scrapes here and there.

It took a few weeks in the hospital to figure it out. The rash vanished, and then reappeared. It came and went seemingly with no rationale behind it. Cora tried as hard as—harder than—the doctors to figure out what was happening to her, but the lack of memory from before Day One didn't help anything. No one thought to record her at first, but the first few videos she had seen after she'd been found were almost painful in how she acted. Cora, in those first few weeks, acted as innocent as a kindergartener. She knew how to speak. She knew her name. She knew things, but her life? Gone. Seemingly in her early 20s, Cora could recall nothing, except a name. *Cora.* Her stay at the hospital became more and more depressing. No family came for her. They put her description on the news, but no one knew her. Even her unique medical condition failed to get a hit on any national healthcare database. It took a bit for the doctors to figure out exactly what her condition was.

One thing tied it all together:

Water.

A nurse during those first few weeks gave Cora an old cell phone—no longer useable as a phone, but the camera worked just fine, along with video functions. Cora began to record her own life for the future, in case her memory vanished again.

She'd watched the diagnosis video dozens of times. It was about the only clue she had for a life which somehow existed before her life at Sheltering Pines.

"You're allergic," she saw the dermatologist say. Cora didn't remember her name—it never came up in conversation during the nearly two-minute video, and those early memories were hazy.

"Allergic? To what?"

"Water. Cora, you're allergic to water."

"What are you talking about? How can you be allergic to water?"

The unnamed dermatologist shifted on the balls of her feet. "It does exist, although extremely rare. It's called Aquagenic Urticaria. I've talked to dozens of other doctors from around the country—shoot, across the world—and it does fit the symptoms. However, yours is the most severe case we've seen."

Cora imagined that she must've suddenly felt a little more at home in the world, which probably prompted the question from her, "Do the others lose their memory, too?"

The expression on the doctor's face turned grim. "That's what's been so baffling. The memory issues are clearly connected, but the amnesia isn't a symptom of the allergy. Frankly, most doctors aren't really sure that Aquagenic Urticaria is actually a reaction to some other allergen in the water, or something toxic already on the person's skin. Because of your memory…uh…issues…we've tested you more than we probably would typically. Best we can tell, your condition is based on the *water itself.* You can still drink, of course. Your allergy affects the skin. However, due to the nature of your allergy, you are officially the first person recorded to have what I'm calling Acute Aquagenic Urticaria compounded with Long-term Amnesia."

The video ended there. Cora didn't recall any more from the unnamed dermatologist, so the conversation probably ended soon afterwards.

One of the first therapists to visit her at the hospital advised keeping a diary, with the hopes it might spur some long-forgotten memory. She dutifully recorded her daily life, as monotonous as it was at Sheltering Pines, with the exceptions of the days when her allergy became too much for her. She left those days purposefully blank in her journal. Flipping through it might remind a musician of a piano with a collection of black and white spaces.

What did she know about herself? Not much. She used the last name the hospital had given her, but it, along with anything else, was just a kind fiction. No one knew anything, but she came to realize people liked to make up the smallest details about someone else's lives to relieve their own ignorance.

Cora's allergy kept her constantly dirty. She rarely had a full bath or shower thanks to the extreme pain and reaction, so unless an orderly shoved her under a faucet, she was always mildly filthy. She'd been given non-water-based deodorants to help control her smell, but there was no easy way to get clean without the intense misery associated with water.

Thus the irony: she was found on the beach, but her body would erupt in a world of pain if she ever set foot in a crashing wave.

~*~

Four hours after Cora stormed out of Dr. Finkle's office, an electronic chime sounded in the hall. Supper time. She wasn't really hungry, but if she tried to hide in her room during meal time, an orderly would drag her out. Well…at least that was what happened last night. When the digital clock on her trusty un-phone clicked seven o'clock, she trudged out of her room toward the cafeteria, along with other residents—a couple dozen in total.

Just ahead, she saw the figure of Rita Evans. Cora sighed and slowed down. If she didn't have to follow Rita in the food line, it would probably be for the best. Rita seemed to have a grudge against Cora. Since she'd first arrived, Cora had been nothing but nice to Rita, but that didn't mean much with Rita around. She muttered off and on about something Cora had done, but she never knew what the woman was talking about. Knowing Rita, chances were good she'd missed a dose of her meds.

Cora ducked into the restroom and hid in a stall for a few minutes, hoping she could stroll into the cafeteria and avoid her adversary. She turned the metal dial and heard a snicker from her right.

"Hey, bitch."

Crap. Rita had followed her.

"Look, Rita, let's just go eat. I don't have a problem with you," Cora said. She hoped her tone came across as a mixture of exasperation and bravado.

"Well I have a few problems with you. First, aren't you gonna wash your hands? You in the can and leaving without some soap and water? *Gross.*"

Cora took a step closer, trying to force Rita to move from the doorway. "I'll use hand sanitizer. I'm sure I've told you before: I can't get wet."

Rita's arm had been propped up against the door frame, but she pulled it down and took her own step closer to Cora. There was a slight path out of the bathroom, but not much. Rita outweighed Cora by at least thirty pounds.

"Yeah…you mighta mentioned that before. Problem is: I don't believe you. I told you before and I'll tell you now, I think you're a lying bitch. You never apologized for five months ago, and someone doesn't just get over that, you know?"

Cora bit her lip. She just wanted to get out of here, but something wasn't adding up. She wasn't here five months ago. She didn't exist five months ago.

"What are you talking about? I wasn't here five months ago. I had amnesia…"

Rita pitched her voice higher, "'*I had amnesia*'…how completely convenient for you. I wish I could just pretend I forgot my life like you. I wish I could just pretend I was someone else." Another step forward. Rita and Cora were less than two feet apart, the door a body length behind Rita, the stalls a few feet to Cora's left and the sinks a few feet to her right.

"I'm not pretending. I…I don't know how to explain it," Cora tried to say.

Another step closer. Rita jabbed her finger into Cora's chest. "You don't have to explain nothing. I know you're a liar, so whatever you say is a damn, dirty lie. Now, what do we do with dirt?"

Cora's chest froze. She tried to run, to dart around Rita and make for the door, but Rita had homecourt advantage. Rita grabbed Cora's wrists as she tried to escape and pulled her sharply off her feet. In a smooth motion, Rita dragged Cora's struggling body to the community shower area. Rita pushed Cora across the tile floor with one hand and used the other to turn on the nearest shower. After a second, she reached over and turned on the next. Cora was still mostly dry, but the path out was now blocked by the moving water cascading down.

Cora was done with logic. In her current state, Rita was not capable of rational discussion. "P…please Rita. What did I do to you?"

Rita ignored the pleas from the corner. There were six more shower faucets and Rita looked intent on turning them all on. She might not believe Cora's words about amnesia, but she seemed to know the water would inflict maximum pain.

And that very pain began to creep up Cora's arms. A flash of fire in the midst of the damp showers. She tried to ignore it, but the rash immediately flared up and the hives sprang up on her skin. They had a shine to them that, for a moment, Cora thought was beautiful.

Then the pain took over.

Fire. Dancing on her skin. Her breath caught in a throat unable to move air out or in. Wave after wave of pain threatened to overtake her, just as she imagined the waves of the Pacific Ocean did on the day she'd been found.

The pain was intense and she no longer heard whatever lunatic ramblings Rita yelled across the spray of the showers. Rita's voice faded somewhere to the back of Cora's mind. Soon, a vision of another woman replaced Rita's watery form. The left side of her brain knew the sight was a mirage, but Cora could no longer maintain the distance between reality and fantasy. The woman dominating her final pain-filled moments shone like a picture of a goddess. Her beauty was unparalleled, gold encircling her body wherever Cora looked. The woman didn't speak, but seemed to just float in the air, her hair swirling in a silent vortex.

"Who are you?" she asked the vision. "Why won't you help me?"

Within seconds, the vision completely faded. Cora's consciousness fled and darkness enveloped her.

~*~

Dana yawned. It'd been a long night. She had missed seeing Cora at the evening meal, so she'd sought her out, finding her unconscious in the showers. The rash snaked around Cora's arms, legs, all the way around her torso and even crept into her scalp. The redness stood out like a beacon and Dana spent extra time putting allergy cream between Cora's fingers and toes where the rash seemed to create rough, almost abrasive blots. She couldn't imagine the pain Cora must've endured to earn the hives. There would be consequences for what happened to Cora, but Dana's first priority meant taking care of her patient. Even though she should have clocked out the previous night, Dana stuck by Cora's side to get her through the worst of her crisis.

She started at a noise next to her.

Cora's eyelids fluttered and she involuntarily reached up to scratch at the hives covering her face.

"Shh...it's okay, Cora," Dana said. She eased Cora's hands back to her sides.

"Nurse Trexler?"

Dana smirked. "I've already told you to call me Dana."

"What happened? Who was she?"

Dana sighed. "It looked like one of the other patients, Rita Evans, trapped you in the showers. Don't worry, she's being transferred away. Anyway, I found you..."

"No, no, no. I knew that. I'm pissed at Rita. I don't want her to get within fifty feet of me again, so that's a relief, but I knew that."

Cora worked to sit up and perched herself on the edge of her bed. Dana reached out and helped her move. Cora's skin cracked near her wrists and elbows, oozing a clear pus. Dana cringed at how it must feel, but Cora didn't seem to react to it.

"Okay...what do you mean, then?" Dana handed Cora a

tube of ointment. She took it and put it on the bed next to her.

"The woman. No, not Rita," Cora said, waving off Dana's attempt to comment. "Sitting in the corner of the showers, the water was all over me. It…burned. I thought it would consume me. I didn't know what to do. I couldn't get out, so I just let it happen. The hives. The darkness. But there was a moment right before the darkness when I saw…her."

Dana leaned in, toward the bed. "Who?"

Cora half-smiled, half-frowned. "That's what I asked you. I don't know. Maybe I knew before. Maybe she's someone I knew. All I know is that she was the most beautiful woman I've ever seen. She stood before me, almost…floating, radiant in the steam of the shower. I nearly cried from her beauty, except then I passed out."

Dana thought it over for a few moments. "Cora, I know you haven't been happy with your therapy sessions with Dr. Finkle. I won't lie and say I totally agree with his methods. He has a belief that the amnesia is all in your head. But what if it isn't…what if the key to unlocking your past is to unlock your Aquagenic Urticaria?"

Dana couldn't believe she even put the idea out there in the ether. To question Dr. Finkle…to doubt the treatments at the facility…she was putting her own job in jeopardy. She didn't have the authority to change treatments and she certainly didn't have the authority as a nurse to suggest a patient seek to harm themselves. The mere idea that Cora's allergy was to blame for her memory loss could be dangerous. Dana was in no position to tell Cora to ignore Dr. Finkle.

Cora interrupted her thoughts when she smiled. "Yes! That's it! Will you help me? Will you be here when I need to"—she gestured to her almost scaly arms—"do this?"

Dana audibly gulped.

"I will."

~*~

She didn't know a thing about herself other than a name.

Cora.

She didn't know anything else. What had she done for a

living? What were her likes and dislikes? Who were her parents? Did they look like her? Did they love her? Did they miss her? Cora looked down again at the hives and ran her hand up and down her forearms. The spots seemed rough at the edges, but smooth in the middle. A twitch of pain erupted when she touched one, but she endured it.

She turned when Nurse Trexler—Dana—knocked at her door. She felt as if she were still trying to hold on to some important piece of information, just for the vapor to dissipate as the knock reverberated throughout her room.

It'd been two days since she had involved the nurse in a conspiracy to push the limits of her water allergy. Dana had said she was committed, but she seemed hesitant. Cora understood, but still refused to budge. It was her life and whatever it was, she wanted to get back to it.

"How's my Aquagenie today?"

In spite of herself, Cora smiled.

"I'm better. The itching has worn off."

"Really?"

"Well…mostly. I'm ready, though."

Dana pursed her lips. "I'm still on my shift right now. Tonight. After supper."

Cora glanced up at a clock. It wasn't even noon yet. She needed answers and wanted to start now. Right. Now.

Dana seemed to sense the urgency in her fidgeting, and walked a little farther into the room.

"I've been doing some thinking about your…condition. We'll test your allergy and the reaction your body has for sure, but maybe there's more. Maybe even the concept of water itself has some hold on you. I've brought you some things that might spur some memories if it really is about the water."

Cora looked through a bag the nurse placed on her bed. A dog-eared paperback of *Moby Dick*, a DVD of *The Little Mermaid*, a couple of children's books centered around a cartoon cat, polar bear, and an otter called *The Octonauts*, a coffee table book with photos and essays by Jacques Cousteau, and a few other science books with barcodes on the spines, evidently checked out from a local library.

"Really?" The sarcasm was thick in Cora's voice.

"Hey, don't knock it. The brain is a strange thing. You never know what might trigger something. Look, I am willing to help you, even if my medical training is screaming in my head the whole time. But that'll have to happen after I clock out. In the meantime, it isn't going to hurt you to poke through a few books about the ocean. See what your brain thinks is so scary."

Cora picked up one of the science books. *The Great Barrier Reef: Coral and the Life Teeming Within.* The title struck her funny for a moment until she realized why. "Look—it's got my name, if you take off the 'l.'"

Dana's cell phone chimed. She pulled it off her waistband and swiped across on the screen. "Nuts. Gotta run—Mrs. McGreevy needs a sponge bath this afternoon."

Cora hadn't wanted to admit it, but the bag of books and movies was a blessing. If her mind was going to be fixated on the ocean anyway, she was thrilled to have something of substance in front of her. She absentmindedly waved to Dana on her way out. Her eyes were already poring over the words about coral and the reef off the coast of Australia.

~*~

The next week was a mixed bag. Dana spent a couple hours each night with Cora, testing her skin and seeing how far her Aquagenic Urticaria would go. First night, just her right hand under a faucet, running luke-warm water. Dana had been content to let Cora set the boundaries and she set the limit the first night just under seven minutes. Her skin blossomed and the hives almost instantly burst out.

The next night, Cora put her left hand in an ice bath. This time the pain tolerance seemed better; the ice soothed the hives as they appeared. Cora kept her hand submerged to her wrist for twelve minutes before she couldn't stand it anymore.

The other nights brought both feet alternately in water for a minute each time, her legs in a room-temperature bathtub, wet towels draped over her shoulders, and her head dunked in a bathtub of moderately cool water. The results left both women a little perplexed. Each experiment brought the expected hives and blisters and Dana had to turn on her nurse training, even though she was off-the-clock. But never did Cora pass out or have any visions. And, most importantly, Cora wasn't any closer to regaining her memory.

Dana almost wanted to call off the testing. Over the course of the past couple weeks, she'd watched Cora's body turn against itself again and again. As a nurse, she hated seeing it, even if it might help in the long run.

As she walked into Sheltering Pines at the end of the week, something felt off. What it was, Dana didn't know, but she immediately headed to Cora's room. The young woman had her knees pulled up to her chest, her head down and sobs emanating from her perch on her bed. Dana softly knocked on the doorframe.

Pulling her head up, Cora looked at Dana with red eyes. Her cheeks were already inflamed from the wet tears. She said nothing, but her eyes told Dana something was wrong.

"What happened? Did you do anything without me?" Dana sat on the edge of the bed, fearful something may have happened without her around. She offered Cora a tissue.

"No. I waited. But this morning when I got up, this letter sat on my desk. They couldn't even tell me in person! I don't know what I'm going to do. Where I'm going to go."

Dana saw the tri-fold of paper on the desk and reached over to grab it. She skimmed through it, getting more and more angry as she went. But this was far from the first time she'd seen government bureaucracy work poorly for a patient. Dr. Finkle had reported to the Oregon Department of Health that Cora was no longer treatable, so Sheltering Pines would no longer be reimbursed for her care through Medicare. Instead, she would transfer to one of a handful of resident facilities across the state. Dana knew from experience this was the moment when a patient fell through the cracks.

She forced a smile and tried to put a good face on the situation. "Okay. This isn't so bad—look, there's a few out near the coast. It's really pretty there."

Dana cringed inwardly, realizing her words espoused the beauty of an ocean Cora couldn't swim in. Thankfully, Cora didn't seem to realize it.

Cora sniffed and looked at Dana with sorrowful eyes, then asked a seemingly strange question. "Nurse Trexler...sorry, Dana...who are you?"

"Who am I?" Dana was taken aback by the question. "Well...I'm Dana Marie Trexler. I am thirty-six years old and a registered nurse."

"Tell me about your family. Your parents."

Dana had no reason to tell her personal information to Cora, but something compelled her. The time they'd spent together testing Cora's skin had been the beginning of the friendship. Over the last couple of weeks, the lines of professionalism had crumbled. The final line had vanished as she read the letter. According to the paper in her hands, Cora was no longer a resident of Sheltering Pines as of tonight.

"I grew up in Vancouver, just across the state line in Washington. My parents' names are Angela and Jim. They've been married thirty-seven years, and live up in Bremerton now, just off the Puget Sound. I have two brothers. Patrick lives in Atlanta and Jimmy is out just south of Chicago. I...why am I telling you this? Why are you asking me this?"

Cora didn't respond with a statement, but another question. "But...who am I?"

Dana opened her mouth, then realized she didn't have a good answer. "You...are Cora."

"That's the thing, Dana. I can go to any of these other facilities, but none of them have what I have here. I don't have a name—not really. I don't have a family, a job, a life of any kind. But I have you. I have a friend."

Again, Dana was speechless. For so long, she came to work and kept relationships with patients at an arm's length. She thought of herself as compassionate, but professional. Somewhere her relationship with Cora had evolved into something else, but as she examined herself, Dana found that she didn't care about what was acceptable. She cared about her friend. Cora.

"What am I going to do? I don't even have a car, or way to get to any of these places," Cora sobbed.

Dana still battled herself. As much as Cora talked about not having a life, Dana's life wasn't one to behold. She clocked in every morning, administered drugs to patients in various states of mental conditions, cleaned all varieties of bodily fluids throughout the day. She didn't have a love life. She didn't even have a friend like what she had with Cora. Her life equaled work and sleep. Cora might not know what her life was, but at least she hadn't stumbled into adulthood and a monotonous prison of a life.

"I'll take you," Dana found herself saying.

The tears stopped. "What?"

"I won't let them treat you like this. I can't do anything about this place and frankly Dr. Finkle is a joke. He couldn't cure a ham," Dana said. Cora chuckled a bit and Dana was grateful to stop her crying. "You're my friend, too. Probably the best one I've had since college. I won't let it end like this. Where do you want to go? I'll take you there myself. Just name it."

Cora had a strange expression on her face, one that Dana couldn't quite read.

"Anywhere?"

"Name it."

Cora pursed her lips for a moment, then blurted it out.

"The ocean."

~*~

Cora was surprised. Dana had calmly accepted her response, yes, but she went a step further by quitting her job. Dana relayed the story as they left Portland heading west in Dana's five-year-old SUV.

"I tried to take a couple vacation days, but my boss wouldn't let me. So I quit."

Cora just stared at her.

"Look, I don't know what I'm doing, but I feel like I have

to do this. I promised I would get you to where you need to go. If that's a new facility that the government will pay for, so be it. If it ends up something else entirely, let's figure it out. I can find another job, but I don't know if you can find out who you are without me. Let's do it."

"The ocean?"

"If that's what you want, we'll go. I don't want you to get hurt, but you feel like you have to go, don't you?"

Cora leaned against the window, the green of the Oregon landscape begging to be seen behind her. "I dunno. I guess? I can't remember anything any other way. Maybe I need to go back to where I was found. I suppose, in a way, I feel the sea calling to me."

Dana sat quietly for a few minutes and Cora could see the nurse struggling with something inside. "I remember a time when I was in high school. My best friend, Vi, had been diagnosed with a rare form of leukemia in October and ended up spending most of our senior year holed up in the Oncology floor at the hospital. I saw the work done day in and day out by the nurses—Vi called them her angels—who took care of her and the other kids on the floor. A day came near the end of the year when I remember feeling a calling to medicine, a need to do something that made a difference."

The SUV was quiet for a few seconds.

"And Vi?"

"She died the weekend of our senior prom. The cancer just ate her from the inside out. It was a horrible way to die, but I wasn't there. I went to prom. I was a selfish teenager at the worst possible time. I don't remember my date's name, but I remember I wasn't there when she needed me the most."

Cora's voice dipped low. She felt tears on the edge of her eyes. "I'm sorry."

Dana kept her eyes forward, clearly trying to keep her attention on the road as she drove. "Thanks."

Cora had no way to repay her friend's generosity, except maybe she was doing exactly that. Dana felt that she was following her calling, but maybe what she really needed was a way to make up for not being there for Vi.

That much, Cora could do for Dana. Whatever came next would no doubt be difficult, but she was sure Dana would remain at her side until it was done.

Emotionally exhausted and lulled by the gentle motion of the car, sleep overtook her.

~*~

Living in Portland, Dana was used to rain. In one form or another, precipitation hit the ground about every third day on average. Rarely did they see what those in the Midwest experienced in the humidity-laced summers, but life in the Pacific Northwest meant a person should prepare, each day, to be wet.

So when Dana pulled into the ocean-front motel near Cannon Beach, she wasn't at all surprised when her windows misted up with a light rain. Still twilight, the sun kissed the horizon of the Pacific on the other side of the Lamplight Inn. A quick look at Cora told Dana the young woman was still sound asleep, so she slipped out of the vehicle to register at the front office. She couldn't have been more than five minutes inside getting registered, but when she stepped outside again, her heart stopped for a few beats. Cora wasn't in the vehicle anymore.

Dana calmed down, realizing Cora couldn't have gone far. She walked around the motel, finding Cora sitting on a wooden bench in a grassy area, gazing out across the waves of the ocean.

Already her skin blossomed with the rash Dana had become intimately familiar with. In the light of the setting sun, there was a certain glow to Cora's appearance. Dana was almost speechless—Cora was radiant.

"You okay, Cora?"

"Do you ever feel like you are destined for something more?"

Dana had a seat next to her friend. "What do you mean? Maybe we should go to our room and get out of this rain…"

"I'm okay. It's just a little fall of rain," Cora said. She still hadn't looked at Dana. Her eyes were fixed on some distant sight across the curvature of the earth. "Have you ever felt like the person you are isn't who you're supposed to be?"

"Every day when I visit Mrs. McGreevy's room for her sponge bath. Seriously, Cora, where's this coming from?"

"I saw her, Dana. The woman in my vision. She woke me up and told me to come to the ocean. It *was* calling to me. I think I know who she is. I think I know who I am."

Dana didn't know what to say. In a way, Cora was speaking a different language. She was almost afraid to ask.

"Who is she?" Dana whispered

"She's my mother, and she's a mermaid."

Something inside of Dana broke. She knew Cora had just watched Disney's *The Little Mermaid*. Clearly Cora had convinced herself she shared the same fate as Ariel. Dana had definitely seen her share of insanity while working at Sheltering Pines, but what frightened Dana even more was if Cora was right.

"Cora…"

"I know, I know. You're seeing a dancing animated crab right now. I swear the movie has nothing to do with this. Not really. I…I can't explain it, but I know that when I was found here, I was literally a fish out of water. Somehow my body changed and I forgot who I was. But now that I'm back, I know who I am."

Dana sat back a bit. This was a lot to take in, but she had pledged to follow Cora and help her find out who she was. Perhaps she hadn't really realized how serious the girl's mental issues were. Perhaps…

"So you've got your memory back? You remember?"

For the first time since they'd arrived, Cora looked away from the beach. She glanced down for a millisecond, then up at Dana. "No. But I believe it. I saw the woman again. Last time I only saw her for a few seconds before I'd passed out and I only remembered her face and how I felt. This time, when I woke up, I remembered all of it, and she was floating. She was a mermaid, Dana!"

"Cora, when I was a kid, I believed in Santa Claus and the Tooth Fairy, but that didn't make either of them real. Just because you want something to be true, doesn't mean it is."

Cora shook her head like a bobblehead on a car dashboard. "No. I know it's true. I was found here. I've felt the ocean pleading with me to return. I've seen a vision with my mother. I am a mermaid, Dana. I need to go. Don't you see, this perfectly explains the Aquagenic Urticaria?"

Dana was taken aback. "What?"

"It just makes perfect sense—if I really am a mermaid, then what better way to punish me for being out of the water? My mother, or whoever, must've made it so my skin would have an allergic reaction. But that's also why it never really made sense. Why was my condition more intense? There's no record of me, even though I have this serious condition. No family. All the pieces just fall into place. You can't deny it."

Dana felt her blood pressure rise. She'd always kept a distance from her patients. She prided herself on the line she drew between her professional and personal life, and she tossed it all away with this...nutjob.

"I...Cora...I have to make a phone call."

"Wait, Dana. Please." Cora put her hand out on Dana's arm. Dana stopped, but not because of Cora's words. The hand on her arm didn't *feel* like a hand. Cold, sticky, rough. Dana paused and looked down at it. The rash still wrapped around her arms, but between Cora's fingers, something had started to grow. A webbing, almost like a frog's. And the softness Dana had observed before in Cora's skin was gone. Her skin was rough, as if slightly covered in barnacles.

"What the hell?"

Cora just smiled. "I was right," she said as if she nearly couldn't believe it.

Dana lifted the hand in the waning daylight and held it up, examining it. Moments before, the scientific side of her brain was at odds with the fantasy Cora was offering. In one movement, Cora's skin destroyed whatever cognitive dissonance Dana had left over. Her eyes lost focus on Cora's hand and went to the beach in the distance. She remembered a time when her parents took her to the shore. Her brothers spent the day splashing in the saltwater, but not Dana. She had the single-minded determination that only a seven-year-old could have while building a sand castle that day, only for the tide to come in and slowly wear away at her creation, eroding the structure with each wave. This felt like that; the wall she'd built up in her mind—all the things she thought she knew—gradually fell to pieces with each minute she spent with Cora. She was that seven-year-old girl again.

"It must be the rain and the salty ocean air," Dana mused.

Cora seemed fascinated by her own body. "It's funny. It still hurts. It's like someone is slowly microwaving my skin, but I can handle it. I think I have to, like I must've done something in the past to deserve it, but I have to endure it to really find out who I was…who I am."

Dana took her turn gazing out over the slow crashing of the waves upon the beach. "You're leaving, aren't you?"

"I don't really know, but I think I have to go into the ocean. I *have* to go. If I don't, I'll always wonder, and I'll never be who I'm really meant to be."

Dana stood, prepared to walk back to the room she'd just registered, or possibly even her SUV. Her mind was swirling; she hadn't yet decided.

Cora's webbed hand was cold on her arm. "I need you now more than ever. Please stay."

The chaos in Dana's mind immediately ceased. This was what she had come here for. She couldn't run away now.

"I will."

~*~

It burned. In the name of everything she ever believed in, it burned.

Cora's skin screamed as the saltwater lapped at her ankles. The pain was too great. She wanted to run back. Get to Dana and spend the rest of her boring life at Sheltering Pines or wherever. Part of her wanted to…

But another part told her this was the only way. One way or

another, she would discover who she really was.

The searing would not abate…it burned…

Like a fire, it licked and raced across her flesh and burned…and burned…

The waves pummeled her knees…her hips. The thin clothes barely helped at all. The water soaked through and the fabric clung to her skin, searing it.

Some new and unwelcome pain burst the skin of her neck. Cora reached up and scratched, feeling as if she were tearing into her esophagus with each scrape of her fingernails.

If she took one more step, she would be in over her head. Water would consume her and may never let her go. She took a deep breath, willing herself to move forward.

She opened her eyes, the saltwater immediately rushing at her pupils. Waves crashed overhead and she lost her footing in the rush of blue. Everything was blue. No up or down. It was all just…there. Surrounding. Crushing. Killing.

She wanted to scream, but the water would force itself down her throat, into her lungs. She would not give in…

She would never give up…

Death may claim her, but it would earn her life. She would fight until the end.

~*~

Dana couldn't help but watch. She'd wanted to beg Cora to stay, but after what she'd seen, the call of the unknown had pulled her in.

Step by step, Dana imagined that Cora hesitated. That she would step backward and forget her foolish quest. Who really knew themselves, anyway? Dana had never really known anyone truly at peace with themselves; why should Cora be any different?

But Cora *was* different. If it had been anyone else, Dana would have stopped her. But deep down, Dana believed.

A mermaid? Dana didn't know, but she wanted to believe it was true. With each step into the ice-cold waters of the Pacific Northwest, Dana hoped Cora truly was who she believed she was. The nurse inside of her wanted to run into the surf, gather

Cora in her arms, and run to the nearest hospital. A few times she even took a tentative step forward. But, as a friend, Dana stayed back.

If Cora could find herself, then maybe there could be hope for everyone else. Maybe there was hope for Dana Trexler.

~*~

The pain was overwhelming, and her skin felt raw and loose. As if she were ready to shed it like a turtleneck sweater on an autumn day. It itched, and she involuntarily ran her hands up and down her body to alleviate the feelings.

Cora hadn't yet committed. She was past the beach, the water over her head, but she still came up gasping for air every few seconds. She needed to let her body be.

With a final breath, Cora relaxed and let herself be swept along with the current and waves, under the surface, until the air begged for escape. She let it go, and with the release something changed. The pain. The burning. The fire disappeared. No longer did she feel her skin melting from the inside out.

Instead, a new feeling replaced it. Completeness. If she'd had a leg amputated long ago which suddenly reappeared, she imagined that would be akin to this feeling. Something had changed, but she couldn't quite decide what it was. She spun about in the water, trying to gain understanding to what was happening.

To what she was becoming.

~*~

Dana wondered how long she should wait. Cora had vanished under the waves about five minutes ago, yet she couldn't bring herself to move from the spot she'd claimed on the shore. If Cora had come up for air a few times, it was hard to tell. Perhaps she would return. Her thumb hovered over the *9* on her phone's keypad as she waited. She wanted to believe, but it was hard. Throwing away everything you'd ever been taught for this.

But what if...

What if her friend had been right? Her mind waged war

with itself over the impossibility of what was happening, but part of her desperately wanted to know that magic really existed.

If Cora was a mermaid, there would never be a reunion. Her friend would be gone forever. Off into the depths of the ocean to find her family, quickly forgetting about the one friend she'd found on land.

That more than anything kept Dana planted. She had already said goodbye, but she refused to believe it was over. She waited for a sign.

~*~

The vision once again came to Cora's eyes. This time, though, the floating woman fit in with the chilly blue of the ever-expanding depths of the Pacific Ocean. She smiled and swam forward.

Cora's body had already grown accustomed to the salty depths, but her eyes were still used to months on land. It burned as she went deeper and deeper. Eventually, the darkness enveloped her.

~*~

Dana sat on the bench, her emotions running the gamut from despair to delight and back again. She wondered what she would do when the police questioned her, but that was a concern for another day. For now, she just worried about Cora.

As if to answer her doubts, in the distance, probably over a half-mile away from the shore, something emerged from the water. Any other day, she would have claimed a dolphin leapt out of the ocean during playtime, or perhaps a small whale breaching.

But she saw the still pale skin in the distance and knew. Cora was saying goodbye. Dana would never see her again. A tear betrayed her stoic face and trickled down one cheek.

"Goodbye Cora. I'll miss you." Dana smiled through her tears. Whatever thread connecting Dana to the sea had been cut at that moment. Her need to stay for her friend had faded with each new wave.

Cora was home.

~*~

A Word from Will Swardstrom

When Daniel asked me to write a story for *Oceans* I was gung-ho until I remembered that I live in the Midwest and have only been to the east or west coast of the U.S. a handful of times. I'm not a scientist, so tackling climate change or some other hard science issue seemed like too tall of an order for me. Eventually I settled on the idea of Aquagenic Urticaria. The water allergy is a real thing, but I definitely treated Cora's condition a little differently than real life. I went down a lot of rabbit holes before I settled on this story line, but the idea that this woman couldn't be in water and couldn't remember her own life had shades of the story of **The Little Mermaid** as well.

I also wanted a story of friendship. Many times romantic relationships are the main focus of a short story like this and I was tempted to go there as well, but I really liked the character of Dana Trexler and wanted to see where the two protagonists went as the story told itself. I hope you enjoyed the story as much as I enjoyed writing it.

About the Author

Like I said, I live in the Midwest, the mostly great state of Illinois to be specific. My wife and I are both teachers in a fairly small school district and we are proud of our two kids. My day job is teaching social studies to high school students and at night I try to write fictional stories like **Aquagenic**. I've been a frequent contributor to the **Future Chronicles** series of science fiction anthologies and have had numerous stories featured in the **Canyons of the Damned** pulp series. I've written four full novels, including two that I share co-writing credits with my brother Paul, who is my first reader and a great encourager.

You can find my website at willswardstrom.wordpress.com

~*~

New Year's Eve

Joshua Ingle

~*~

"Nobody made a greater mistake than he who did nothing because he could only do a little."

—Edmund Burke

BLOOD, SWEAT, TEARS. As Nicole tried not to freeze to death, the phrase swam around her semiconsciousness. *Blood, sweat, tears. What are they good for?*

She'd given plenty of sweat and tears, but never much blood, not until now. A thin trail of the dark red stuff snaked off into the darkness before her, quickly erased by the snow in the katabatic wind blasting down from the mountains. She could only see it by the dim light of the aurorae overhead, which were almost as obscured by the snowy wind. The blood offered tepid warmth. Most of it froze in her hair before it found its way to the snow-covered ground.

She was moving, somehow. Her arms had been slung through two of the holes in what looked like a piece of net cut out of a trawl. She lay supine on it, staring up at the glowing green bands of the Northern Lights and—if she ignored the pain and tilted her head upward—at a man who was dragging her through the gale.

143

Is this the end? Is this how I die? She couldn't remember how she'd come to be here, but it felt final, like her long-dead parents had been right after all, and the whole enterprise of her life had been fruitless. *There was so much to do, and I'm only one person. Surely no one expected more of me than what I did.*

No one but herself, at least.

And it hadn't been enough. The oceans were still in shambles, dying just as fast as she was. Years, decades, and what had she accomplished? Only failure after failure…

She groaned in pain more mental than physical, and the man dragging her stopped. He set her down. The back of her parka's hood touched snow, and then he stood over her, a young man, face bearded, eyes squinting.

"Nicole!" he yelled over the gusts. "You're alive! Are you okay?"

The numb insides of Nicole's nose and mouth were frozen dry, but she managed to croak out a weak, "No."

The man frowned. "How many fingers am I holding up?"

"Six."

His frown deepened. "Nicole, do you know what year it is?"

She stared for what felt like minutes before she remembered. "2077."

"That's right!" He grinned, slid his arms back through the net, and started dragging her again. "You fell and hit your head pretty hard, but we're gonna go find Doc Santillan and get you all fixed up. You keep talking to me, okay? What's your favorite color?"

"Blue," she said without hesitation.

"Mine, too! Do you know how old you are?"

"I'm, uh…Eighty-three?"

"Yes you are. And do you remember what your favorite holiday is?"

"New Year's Eve." These questions were so easy. *I must really be in bad shape for him to keep asking such easy questions.*

"Good, good. Keep talking," the man said. "What else do you remember?"

What else do I remember? She couldn't recall the man's name, or why they were here, or where here even was.

She remembered New Year's Eve, though. Was it New Year's Eve tonight? Was that why he'd asked? If it was, then why wasn't she with Terrance?

Terrance. The name grounded her, brought her back to herself, and she could almost hear his voice singing in her ear. Now *that* was a New Year's Eve she remembered well...But had it mattered? Had anything she'd done mattered?

~*~

The waters should have been pitch black a mile under the Pacific Ocean. They should have been. But a grand light show danced before Nicole and her tiny submersible, rivalling the most extravagant human-made spectacle. Lanternfish, atolla, tomopterises, and smaller creatures likely unidentified by science flickered on and off in the depths. Nicole had been hoping, if not expecting, to see some of these bioluminescent creatures, but nothing in her life as an oceanographer had prepared her for just how *many* of them swam in just the small space she could see from behind her thick window. Thousands of living things blinked out and in, jumped playfully, radiated reds, greens, and blues down the length of their bodies in the deep sea's closest imitation of a fireworks show.

Has anyone ever tried LSD at this depth? The seriousness of her mission aside, Nicole marveled at the diversity that still existed down here. She was tempted to bring the sub into neutral buoyancy and lose herself to the light show in an hour of pure Zen.

Just when she was wishing she'd brought along some music, a deep male Australian voice swelled from the speaker set into the wall. Terrance, singing *Octopus's Garden*. Nicole chortled at the timing.

"How's the typhoon?" she asked.

"Not here yet; forecast still says it should curve north and miss us. Waves are getting bigger, though. Won't be dropping the CTDs today. I can't believe you talked us into doing the dive in this weather."

"Relax. It's peaceful down here."

"I'm jealous. See anything good?"

"Oh, yes." On a whim, she flicked a button, and the depths around her lit up. She checked each window and at the third found what she thought was a creature drifting just a meter away. But on closer inspection it turned out to be a plastic bag from Walmart.

Depressing. Walmart had done away with plastic bags decades ago, but here, at sixteen hundred meters, one remained. At this depth, the hull could collapse, the CO_2 scrubber could fail, or the ballast could get stuck, trapping her at the bottom of the Pacific, but that Walmart bag seemed a far greater threat to Nicole than any of the more immediate dangers.

In truth, this wasn't a leisure trip. She had two goals down here, and the first was to check the ocean floor for signs of illegal mining. Diving to the bottom grew cheaper every year, and the greedy hands of the world had been increasingly bold about trawling the ocean floor for pricey manganese nodules— never mind that they were extracting those nodules from beneath the open sea, where no country reigned and no company held mining rights. *But who could possibly enforce the mining ban? Nicole and Terrance and their little crew?*

The Institute had also tasked her with grabbing some samples of sea creatures so they could be tested for mercury. Terrance hadn't believed her when she told him that pollution from coal plants could work its way down so deep. But food webs overlapped, so wherever there was life in the sea, there was mercury.

So now she was on her way down. No human had ever been to her particular destination, which wasn't uncommon for dives like this. Before the dive she'd ranted to Terrance that humans had seen only ten percent of the ocean, much less mapped it, and that when they retired they should become explorers of the abyss. Terrance himself longed to visit the Mariana Trench, where life subsisted under inconceivable pressure at the ocean's lowest point, and then *deeper still*, in long water-filled cracks piercing several kilometers beneath the ocean floor. Germs, it seemed, were the world's true pioneers of the frontier, surviving deeper in the crust than Nicole could ever hope to visit to sample them.

Shivering at the cold, she huddled into her thick jacket and turned off the exterior light. Immediately, beyond the window and darkness, she saw a constellation of shapes drifting in the deep. Tens of thousands of comb jellyfish, their multicolored bodies pulsing with light, stretched for what seemed like infinity. Ghosts in the dark.

For all the difficulties Nicole had connecting with people, she felt completely at home with these exotic fish. The family of ctenophora outside could never substitute for a real family. But she did have Terrance, though he couldn't be considered a romantic attachment by any stretch of her imagination. If only Ian had stayed. Or if only Dr. Ernst were still alive to share this moment with her. *Sloane, did you ever see anything like this?*

"It's officially the new year," Terrance's voice said from the speaker. "Happy 2069." He started singing again, and the frenzied light show of transparent creatures mating, preying, and eating strobed ever on.

~*~

"HAPPY NEW YEAR 2060!" read the sign in the local Sinama language. But this last day of the 2050s was not a happy day for Nicole. She led Terrance Hawthorne, the ocean chemist she'd just started working with, down the hill from the amphitheater where she'd given her failed speech. In an alley beside the path, barefoot preteens in shorts and T-shirts danced to rap music playing from a thirty-year-old party drone, its strobe lights long since broken. Overhead, inverted rainbows of multicolored clothing hung drying between buildings all the way down to the shore, where stilt houses, lipa boats, and houseboats extended half a mile out to sea. Terrance's catamaran—their destination—lay anchored at the end of the stilt houses, floating above the ruins of past generations' homes that had been submerged by gradually rising seas.

How can I convince these people to stop blast fishing? These desperate people whose only source of income is fish? Who get landsickness the way other people get seasickness? They certainly hadn't liked her ardent plea to stop blowing up ecosystems. The waters had been depleted so thoroughly they needed to use explosives to net decent catches. Half the audience had left the amphitheater before she'd finished speaking.

Maybe I should've tried a different approach. The extreme fish stock depletion here was the government's fault anyway. Nicole had thought to appeal directly to the people here in Basilan since the Philippine authorities would do nothing to stop the big commercial operations from fishing their oceans dry. *I should have made a personal appeal. I shouldn't have started by blaming their own ways of fishing, speaking a bunch of science gibberish.*

And now *Spondylus vastataprope*, the mollusk that had started this whole adventure, would probably die off. Once a cornerstone of the Celebes Sea ecosystems, *S. vastataprope* now lived only in this bay, among these people, who were slowly eating the last of it. What the fishing companies and the ever-acidifying oceans had started, the Sama-Bajau people would finish.

Five years of trying to save this thing, only to stumble at what could have been the turning point. She chastised herself for spending too much time at the Institute, too much time chatting with science and corporate bigwigs. She needed more trips like this. She needed to reconnect with the people she was trying to help.

"Hey!" someone called as Nicole stepped into the surf, a few meters short of the ladder up to the stilt-house labyrinth above. She turned to find a man pacing toward her wearing an old straw hat, his clothing faded and torn. Two women, three other men, and eight children trailed behind him. *His family?*

"Hello," Nicole said, trying to assess his intentions.

"Hey!" the man said again, stopping at the water's edge and continuing in heavily accented English. "You trying to end my livelihood? The way I feed my family?"

As a young woman, Nicole might have balked at the man's

hostility, but now she relaxed into a familiar hardened calm that came from decades of arguing. Sometimes she felt like she argued for a living.

"No," she said, taking a step toward the man as shallow waves washed over her heels. "I'm trying to *save* your livelihood, in the long term. If you kill all the fish in your sea, you won't have any left to eat, and every fisher on this island will be out of a job. I've seen it happen over and over again in other places."

He vigorously shook his head. "I think you lying. I think you just want to control us."

Nicole felt Terrance's hand pulling gently at her shirt. "Let's go," he mouthed when she turned to him. But seeing a second chance to convince the Sama-Bajau, she shrugged his hand away.

"What's your name?" she asked the local man.

"Angelo."

"Angelo, I'm Nicole. It's nice to meet you. I'm an oceanographer, which means that I study the oceans. And I don't want to control anybody."

"You want to stop us from fishing! Look right behind you. Whole ocean of fish. And you want us to stop getting food! Would you tell a farmer not to eat cows and chickens?"

She spoke carefully. "Angelo, fishing isn't farming. When we eat meat from cows, pigs, and chickens, that meat is farmed specifically for humans to eat. Fish aren't. For most species of fish, there's no farm that will create a new supply for us if the supply in the wild runs out. Imagine if we only relied on *wild* cattle as our sole sources of cow meat! We'd run out pretty fast."

Angelo spat into the water. "You got lots of fish. If you want us to stop fishing so bad, why you don't give us some of the fish you catch, huh?"

"I study fish. I don't catch any fish except the ones I need for my research."

"Yes you do! I see you all out there on the water. Big boats with more fish than I catch in my life. And then you rich white people come here and try to tell us you know better than we do? No, no, no. It's our *right* to fish here because we live here. It's our way of life."

Nicole's gaze dropped to the water lapping at her pants. He was right, of course. If not about her motives and allegiances, at least about his culture being a victim of hers. It wasn't local fishers who'd killed eighty percent of the world's fish. It wasn't local fishers who threw away a fourth of all they caught just because they couldn't sell it, whittling away at the planet's biodiversity.

"The companies that are overfishing your waters, Angelo, are the companies I'm fighting. They don't care about you or your job, or even about their own people's jobs in the future. All they care about are this quarter's profit margins. They bribe governments to pay subsidies to strip your waters bare, when that subsidy money could be going to you and to helping build back your fish stocks instead. Please believe me when I tell you I am *not* on the same team as them. Here, look." She removed the *S. vastataprope* shell she'd used in her presentation from her pocket. "This is a shell from the species of oyster that I'm trying to save. My culture has made the water so acidic that the calcium carbonate shells degrade. So they've been dying off, and the companies have been harvesting them, too. The reason I'm here is because the last of these oysters live here in your bay, and I need your help trying to keep them from going extinct."

Angelo didn't skip a beat. "You think an oyster is more important than my family?"

Nicole blinked, stepped backward. Had he listened to anything she'd said? "Angelo, this isn't just about saving nature. It's about saving us. The ecosystems we rely on are so fragile, and so many of them have already collapsed. I'm not someone who devotes her life to saving oysters because I think oysters are more important than people. I'm someone who saves oysters because I want my grandkids—hypothetical, nonexistent grandkids—and your grandkids to have food."

Angelo spat again. "Hot air. My grandkids cannot have

food tomorrow if my kids have no food today. I think *they* give you money. The Chinese and the Americans. You cannot get money if you do not tell them what they want to hear. And what they want to hear is that the world in danger, and it's my people's fault."

"It's everybody's fault. Including mine."

"You trick them or they trick you. Either way, you make all this up."

The accusation stung, and it echoed another word with which she'd been incessantly slandered back home. *Alarmist.* As if nature wasn't sounding a thousand alarms every day, and humanity wasn't choosing to ignore them. *How could she possibly fight this man's worldview and hope to change it?*

Terrance tugged at her shirt again, and this time she let him pull her back toward his boat. "I'm sorry you feel that way," she said to Angelo. She left him standing there, his family silently accusing her behind him.

Condescending. I was so condescending. How can I expect anyone else to change if I can't? Holding back a frustrated yell, she snatched a random Diet Coke bottle drifting in the surf, planning to recycle it later, and climbed the ladder to the stilt house.

~*~

While the rest of the world was celebrating New Year's Eve, 2051, Nicole dived alone in the Belize Barrier Reef.

It was a graveyard. The fish had all fled or died, the coral had expelled their algae and starved. The vibrant, colorful ecosystem she remembered from years ago had been replaced with a battlefield littered with coral skeletons, slaughtered after a valiant war against water with a pH of 7.9. So much death, and all within her lifetime. Within just a part of her lifetime.

Didn't I fight to prevent this? If dedicating my entire life to stopping this wasn't enough, how can anyone ever hope to stop it?

She swam among the dead things, spotting some glass plates, a lone shoe, and a lawn chair among them. The refuse of the living had rained down upon the refuse of the dead. How many fewer fish now lived in the Gulf of Mexico because of this destruction? How many species unique to this particular reef would Nicole never see again? The company that had sent her here to research food security would certainly be disappointed to learn that the food supply from the gulf was not secure.

And in the back of her mind for the entire dive: Ian and the ultimatum he'd finally given her. No more on again, off again. No more "casual love," because apparently all love without marriage was casual. He was in his late fifties now, and he suddenly wanted to get married, buy a house, get a "real" job at a university. He wanted to settle down.

She'd imagined staying with Ian forever, but the lifestyle he wanted her to adopt was one of immobility. It meant no more traveling the world, helping where help was needed most.

So instead of starting a new life with him, she'd left to come here, to the dead reef. He'd find another woman who could give him what he wanted, and she'd find another reef to try to protect. Other reefs did still live, after all, in other waters.

But it was too late for this reef. Her favorite reef.

~*~

At a beachside fundraising party at the end of 2042, Nicole mingled with the Institute's patrons, gave a short speech, and ate from bountiful platters of food. The festivities dwindled as the guests grew tired but couldn't yet leave—midnight hadn't arrived.

Most of the guests were strangers to her. They could drink and laugh and flirt, but to Nicole, this was *work*. The Institute's finances and the urgency of its missions seemed to vanish in the minds of everyone here but her. She both envied and pitied them. But then again, maybe they envied and pitied her, too. Both possessed something valuable the other didn't.

Or maybe she was just in a funk because only half of the fundraising goal had been met so far.

She wandered out to a solitary beach where Caribbean monk seals might once have lounged before humans had hunted them to extinction in the 1950s. She covered her nose at the faint, musty, fecal smell out here. Fertilizer runoff from the mid-state sugar farms had clogged the Caloosahatchee

River with an algal bloom, which had blossomed down the coast and caused the worst red tide in forty years. *The Gulf of Mexico, our eternal sewer.*

When she noticed blue light in the water near a mangrove forest, she flicked off her sandals and waded toward it, the stink in the air be damned.

Noctiluca scintillans and its coconspirators didn't smell great, but as the water lapped against the mangroves, the tiny dinoflagellates lit up in small ripples of bioluminescence. The alien sight of trees with glowing bases evaporated, though, when Nicole realized she could see the stars and the moon through the branches. The mangroves here were leafless, dead.

"It's your favorite holiday," said a voice from behind her. Dr. Ernst's voice. "Why aren't you celebrating?"

"Oh, I am. In my own way." Nicole picked up a rock and threw it into the ocean. Blue light exploded and a shockwave spread outward.

Sloane sipped some champagne, then set her glass on the sand and kicked off her own shoes. Her hair shone white in the moonlight. "You don't sound very celebratory."

Nicole watched the waves break, each crest a riveting blue comet sweeping across the water. "I don't know. I just wonder sometimes why I'm doing this. Risking every relationship I've ever had. I'm almost fifty and I'm still flying around the world to do science, and I just...I just don't seem to be accomplishing much."

"You're an inspiration to the rest of us. You really are."

"Well, thanks, but even if that's true, that's just *us*. Just oceanographers. There are, what, a thousand of us in the world? No one else seems interested. When we gave our speeches in there, people's eyes were glazing over. Especially the young people."

"We did raise some money."

"But not enough. It's like other conservationists don't care as much about the ocean because they can't *see* it like they can see the land. Whether it's healthy or not, it's just a big blue expanse to them. The ocean could be empty and dead and it'd still look the same."

Sloane Ernst, the legendary oceanographer, waded into the water next to Nicole. Together they watched a dolphin swim inside a cresting wave, silhouetted by the blue glow of the dinoflagellates.

Ugh, it must be sick or dying, swimming in this oxygen-depleted water.

"One day I'd like to be able to be a real oceanographer," Nicole said. "Like you. I want to just study the ocean for once. Learn about the things living in it, how the currents operate, what medicines we can find in the life down there. I mean that's why I got into this. Because I love the oceans. I never signed up for ripping my hair out trying to save them."

Sloane patted her on the shoulder. "This burden was placed on us. We can't deny it. If we don't succeed, future oceanographers may not have much left to study."

"I don't feel like an oceanographer anymore. I feel like a coroner." *Like a salmon butting its head against a hundred-year-old dam in a futile attempt to swim upstream.*

The silence that followed spoke Sloane's response as loudly as if she'd said the words. *Me too.*

"My parents have finally stopped pestering me about settling down, having kids. I guess they realized I'm probably too old now. But sometimes I wonder if there's still time. If I want to."

From a distance, a chant coalesced. "Forty-one, forty, thirty-nine…"

"Why is New Year's Eve your favorite holiday?" Sloane asked out of the blue.

Nicole glanced down at a glowing blue blob at her feet—a floating plastic fork—and considered the question. "Because it celebrates the passage of time. Both an ending and a beginning. It reminds me there's a future on its way, and the more I prepare for it, the better it'll be. Sometimes I get scared in December, knowing the end is coming."

"Eighteen, seventeen, sixteen…"

"And also…it's the one holiday where you get to be with

the family you choose for yourself. Not the family whose genes you happen to have." She lightly kicked the water, sending blue sparks flying. "But here I am, alone in the ocean on New Year's Eve."

Sloane's hand, still on Nicole's shoulder, squeezed.

"You're not alone," the older woman said.

Party horns honked far away, and calls of "Happy New Year!" resounded through the night.

~*~

And then she was an old woman again, remembering, pondering blood, sweat, and tears. The sweat grew thick beneath her layers of clothing. Cold sweat. An emergency symptom.

"Hey Nicole!" said the man who'd been dragging her across the Arctic ice. "You stopped talking. I need you to keep talking to me. Do you remember my name?"

She tried, and the name Chen came to mind, but her throat had grown too numb to speak it, and then it slipped from her memory again. Her mind was too busy skimming her mental to-do list, which stretched for another twenty years at least. So many important things would never get done with her gone. She'd meant to do something about all the plastic in the oceans, the nine million tons of trash dumped into it each year. Perhaps she could have found a plastic-eating microbe and dispersed it en masse. Clearing humanity's rubbish from the seas remained a huge, vital area of ocean preservation where Nicole had done nothing at all. And if she died now, perhaps no one would ever get to it.

How can one person ever hope to make a difference? She didn't want this dismal thought to be her last, but it wouldn't go away.

"Hang in there, Nicole! Not much farther!"

~*~

Her fading mind retreated to Florida. To the *other* Florida, the one that only she and a few others knew. The Florida that stretched west of Tampa for a hundred miles, where mastodons and giant sloths had walked long before dolphins and manatees reigned. Slipping down into the Gulf of Mexico basin, her mind went past the Campeche Bank, down into the western Caribbean Sea, and it was New Year's Eve, 2033. She was thirty-nine years old.

Tomorrow she and Ian would harvest coral colonies from a thriving ecosystem to transplant into struggling, bleached reefs elsewhere. But today...today was for fun.

They arced downward toward the coral and the undulating, shapeshifting masses of sea life that lived because of it. In front of her, Ian swam past long transparent bands of salp, decorating the water like nature's own Christmas-tree garland.

Rays glided between a thousand different colors of coral, schools of parrotfish traveling in their wakes. Some of the fish stopped briefly to inspect Nicole, perhaps wondering who she was and how such a big fish as her had sprouted arms and legs.

While examining some shark eggs she found tucked into a crevice in some coral, she spotted a hermit crab scurrying along the sand, using an orange medicine bottle as its shell. Starfish also abounded here, slowly shuffling along the floor, looking for food. The sheer number of organisms here, many likely unknown to science, overwhelmed her. Oceans were home to three-fourths of all life on Earth, and it seemed like all three-fourths of it was standing right in front of her.

Resting on the floor of the Caribbean Sea, she felt a tickling sensation on her hand and instinctively jerked it away. But it was only a curious spiny lobster probing the strange human in front of it. She reached her hands cautiously toward it, and it stood on its hind legs, every other leg quivering in front of it— whether as greeting or warning, she didn't know. But for a moment she saw her ten fingers in front of the lobster's own ten appendages and contemplated their shared genetic kinship, and unnecessary rivalry. Had their roles been reversed, would this lobster's kind have harvested millions of humans from their home, keeping them in grocery-store tanks and boiling them alive?

The lobster backed away and disappeared into a bed of seagrass, the grass itself threatened by human eutrophication, thus decimating populations of manatees who ate the stuff.

Ian pointed out some spotted cleaner shrimp nibbling at the sides of several larger fish. Nicole was in a showoff mood, so she swam right up to them, breathed in deep, and removed her mouthpiece. Holding her breath, she grinned at Ian. He looked confused, until several of the cleaner shrimp gathered at Nicole's mouth and started to clean her teeth, wiping away her mouth's bacteria like the world's most unlikely dentists. She'd brushed and flossed thoroughly this morning, but apparently enough morsels remained for the shrimp.

Ian pantomimed clapping at the goofy display.

Later they found an abandoned fishing net eighty feet under the surface. Long ago discarded by humans, it continued its job of catching fish. Their skeletons littered it. Nicole liberated a barred hamlet, a highhat, two triggerfish, and several ceros.

Bribed by fishing companies, the Belizean government had downgraded the reef from a marine reserve to a mere marine sanctuary three years ago. *Some sanctuary if I can find nets, medicine bottles, and car tires down here. Ah, the language of politicians.*

She balled up the net to take with her, and they were about to leave when the unthinkable happened. Ian didn't notice it at first, and she had to physically grab his head and turn it so he'd see.

A hundred meters away, in deeper water, two blue whales swam. Ian's eyes went wide. Sighting the immense creatures was rare enough in their normal habitats, but they almost never swam into the Gulf.

The two humans approached cautiously, in awe. The 150-ton beasts were as big as airplanes, their undersides dotted by callosities. As Nicole watched, one of them opened its great mouth and gulped seawater, filled with zooplankton she couldn't see that its baleens filtered from the blue. She felt like an ant next to them, and yet they wheeled through the water with far more grace than she.

Astonishingly, she shared a mammal brain with these giants, who themselves shared a common ancestor with hippopotamuses. *And what a different life they live than us.*

If only everyone could come down here and see this. Get to know the creatures here and know that they're worth saving. Nicole could take pictures, could give speeches, could even rush up to the nearest person on the street and gush about enormous whales, curious lobsters, and shrimp that clean your teeth. She could rant about how it was all in danger. But without a common frame of reference, the paradise that was the ocean remained abstract to those who hadn't physically been there.

If only.

But time remained. Certainly all the excess CO_2 falling into the oceans was acidifying them to their breaking point, but for now that point seemed very far away. For now, the Belize Barrier Reef yawned around her in all directions, an infinity of life.

~*~

"Artificial. Lab-grown. Meat."

Dr. Ernst spread her arm before her as she made her pitch, stopping her hand at each word for emphasis.

"It's cheaper than real meat, even more nutritious, and keeps fish stocks from being depleted, not to mention taste testers can't tell the difference between it and real meat."

Nicole scanned the Kenyan restaurateur's face for a reaction, but all she found there was a slight scowl. He sat with them at a table beneath slow-turning ceiling fans, sipping occasionally from his bowl of shark fin soup.

"All the rage in China," he'd explained of the soup, oblivious that cutting fins off of sharks and dumping their bodies back in the water to die was the singular reason why most shark species—which almost never harmed humans—were now on the verge of extinction. John Mwangi may have owned half the high-end restaurants in Mombasa, but he didn't seem to know much about the food he served. That or he didn't care.

"Fake meats?" Mwangi said when Dr. Ernst had finished explaining. "It's unnatural. Customers wouldn't buy it."

"Give them the option and some of them will. Most of

them will, as the idea catches on. And you can advertise that you're helping to save the oceans."

Mwangi savored a spoonful of soup, swallowed, then gestured out the window, past the giant iceberg looming offshore, to their grand view of the Indian Ocean at dusk. "The ocean is so big, though. Does it need saving? The fishes I serve to my customers are but a small fraction of the fishes in the sea. The ocean is boundless, infinite."

"Fish stocks have declined by—"

"Yes, yes, you keep saying all the fishes went away. Where did they all go?"

"Well, frankly, we ate them."

"Ha!" He pointed at Ernst in a *you got me* gesture that indicated a good joke, not a sobering reality.

"That's why only higher-end restaurants like yours still serve fish," Ernst continued. "The oceans contain so few fish that cheaper restaurants can't afford them."

Mwangi took another sip and shrugged. "So I charge higher price for fish, and I make more monies. This is a bad thing?"

"Yes!" Ernst said, getting flustered to an extent Nicole had never seen in the usually calm woman. "Because when you charge a lot for fish, that's a market incentive for fishers to poach the last fish out of existence."

"And then," Mwangi said, raising a finger, "when the fishes are gone, imagine how much forward thinkers that kept tons of them in frozen storage will be able to charge for them. Like storage I have at my warehouse."

"Imagine. Exactly," Ernst said coldly.

Mwangi winked at her and tapped his finger to his scalp. "You can't have an economy without forward thinking."

"No," Ernst said. "You can't."

When Ernst glanced at her recently graduated protégé, Nicole nodded toward the exit. They'd made a mistake by trying to appeal to Mwangi in person. Maybe the Kenyan government would still listen to their pleas, force Mwangi's hand.

But the humongous iceberg outside told Nicole this was

unlikely. If the government would let companies tow icebergs from Antarctica so they could charge a premium for fresh water in the midst of the worst drought in Kenya's history, they wouldn't regulate fish.

"Pardon me, ladies," Mwangi said, rising. "I have New Year's party to attend. 2028. Can you believe we've come so far?"

As they exchanged goodbyes, Nicole pondered how humans could be so avaricious, so predatory that they'd kill countless other species just to make a buck off of their own. Especially when most of their own couldn't even afford it.

Throughout the conversation, a landfill by the shore had drawn her eyes, marring the majestic view of the iceberg with its copious trash overflowing and falling into the ocean. Families with young children stood atop the rubbish, digging through it. Even now, an old man was trying to free a bicycle tire, and a teenaged boy victoriously thrust a dirty shirt he'd just uncovered into the air. Immediately beside the landfill stood high-rise condos for the rich.

How can we possibly come to care about the living things in the sea when we can't even take care of our own? Are our instincts so cruel? Are we really just killer whales, stealing seal pups from shore only to toss them back and forth like footballs, battering them, toying with them while they're still alive, eating parts of them then leaving their bodies to rot? Predator and prey?

~*~

The inquisitive penguin, finally tired of pecking at Nicole's shoelaces, stood up straight and trilled at her.

"I don't know what it is, either," she told it. "It's on my foot. There must be a reason for it. I heard that guy over there calling it a 'boot.'" She pointed to Ian by the tent, his head covered in a trapper hat. He waved and took a big bite out of an icicle in his hand, munching it like a carrot.

In response, the penguin grabbed her shoelace in its beak and pulled like it was trying to strip it from her boot. When it failed again, it squawked.

Nicole laughed. "You're not afraid of me at all, are you?

Nothing's ever hunted you on land, so you think you're the king up here."

The penguin brayed. She stuck her tongue out at it.

"Better watch out, kid. Next time you see someone who looks like me, they may not be so friendly."

When she stood, the penguin abruptly retreated, waddling away toward who knew where.

It had plenty of new territory to explore. Each spring now—spring here being October and November—thousands of waterfalls stretched down the ice shelves, carving chasms in the ice until no ice was left, exposing innumerable square miles of the most astonishing sight seen here in a hundred thousand years: land.

Lots and lots of land.

And where there was land, there were developers. And those developers were trying to get the Antarctic Treaty changed so they could develop resorts on newly green Antarctic terrain. *The premiere vacation spot of the Southern Hemisphere, a must-see for anyone who's anyone. Never mind the oil and coal deposits on our land purchases. That's entirely coincidental.*

And the continent was *saturated* with coal. The place used to be covered in lush tropical jungles, after all. Now those jungles lay deep underground, compressed into combustible rock.

But where other humans had set up camp—humans like Nicole and Ian—those companies couldn't go digging, drilling, building, and destroying animals' habitats. Or so thought Greenpeace. "Until they get the treaty changed, you have just as much a right to be there as they do," their team leader had explained.

So here they were, waiting for spring to begin and the speculators to arrive. With hundreds of other activists spread across the continent, they would follow, spy on, and pester the speculators, noting their locations and erecting camps there after they left, permanently occupying the very land they wanted to use until somebody's government kicked the companies out.

Or the activists.

"No need to thank us, little penguin," Nicole said as the bird wandered off into the bright white snow. "Just go and live your life."

She walked past a pine tree, crossed onto the frozen bay, and reentered the tent. Inside, Ian was cooking what smelled like baked beans in the little solar toaster oven they'd brought with them.

"Making dinner?" she asked.

"Dessert!" Ian said.

"Dessert?"

"It's tofu, avocado, and black bean cupcakes."

The sound that came out of Nicole's mouth was half laugh, half disgusted groan. "Dessert?"

"Trust me, they're delicious. You'll love 'em."

"You really are vegan, then, huh?"

"Super vegan. Why aren't you?"

"And a vegan evangelist, too! I'm so lucky."

"That you are, milady," Ian said, plopping down into a pile of snow at the back of the tent. "I figure we deserve a New Year's Eve feast, and what better food to snuggle up and watch *Battlestar Galactica* on my cell phone with than super-vegan cupcakes?"

Nicole snickered and studied this unusual man with whom she'd be spending the next several months. Ian was thirty, a few years older than her and sexy in a geeky sort of way. The chemistry was certainly there, but they hadn't so much as held hands yet, and she kept wondering if she really wanted to hook up with this guy who regularly talked to himself, licked the flavoring off potato chips before eating them, and liked to bathe nude in freezing ocean water.

As was said of women dating in the male-dominated Antarctic continent, "The odds are good. But the goods...are odd."

"Your family approve of you coming here?" Nicole asked.

"I'm worried they'll hang me when I get back. Yours?"

"Same. But they disowned me years ago as an eco-terrorist. They say I've been brainwashed by Al Gore."

"Haven't we all?" Ian took a ponderous bite of his icicle.

Nicole laughed. "When they find out I'm not even getting paid for this, they'll probably hang me, too."

"Yeah, it doesn't exactly help the student loan balance, does it? I'm starting to think that oceanography degree wasn't worth the trouble."

That perked Nicole's attention up. She leaned forward. "You have a degree in oceanography?"

"Indeed I do. And yourself?"

"I, uh, never went to college," Nicole said. "But I've been thinking about going to school for oceanography."

"You should! It's absolutely worth the trouble."

"But didn't you just say—"

"Shh. Student loans, student schmoans. We need more trained converts to the cause. Al Gore's orders."

Nicole rolled her eyes.

After dinner and a surprisingly not-awful dessert, the pair settled into their sleeping bags with the sun still high in the sky, where it would remain for the next several months. The ice on which they'd raised their tent lay near the Prince Olav Mountains, near the southern starting point of what was left of the Ross Ice Shelf, so the ice hadn't thawed for the summer quite yet. Tonight would be the last night they could safely camp on it, though.

When Nicole was almost asleep, Ian whispered something to her.

"Huh?" she said, rousing to partial wakefulness.

"Listen."

She didn't hear it at first, but soon it came to her: faint whisking noises, each like an electric zapping sound extended over several seconds, sometimes rising from low to high pitch, sometimes the reverse. They sounded artificial, like a synthesizer sound effect from a 1980s rock album.

"It's seal calls," Ian whispered. "From beneath the ice. That's the sound of males challenging each other to battle."

Nicole took her head off the pillow and lowered her ear to the ice. The noises grew clearer, even more otherworldly. She felt the rise and fall of the sea ever so gently from beneath the ice. *A whole other realm exists below.*

The tent walls flapped in a gentle wind, faraway seabirds cawed, and together the two isolated activists listened to the sounds of mighty Antarctica, the last great refuge of nature, where humans had treaded lightly enough to leave only a vanishing trace of a footprint.

~*~

New Year's Eve, 1999. The new millennium beckoned with promises of hope and progress, and for five-year-old Nicole, of a long and happy life.

At a resort near her home in Tampa, adults chatted up by the gazebo, and older kids frolicked with sparklers. Waiting for the fireworks to start, hundreds of beachgoers watched the last bit of dusk slip away behind the clouds on the horizon. Nicole spent the time jumping in puddle after puddle near the water, splashing passersby and laughing giddily.

Suddenly, she came upon something horrifying.

"A fish! Daddy, Daddy, Daddy! There's a fish! A fish!"

After a minute, her dad sauntered over, a bottle of his adult drink in one hand. "What is it you're screaming about?"

"Daddy, there's a fish. Look!"

In one of the puddles, a fish lay twitching. Its body was bent in half, and Nicole couldn't wrap her mind around how it had gotten to be that way.

"It broke," she said sadly. "It needs our help."

Her dad laughed, downed the last of his adult drink, then lobbed the bottle into the surf. "If you want, there's about ten more fish just like it on the grill. We can take this one up and fry it, too."

Nicole was torn between two next steps, each equally important for helping nature: pleading with him to save the fish or running to go get his bottle back. She chose the latter, because the bottle would be gone soon. Waves drenched her, threatened to knock her over as she struggled out into the water. Her dad was yelling behind her, but instinct was driving her now, and her fist closed around the discarded bottle just as her dad's arms closed around her.

"Hey! What do you think you're doing?" he bellowed.

Nicole tried to slow her breathing, but her words came out piecemeal. "You're not...supposed...to put trash...in the water. You're supposed...to recycle."

Her dad seemed winded, too. He frowned at her, perplexed. "You get that idea from your mom?"

"No...from the TV."

Her dad scoffed, pressing her to him, keeping her from breaking free or from moving much at all. "What's the point?" he asked almost teasingly, snatching the bottle from her. "It's just one beer bottle. It's just one little thing."

Nicole gazed up at him. She'd found her breath. "Little things add up to big things," she said. "You have to keep trying."

Her dad snorted, drew one arm back, and hurled the bottle far, far out to sea. By the time Nicole returned to the fish, it was dead.

~*~

Blood, sweat, tears. Nicole's whole life narrowed to this last moment, her eyes watering then overflowing as her life's failures ebbed into sad oblivion. The man dragging her through the snow had been fading, too, his strength nearly exhausted. Would *he* die here as well? Would the Arctic serve as both of their graves? *The Arctic. Fitting that I should die along with it.*

But he wasn't dragging her through the snow anymore. In fact, the light above Nicole was no longer dim aurorae, but a piercing incandescence beaming down like the sun. Where had her parka gone? Where had the cold gone? Her fading memories suddenly struck her not as the unconsciousness before death, but as the subsiding of a sickly delirium. Her vision grew clearer and her head stopped pulsing with pain.

She lay on a bed in a doctor's office. A small office cluttered with equipment. The whirlwind still raged beyond the thick windows but in here, it was warm.

"Hi, Nicole," said a woman standing over her. "Do you know where you are?"

She didn't, but the face before her stirred her memory. "Santillan. You're Dr. Santillan."

"I am. And do you know who this is?"

Face red from cold exposure, snow still melting in his beard, the young man who'd dragged her through the gale stood behind Santillan, his eyes worried.

"Chen," Nicole said. "My friend. From Beijing University."

Both Chen and Santillan smiled. "You remember what we were doing before you hit your head?" Chen asked, the same way he'd asked those questions about her favorite color and holiday.

"Occupying," Nicole said, guessing based on the flimsy wisps of memory dancing before her. "We set up a tent…We were gonna spy on the…on the corporations. Keep them from building resorts."

Her colleagues exchanged a confused glance. "I don't think building resorts here is legal," Chen said. "The Antarctic Treaty forbids it. Greenpeace stopped all that resort nonsense fifty years ago, Nicole."

Now it was Nicole's turn to be confused. She tried sitting up.

"No, no, lie back," Santillan said. The doctor clutched Nicole's arm with a firm yet gentle hold and eased her back onto the pillow. "Just rest for now."

"But they want to build cities here, destroy ecosystems—"

"Nicole, you're in the biggest city here, and it's good old McMurdo Station, population four thousand."

"But this is the Arctic."

Santillan chuckled. "This is the Antarctic."

Antarctica? But of course. They'd trekked across ice, and no ice remained in the Arctic. Only ocean. Of course they'd been in the Antarctic the whole time. Her and Ian.

Confusion kept clouding her mind, and she grappled with it. "But isn't it New Year's Eve tonight?"

Her companions looked at each other again, as if Nicole had spoken a foreign language.

"It's the middle of June," said Chen.

"June?"

"We were collecting samples of marine life under the ice. You just slipped all of a sudden. Do you remember?"

Nicole remembered drifting near Ian in the shadow of a blue whale, remembered Dr. Ernst's kind words in the water of the Everglades, remembered countless others who'd helped her along her path through life. If she could remember all that, why couldn't she remember the last few days? The last few years?

Or maybe she could…

"We were measuring mercury levels," she said.

"We were!" Chen said.

"The levels were…" She knew what they'd found. Could it be true? Was her memory tricking her? "They were going down. Because there's no more coal power anywhere."

"I think you'll make a full recovery," Santillan said, peeling something off Nicole's head and replacing it with something else warm and sticky. "Your memory should come back within the hour as the treatment repairs your skull and the pressure in your brain normalizes. You're very lucky, you know. The treatment that just saved your life is brand new—we just got it in last month. It actually comes from my home city, from a mollusk called *S. vastataprope* that almost went extinct at one point."

The doctor disposed of some supplies in a biowaste container and started wiping off the countertop. "A few months ago *Popular Science* did a profile on this fisherman who lives in the last bay where they're found, a guy named Angelo Melcito. He set up a marine reserve in that bay, extra-governmental, policed by the local community. He didn't even know about the medical benefits. Just said the bay was almost fished clean until some lady changed his mind about how he ran his business. Now he fishes just outside the reserve and catches more fish than ever. Kind of a cool story."

"Nicole!"

A blast of chill air blew in from outside as Terrance swung into the room, carrying a bag. He bolted the door closed and ran to Nicole's bed. "Are you okay? What happened? Will she be all right?"

Still too shocked to respond, Nicole just stared at him. Terrance had witnessed her exchange with Angelo, years ago. Did he know the story Santillan had just relayed?

He kissed her hand. "I'm so, so glad you made it back safe. I love you so much. I'm so sorry I wasn't there."

Terrance is my boyfriend, Nicole remembered in a pleasant rush of nostalgia. *Has been for years.*

"Here," Terrance said, removing a container from his bag. "You'll need protein. I brought you some salmon. Eat, eat."

"You want me to eat *fish?*"

The disgust showing from her own face reflected as compassion on Terrance's. "Of course not," he said. "It's not real meat. Who eats real meat anymore?" He glanced up at Chen. "Just how hard did she hit her head?"

Nicole's head was certainly spinning. *What world have I woken up to?* She remembered more every moment, and this was indeed the world she'd lived in before her fall. It just seemed so divorced from the world of her past—the world that had crushed every dream she'd had since childhood. Experiencing the world before her now, the world she'd worked to build, as if for the first time…It threatened to make her pass out again.

She spied a computerized map of the world's oceans on a wall, complete with shading for coral reefs, dead zones at the mouths of rivers, deep-ocean mining areas, and other areas of interest. There seemed to be many more reefs than she remembered from when she was middle-aged, and far fewer of the dead zones and mining areas.

The snowy wind outside subsiding, McMurdo Station came into view. Though the sky remained dark save for brilliant green aurorae, bundled workers trod between the buildings in what appeared to be the early-morning rush hour. All vehicles on the roads were electric, and the roads themselves, she recalled, were made from bioasphalt instead of petroleum. Not only here, but worldwide. A lack of plastic products in the room also brought to her mind the global moratorium on plastic.

No asphalt, no plastic, no gasoline…No more need to drill for oil.

"No, don't cry, Nicole," Chen said beside her. "Why are you crying again? You're okay now."

She clasped his hand, this new collaborator who'd just saved her life. At forty-six years of age, Chen's eyes were the eyes of youth.

"It's been hard," she said in a wavering voice. "It's been *so* hard."

"I know. I know it has," Chen said, gently gripping her hand in return. "It's been hard for all of us."

"I thought I'd failed."

"Whaaaaaaat?" Chen jokingly stretched out the word. "What are you talking about? You're Nicole Olson! You're a legend! You're the whole reason I became an oceanographer. In school, I saw an online talk you gave for kids and I was hooked for life."

"I'm just a normal woman. I'm just one woman."

"You're not, though. We're your family. We're all here with you, backing you up. We always have been."

As Nicole thought back through past New Year's Eves, she considered that maybe Chen was right. She'd always worked through holidays—every holiday, not just her favorite one. But even then, her memories of those days dwelled not on the work she'd been doing, but on the people she'd been working with. And the countless others who they'd been working to help.

Nicole wiped away the last of her tears. She flung her bedsheets aside, swung her legs over the edge of the bed, and stood on the cold ground, wet from melted snow someone had tramped in. The water was freezing, but it felt marvelous against her feet.

Terrance and Santillan immediately moved to stop her.

"Ms. Olson, I have to insist that you lie back down until you're healed."

"Dear, please, listen to the doctor. You need rest. You're not as young as you used to be."

Nicole waved their concerns aside. "I may be eighty-three, but it's only June now. There's still plenty of time. And plenty of work that needs doing."

~*~

A Word from Joshua Ingle

Hi, I'm Josh. I'm a pathologically curious fantasy, horror, and sci-fi geek who moonlights as a film/TV enthusiast and wishes I were a scientist. I'm a big fan of this awesome and mysterious universe that we find ourselves in, and one of my favorite things to do is learn as much about it as I can and share my findings with kind gentlefolk such as yourself. In both my own work and in the stuff I read, I gravitate toward envelope-pushing, mind-bending ideas that challenge common assumptions.

Every story I write is a story with a purpose. I write to entertain you with ethical and philosophical crises, packaged in nail-biting thriller and mystery story lines, taking place in super-detailed story worlds. And I write to open your mind, and my own mind, to new ideas. Many, but not all, of my stories feature dark and ominous atmospheres, which is basically the opposite of my real-life personality.

Writing fiction is my passion in life, and I'm thrilled to have this opportunity to share my stories with you. To see some of my other work, check out joshuaingle.com/books.

~*~

Turtle:
An A.L.I.V.E. Story
R.D. Brady

~*~

"Tolerance and apathy are the last virtues of a dying society."
—Aristotle

Diego Island
Off the Coast of Washington State

NORAH TIDWELL LENGTHENED her stride, keeping her breathing in time with her footfalls. God, she loved to run. Every morning, rain or shine, she hit her five miles. She had been at the R.I.S.E. base for the last four months. The base covered the entire island, with a rocky shore that made any approach by boat daunting, even the sanctioned approaches.

She hadn't stepped foot off of it in all that time. Now, Norah never really thought of herself as someone who got stir crazy. Even back at Quantico, when training with the Marines at Officer Candidate School, she hadn't been itching to get off the base like most of her fellow candidates. But here, she would trade almost anything for a little time off this base.

Because this base was nothing like any of the military bases she had spent time on. When she'd been a Marine, she'd known what her objective was, and the objective of every last person around her. Here, she was still unclear what the base's purpose was. She didn't even know what R.I.S.E. stood for. And she had no idea how many people were on the base. She'd met maybe half a dozen people so far, but from a distance she'd seen dozens more.

She along with the rest of the refugees, as they'd come to think of themselves, resided on only one quarter of the base. The rest was strictly off limits, adding to the prison like feeling. Oh, the guards in their fatigues were polite about it when they intercepted Norah or one of the other refugees who wandered too far afield, but the message was clear nonetheless: stay in your section.

She ran along the fence line now and was happy to see the path she had created in the grass, evidence of her early morning habit. She was working on getting her time down to thirty-five minutes for five miles. She was at thirty-six and she was sure with a little more of a push, she could trim off the last minute.

Norah reached the end of the path and slowed to a walk, her hands on her head as she tried to calm her breathing. A short two minutes later, Maeve Leander—with her dark hair pulled into a ponytail, her long lean frame showing the results of her own morning workout routine since she'd arrived at the base—came into view. Maeve slowed to a walk, joining Norah.

"You good?" Norah asked.

Maeve doubled over, taking in a deep breath while holding up one hand. Maeve had been joining Norah for runs for the last two months. She'd really come a long way. But she wasn't quite as fast as Norah yet. Norah smiled. The good doctor might not be naturally athletic, but she definitely didn't hold back.

Maeve straightened, her breathing still uneven, her breaths coming out in pants. "How—do you—speed up like that?"

"I always picture something important I need to get to or someone to save. It makes me move even when everything is telling me to stop." Norah grinned. "Plus, I figure the faster I run, the sooner I can stop."

Maeve gave a little laugh. "Now that's a reasoning I can appreciate." But Norah saw the understanding behind Maeve's eyes and knew for the next run, Maeve might not be so far behind for the last lap.

Norah had met Maeve four months ago when Norah had been the Department of Extra-terrestrial and Alien Defense (D.E.A.D.) representative on a Presidentially appointed committee on the dangers of the aliens who'd escaped Area 51. Maeve had been the government's expert. But that meeting wasn't what had led Norah to track down Maeve just a few days after their first meeting. No, that explanation had to do with a little guy named Iggy.

The two women headed back toward the barracks. They stopped at the edge of the single road just as the four buildings that made up their section came into view. Each building was almost identical to the next. The only way to tell them apart was the signs next to the main doors: barracks, mess hall, rec center and headquarters.

Norah watched with narrowed eyes as a large, green panel truck rumbled by. "Any idea what's in *that* truck?"

Maeve shook her head. "No more than I know what's in the other trucks."

The two of them exchanged a look, then kept walking. Both of them were voluntarily on the base, as Tilda Watson, the base commander, reminded them. But that wasn't entirely true. Both Maeve and Norah were responsible for the lives of other beings who quite literally had nowhere else to go. Alvie and the triplets were alien-human hybrids the government were trying to track down. Iggy was a Maldekite, a survivor of the planet Maldek that had been destroyed billions of years ago, back during a time when Mars had an environment more similar to Earth's. While different species, all five had been recreated in U.S. government labs.

And all five were currently being hunted by the U.S. government.

Tilda Watson was the only person with enough resources to

keep them hidden. But it was a double-edged sword because Tilda's exceptional ability at hiding things extended to the reason why, exactly, this base existed.

The woman in question stepped out from the cafeteria, her thick white hair pulled back into its usual braid. Tilda was seventy-four and yet Norah was pretty sure if she joined Maeve and Norah on their morning runs, she would leave both of them in her dust. Behind Tilda came a tall grey alien, dressed incongruously in green camouflage.

Agaren.

When Norah had first seen Agaren, his appearance had been unnerving. He had a large, almost triangular head that came to a rounded point at his chin. Wide black eyes scanned the area as he walked, his neutral facial expression in place. His back ramrod straight, Norah knew very little about him but the way he held himself reminded her of aristocracy.

"And do we know why *he's* here?" Norah asked.

Maeve shook her head. "No. But Alvie defers to him, the triplets as well."

"So does Iggy. But who is he?"

"I don't know but I'm pretty sure Tilda does."

Norah watched the septuagenarian walk across the gravel drive, deep in conversation with Agaren who walked silently next to her. She disappeared into the office and Agaren paused at the door, turning and catching Norah's gaze before he disappeared inside as well.

"I'm going to grab the gang for a picnic. Do you and Iggy want to join us?" Maeve asked.

Norah pulled her gaze from the building that housed Tilda's office. "That would be great. I'll see—" She cut off as she noticed a tall muscular man with shockingly blond hair and sunglasses heading toward them.

Adam Watson, Tilda's grandson, stopped in front of them. With a curt nod to Maeve, he turned his attention to Norah. "Your excursion has been approved. I'll meet you at the dock in fifteen."

"Meet me?"

"Tilda thought it was best if you had—" he paused.

"A chaperone?" Maeve suggested.

"A guard?" Norah said simultaneously.

"Some company," Adam said smoothly.

"Yes, your grandmother seems big on making sure everyone's emotional needs are met," Norah said dryly.

Adam merely raised an eyebrow. "Fifteen minutes." He strode toward the barracks.

Norah watched him go with a frown on her face. There was something up with that guy but she just couldn't put her finger on it.

Maeve nudged her shoulder. "You better get going because when Adam says fifteen minutes, I'm pretty sure he means exactly fifteen minutes."

Maeve was right. Norah tore her gaze away and nodded. "Quick shower, grab my pack, and I'm out of here."

"Enjoy your freedom. I'll keep an eye on Iggy while you're gone."

Norah paused before nodding. "Great. Thanks."

~*~

The SDX 240 Sea Ray cut through the waves, sending up sprays of water. With Adam at the wheel, Norah was free to sit along the long bench at the stern of the boat and enjoy the ride. Occasionally, a spray of water would waft over her. But instead of re-positioning herself to avoid the dampness, she shifted closer to the edge. She breathed in deep, soaking it all in. For the first time in months, she felt a little sense of freedom.

She glanced back at the island they'd just left. It was set on its own with a few smaller islands in the distance. Diego Island was not part of the San Juan Islands, but the larger island chain sat north of them.

Norah squinted and could just make out the large radar arrays on the other island surrounding Diego. She wasn't surprised. Tilda would never allow the chance of their enemies being able to get too close, which meant Tilda and R.I.S.E. controlled those islands too.

But exactly how had this woman amassed such resources? And what was her end goal?

She shook her head, chasing the question away. *No, not today.* She'd spent the last few months wrestling with variations of those questions. She was not going to spend today doing the same.

Today was about—

"Ig! Ig! Ig!"

Norah cringed, glancing at Adam even as she reached for her backpack on the seat next to her. *Crap.*

Adam didn't change his speed or swerve at the sound. He didn't seem to react at all. He *had* to have heard that, even with the loud, droning engine.

Norah unzipped the bag. A small green head popped out. Freed from the bag's confines, his pointed ears, which stuck out on either side, wiggled. He reared back when he caught sight of Adam. "Ig," he squeaked.

"You were supposed to stay quiet until we got to the beach," Norah mumbled.

Iggy looked up at her. "Ig?"

Adam glanced back at her, a small smile on his face.

Norah frowned. "You knew he was in there the whole time, didn't you?"

Adam nodded.

Norah shook her head. She'd been wracking her brain trying to figure out how to sneak Iggy off the base with her. *Apparently, I could have just told Adam my plans.*

Of course, there was no way for her to have known that. To say Norah was out of the loop was a severe under exaggeration. The base was a military base but not a government base. Norah still wasn't sure who, exactly, the base was aligned with. But since they kept her and Iggy hidden from the branches of the U.S. government trying to catch them, she couldn't ask too many questions.

They had taken care of Iggy, who'd been seriously hurt protecting Norah. And for that, Norah would always be thankful. But that gratitude didn't do anything to reduce the need to get out, for just a little while. "Well, come on out Iggy."

Iggy squirmed from the bag. His feet were disproportionately large for his two-foot stature, as were his hands with their enlarged knuckles. When she'd first seen his hands, they'd reminded Norah of tree frog hands. He was wearing little red pants with big yellow buttons. Norah wasn't sure where the pants had come from, but she had a sneaking suspicion there was a pantless stuffed Mickey Mouse somewhere on the base. His little belly stuck out. Combined with small curly hair on the very top of his head, it gave him the appearance of a little old man.

A small white bandage covered half his chest. It was only a precaution. The wound had healed nicely but no one really knew how Iggy healed. As Norah had painfully learned over the last year, Iggy was only one of dozens of alien creatures that the United States government had recreated from their DNA.

Iggy climbed onto the back of the seat, then reached for Norah. Norah picked him up and held him to her chest. She glanced over at Adam. "Thanks."

He nodded.

Norah walked to the bow and took a seat, Iggy facing forward. He let out a happy squeal each time the ocean spray touched him.

Norah leaned back and smiled, feeling relaxed for the first time in months. *We both need this.*

~*~

The beach was only a twenty-minute drive from where Adam docked the boat along the Washington shore just outside of Blaine, Washington. There was no one around when they stepped onto the metal docks, but Norah knew they were being watched.

"What is this place?"

"Technically it's part of the R.I.S.E. base, although it's not listed on any documents that way."

Norah glanced at him from the side of her eyes. "Exactly

how much 'property' does R.I.S.E own?"

Adam just smiled and pointed toward an old Ford Explorer. "We should get going."

With a sigh Norah followed. While she had expected the non-answer, it did nothing to tamp down her frustration. After four months, she figured they could share a little.

Iggy bounced ahead of her behind Adam looking happier than she could remember seeing him, which only reinforced the need for this outing. He'd seem to be becoming more withdrawn and nervous over the last month. She knew it was due to the stares he received on the base. He seemed more sensitive to them than Alvie and the triplets. They couldn't go into a city or more populated area without Iggy causing a stir, but a deserted beach could give him a little taste of freedom. And, if she was being honest, there was some serious appeal to feeling the sand between her own toes.

Thirty minutes later, Adam pulled over to the side of the road. He nodded toward the path that jutted out through the rocks. "That leads to the beach."

"You're not coming?"

"I'll make sure no one intrudes on you two."

She glanced out the window. "Shouldn't we check if anyone is there first?"

"There's no one there."

She frowned. "How do you—" Then she shook her head. "You guys own the beach, don't you?"

Adam smiled. "No one will bother you."

Iggy, who'd crawled out of the backpack as soon as the car had started moving, bounced up and down in Norah's lap, his excitement contagious. Norah grinned at him, feeling her own excitement build. "Well, we'll see you later."

Adam nodded, his gaze returning to the road. Norah opened the door and Iggy scrambled off her lap, making a beeline for the path between the tall rocks.

"Hey, wait up," Norah called, grabbing the backpack and hurrying after him. Iggy disappeared from view. Norah jogged behind him down the winding path. The sound of waves reached out for her and the scent of salt water carried toward her. A smile crossed her face and wouldn't leave. She picked up her pace. She jogged out between the last of the rocks and stepped onto the beach.

Pale white sand stretched along the water line as far as she could see, dotted with rocks but not too many. And beyond it, the Pacific Ocean rolled, waves crashing down on the shore with a ferocious energy. Iggy stood transfixed a few feet ahead. Norah stopped next to him, just as amazed by the power of nature. Waves tossed, sending plumes of water up into the air as they crashed down. There was something so wild and freeing about an ocean. She stood there and all the modern conveniences of life disappeared from her mind. All she could focus on was the beauty of what was in front of her.

Iggy reached up and slipped his hand into hers. Norah squeezed his hand in response.

She looked down at him.

A single tear rolled down his cheek.

She swallowed hard past the catch at the back of her throat. She couldn't remember ever seeing a sight more beautiful. She breathed in deep, feeling a peace that had alluded her these last few months.

There was nothing better than this moment.

~*~

Two hours later, Norah was lazing on the beach, using her backpack to prop herself up. She and Iggy had filled their time with a days worth of activities: a walk along the shore, newly collected shells, a few inching trips into the water, and a little picnic. She smiled as his expression when the water had first touched his feet wafted through her brain again. After lunch, she had shown him the joy of building a sandcastle, with the small buckets and cups she'd brought from the camp.

The sand castle she and Iggy had made now stood guard next to Norah as she finished up her snack. Iggy's snack was long since finished. He was busy finishing up his own sand creation, and Norah was not afraid to admit she was woefully outclassed. Iggy's creation towered over the small castle Norah

R.D. Brady

had helped him build. There were multiple turrets, an outer wall, even a drawbridge. No one was really sure what role the Maldekites played in their original society, but watching Iggy create, Norah was pretty sure construction was part of it.

She smiled, glancing at the horizon. They had needed this—the peace, the quiet. The sun was dipping toward the horizon now, their day coming to a close. But she promised herself she would bring Iggy back. The happiness exuding from him made that an absolute necessity. Maybe next time she could find a way to bring Maeve and her gang as well.

Iggy hopped off his castle, which now stood four feet tall, and looked over at her.

"That's great, Iggy."

"Ig." He smiled, but then his head whipped toward the water.

The hair on the back of Norah's neck stood straight up. She scanned the water but couldn't see anything wrong. Iggy let out a cry and raced toward the water's edge.

Norah scramble to her feet and gave chase. "Iggy!"

Iggy sprinted to the water's edge and waded in. The water quickly reached his chest and then he was under. Norah charged forward to where she'd seen the water cover him but she didn't see him. She reached around but couldn't feel him.

A squeal erupted from her right and Iggy's head popped up before he went under again. She dove for him, catching a hold of his arm and pulling him up. "Iggy!"

She held him to her chest, stumbled under the weight. *What the—*

She nearly dropped him in surprise as she saw he too had something clasped to his chest. It was a two-foot long green sea turtle with large flippers. Shaking hard, Iggy let out a mewling sound, his arms protectively wrapped around the turtle.

She quickly hurried back to the shore as Adam came racing across the beach. "What is it?"

"I'm not sure." Norah lowered herself to the ground, placing Iggy in front of her. Iggy rocked back and forth with the creature, a small strange hum emanating from him.

"It's an olive ridley sea turtle," Adam said. "They've been beaching around here, driven from the warmer water by the hotter zones."

"This one didn't beach. Iggy fished him from the water."

Tears were in Iggy's eyes as he held the turtle toward her. Norah gasped as she got her first clear look at it. A plastic ring had wrapped itself around the turtle's shell. It must have happened when the turtle had been very young, because his shell had grown around it, cinched in the middle by the plastic ring, which was attached to another five plastic rings. It was a six-pack plastic holder. "Oh my god."

A sense of sadness, along with heartache wafted over her. Norah gently took the turtle from Iggy's outstretched hands. "I—I don't know what I can do."

The poor turtle was so misshapen—its shell in the shape of an hourglass—she didn't know how the poor thing could still be breathing. The plastic must have been compressing the poor creature's organs. Iggy was mewling softly, his fear for the creature's wellbeing heartbreaking as he placed a gentle hand on the turtle's back.

"How does this happen?"

"Humans," Adam said, disgust lacing the single word.

Norah's gaze jolted up, but with his sunglasses on she couldn't read any expression on his face. And for the first time, she turned and really looked at the beach and the water. The beach was covered in white sand, true. But now she could see the careless disregard—a bottle cap here, a small plastic tab there, a handful of cigarette stubs casually tossed. A wave crashed down and Norah watched the water race forward. Objects from the receding water littered the shoreline: a beer can and a piece of plastic from God knew where, along with other little pieces that were obviously manmade. Small pieces of garbage littered the whole beach.

Adam was right. Humans had caused this poor creature's suffering. She stood up. "We need to get him some help."

~*~

Adam had driven them to an animal hospital fifteen minutes away. He and Iggy stayed in the car while Norah carried the turtle into the Seas the Day Veterinarian Hospital.

The receptionist only raised an eyebrow before sighing when Norah presented the patient. Apparently, this was not the first time a creature carelessly re-designed by humans had been here.

After the turtle was taken for x-rays, Norah stood across the steel table as the blond veterinarian, Dr. Teel, shook her head, examining the creature. "God, I hate this. The band's compressing the creature's stomach, intestines, liver—basically all of its internal organs have been rearranged and shoved together."

"Will it survive?"

"It's amazing it's survived this long. If I snip this band off, it could help or it could make it worse."

"There's worse than this?"

The vet nodded. "Yeah."

"You've seen this before."

"I've seen everything before. Our oceans, they're turning into junkyards. Sea creatures, if they're not getting wrapped in the garbage, they're eating it." Dr. Teele gestured to the X-ray view box.

Norah stepped forward, squinting, trying to figure out what she was seeing. "Is that a bottle cap?"

"A few of them. His stomach is full of plastic, metal, garbage."

"What? How?"

"There's so much garbage in the oceans and sea creatures can't tell the difference between garbage and food."

"How is this possible?"

"People don't care or at least don't think through what they're doing. Dumping trash on the beach—plastic bags, aluminum cans, all the things we think of as disposable. But those things don't just disappear. Most take decades to decompose. Which gives them plenty of time to wreak havoc with marine life."

Norah had never really spent much time thinking about ocean pollution. The oceans seemed so vast. It was amazing that anything humans did could hurt it. "But surely it's not that large of a problem—"

"I wish that were true. People don't realize that most of the garbage we generate eventually touches the water. From plastic to pesticides, it's in there and it's killing the oceans. Hundreds of different species are harmed or killed annually. I volunteer down at the Pacific Coast Marine Animal Rescue. Every single sea animal they take in that I have worked on has had manmade objects in its stomach. Turtles mistake plastic bags for jellyfish. Dolphins get caught in discarded nets. In other parts of the world, the oceans are heating up, killing off species upon species. And we act like it doesn't matter. Like destroying the world around us won't have any effect, but it will."

Norah felt overwhelmed by the sheer scope of the problem.

Dr. Teel looked at Norah and winced. "I'm sorry. It's been a really long week of cases like this. But I shouldn't be—"

"No, no. You have nothing to apologize for. The fact that you're not screaming in frustration is pretty surprising."

The vet smiled. "I save that for after hours when no one can hear me."

"So what's verdict?"

"He's survived this long, he'll hopefully survive a little longer. I'll contact the rescue group and see if they can take him. Once I've got that set up, I'll remove the band and set him up for the recovery."

"Thanks. Is there anything I can do?"

The vet carefully gathered the turtle in her arms. "Not to sound like an old commercial, but if you give hoot, don't pollute."

~*~

The car ride back to the dock was quiet. Norah wasn't sure what to say and Iggy, who'd been so happy earlier, seemed to have sunk into himself. He lay curled up in her lap, his breathing even as he stared straight ahead. She rubbed his back, which normally made him purr. But right now, he looked so lost. She felt like she had let him down, like humanity had let him down.

She'd borrowed Adam's cell phone when they'd gotten into the car to do a little research and the more she learned about what was happening to the oceans, the more her stomach turned.

"What are we doing to our planet?" she whispered, not sure if she was talking to herself, to Iggy, or to Adam.

"We're killing it," Adam said. "Each year we lose more and more animal species. The ice is melting. We're in the middle of the sixth mass extinction event and people are just going around as if none of it is happening."

"Extinction event?"

"Within the next two to three centuries, the Earth will lose two-thirds of its species. And the species that exist are already showing huge population decay and the loss of territory, suggesting the extinction event may be even worse than feared. We've already wiped out fifty percent of the world's wildlife in the last forty years. Can you imagine how little will be left in another forty and then another?"

"But species go extinct all the time."

"Yes, but the rate is currently 100 times the normal rate. Humanity is driving this extinction through climate change, the destruction of natural habitats, and consumption. We are fueling this extinction cycle." Adam shook his head. "Humanity has been given the gift of this beautiful planet and in return has destroyed it."

Norah stared at the man sitting next to her. In the short time she'd known him, he'd said maybe a half dozen sentences during any one conversation. The impassioned speech she'd just heard was all the more influential because of the usual reticence of Adam to say anything.

The boat ride back was a silent affair, everyone lost in their own thoughts but Iggy just seemed lost. As they stepped off the boat, Norah took in a deep breath, the tension in her shoulders and chest easing. Here, she was safe from all the crazy that was out there. She could pretend they hadn't just seen a turtle who'd practically been cut in two by garbage. She could shove away all thoughts of how humans were destroying this planet with their carelessness.

And then I can be part of the problem instead of part of the solution, she thought.

Because that was exactly what humanity had been doing. There was no debate that temperatures were rising. Parts of the world, particularly the Middle East, were going to be so hot in the summer that by 2100 they would be completely unlivable. The rising sea levels were going to completely destroy some small island locales, like the Marshall Islands, and even major cities within the next fifty years.

And mankind was responsible for it.

Oh, there were people who argued that the planet naturally went through cycles. Which was true. But the temperatures were rising too fast. The carbon monoxide levels were too high. And our concern was too low to think that an answer was right around the corner.

Exhaustion weighing her down, Norah opened the door as Adam brought the car to a stop in front of the barracks. Iggy had fallen asleep in her arms and was jarred awake by the light from the car's interior. He started and Norah rubbed his back. "It's okay. Shh, it's okay."

Iggy snuggled in closer to her as she stood to carry him inside. Maeve and Alvie were stepping out of the barracks as Norah approached. Alvie went still for a moment and then hurried over to Norah. He lay a hand on Iggy's back.

Norah stopped, letting the two of them communicate. Neither talked in the conventional way, but from what Norah understood, Alvie could share his thoughts and feelings, sometimes in images. Norah hadn't been on the receiving end of such a vision yet, but Iggy had.

Sadness wafted over Norah and she knew it was Alvie's. He was such a sympathetic little guy. He looked at Norah. "I'm not sure. The vet is taking care of him."

Alvie nodded but he kept his gaze on Norah. And Norah was the one who broke the connection, guilt along with shame forcing her to look away. How could she explain to Alvie that humans didn't mean harm even though they knew harm could be caused by their actions? Alvie thought out each step, each move. He was incredibly empathetic. He wouldn't be able to understand it. Now that Norah was stepping back and looking at it objectively, she wasn't sure she could understand it in any way that did not make humans look awful. She was part of the species responsible for the turtle's pain and now for Iggy's. She was part of the species slowly destroying this planet.

"Hey, how was the beach?" Maeve asked as she joined them.

"It started better than it ended. I need to get him inside." She nodded toward Iggy.

Maeve's brow wrinkled. "Is he okay? Did he get hurt?"

"Not physically."

Maeve opened her mouth but then closed it, sensing now wasn't the time for conversation, for which Norah was grateful. Instead, she walked with them to the door and held it open. "Take care of him."

"I will," Norah said as she slipped past her. She headed for her and Iggy's room but stopped just inside the door. She'd left the light on next to the double bed because Iggy didn't like the dark. The room had no personality. Just the bed, a desk, and a small attached bath. Her gaze shifted to the flowers on the desk that were beginning to droop. The triplets had given her the flowers just yesterday.

Suddenly, she just couldn't be in here. She didn't want to be inside. She didn't want to look at the flowers that would be dead by morning. She didn't want to be in the sterile room. She wanted to be outside, to feel the air on her face.

She dropped her backpack on the desk, deposited the flowers in the trash, and grabbed a blanket from the end of the bed. Wrapping the blanket around Iggy, she headed back down the hall. She stepped out of the barracks at the other entrance and headed around back. A small fire pit stood, surrounded by half a dozen Adirondack chairs. She was relieved to see no one was there. She just needed a little time by herself with Iggy to decompress and hopefully to shake this pall that had stolen over her.

She slunk into one of the Adirondack chairs, snuggling Iggy close. She was worried about him. He'd barely moved since they'd left the vet's office. Today was supposed to be a chance for him to have fun, to feel free. She hated that it had ended the way it had. Iggy's pain was a tangible thing. It was as if he himself had been squeezed by the plastic. And it wasn't just that he felt the creature's pain. He'd been appalled that the creature had gone through that. And all due to the carelessness of humans. Truth was, she was mad at herself and every other human on the planet.

He let out another little whimper. Norah rubbed his back. "It's okay. It will be okay."

But even she knew that wasn't true. Iggy was heartbroken about the turtle. *Shouldn't I be? As a member of this planet, shouldn't I be angry that an innocent creature was treated that way?* But she wasn't. She was more worried about Iggy. Even with all she knew about refuse that had been tossed into the ocean, all she read, her mind was still coming up with ways that it wasn't her fault. After all, she was one person. What could she do?

But wasn't that the point? Billions of people thought, *Hey, I'm just one person.* And so billions of people tossed their trash without thinking. Or used a plastic bottle instead of a reusable one. Sometimes it was ships that lost big containers, but eighty percent of the garbage came from human carelessness. And there *was* something she could do. She could police herself just as everyone else could, and maybe just maybe eight million tons of plastic alone wouldn't end up in the oceans every year.

All the stats she'd read today rolled through her mind. Plastics threatened at least 600 different sea creatures. Plastic now made up a considerable part of some animals' diets. Creatures who were washing up on the shore had bellies full of garbage.

Which means that when we humans eat fish, it makes up our diet too.

There was even a garbage dump in the ocean. The Great Pacific Garbage Patch was actually comprised of two patches, one on either side of the Pacific. Garbage got caught up in the movement of the water and ended up trapped in a spinning vortex. The center was stable, trapping the garbage inside, and the swirling exterior pulled in more and more every day.

Norah vaguely remembered hearing something about it, but like with every other large societal problem, she assumed someone would do something about it. But in the car today, she'd learned it had been discovered in the late 1980s. It had been a full thirty years and the garbage patch was only getting larger. Nature was doing its part breaking it down. But that opened up a whole new problem. As the plastic breaks down, sea creatures eat the smaller pieces.

But the vortex, besides being essentially a floating junkyard that marine animals were feeding on, was also causing another issue. With all the garbage floating on the surface, sunlight was unable to break through to the lower depths, meaning plankton and algae couldn't grow. So not only were humans providing them garbage to feed on, they were removing a critical food source by doing so.

Seventy-one percent of the planet was covered by oceans but we get ninety-seven percent of our water from them. Even the air we breathe is in large part the result of the ocean. Seventy-percent of the oxygen we breathe is produced by marine organisms. The oceans absorb thirty percent of the carbon dioxide we produce. Norah took in a shaky breath. *The oceans are critical for humanity's survival and we are destroying them.*

She knew that thought wasn't hyperbole. Over 415 dead zones, areas of the ocean so lacking in oxygen that any sea animals unfortunate enough to swim into them would suffocate, had been found. Dead zones were naturally occurring, but the rate of them was far beyond what nature can devise. The Gulf of Mexico had a five thousand square mile patch completely empty of life due to such a dead zone. Norah hadn't even realized you *could* remove oxygen from water. The effect was to drive ocean animals away from these zones, changing behavior and food patterns and, in essence, shrinking the useable ocean.

With effort, she pulled herself from her thoughts. She

looked down at Iggy, whose chest rose and fell in an even rhythm. He had been brought here years ago. They believed whatever alien had brought him had either used him as a pet or even just a DNA sample. But he wasn't the only visitor. Between 1948 and 1969 alone, there had been over twelve thousand reported sightings, almost exclusively by military personnel. Even assuming a tenth of that was real and extrapolating over the years, that meant in the last eighty years, there should have been something like four thousand visitations. But why? Why this planet? Especially since it was slowly being destroyed. *Or maybe that is the reason…*

The door to the barracks opened. She hoped whoever it was was heading somewhere else. She didn't hear any footsteps and let out a breath. Good. She still needed a little time to—

Good evening, Norah.

Norah's head whipped around as Agaren sat down next to her. Her heart began to pound. Agaren had been rescued along with Alvie from the base at Dulce, New Mexico. But according to the bits and pieces of conversation Norah had overheard, he'd been in custody of the U.S. government for decades.

Agaren's grey skin looked almost white in the moonlight and his long, thin arms ended with hands with only three fingers. Unlike Alvie, he was a full-blooded grey and also unlike the other creatures in their custody, he had not been created in a lab. He had been working with the U.S. government until, somehow, he had shifted from colleague to prisoner. Norah hadn't been told much more about him. But she could tell there was something special about the large grey, an aura of authority surrounded him.

He communicated mentally, not physically capable of speech. It still surprised Norah when he spoke with her. But so far, those interactions had been casual. Agaren had never sought her out.

Until now.

"Good evening, Agaren. How are you?"

I am well. Agaren nodded toward Iggy. *But I see our friend is not.*

Norah pictured the turtle and swallowed. "It was a difficult day." She had the sense of something fluttering on the edge of her mind before Agaren's thoughts appeared. *I see.* There was a pause. *And how are you handling it?*

She opened her mouth, then closed it. The shock of knowing Agaren had just read through her memories left her momentarily stunned.

She took a breath, ignoring the sense of violation, and focused on his question. How *was* she handling it? Normally, she was like everyone else—she felt horror for a moment when she thought about how the planet was being treated and then shoved the thoughts aside, real life more important than abstract doomsday scenarios for the environment.

But ever since Iggy had found the turtle, she'd been unable to shake the fear and almost sense of desperation she felt at what had happened to the turtle and what was happening to animals across the ocean. "I don't know how to answer that. I'm scared, I'm angry. I feel hopeless."

Reasonable responses. So what are you planning to do?

Norah felt herself become defensive. "To do? What can I do? I mean, I'm not one of the people dumping garbage into the ocean. I'm not a big corporation that can make a dent in carbon emissions. I mean, what can I do?"

Agaren's sense of sadness hit her.

"What? You don't like that answer."

No, I do not. You humans, you are capable of much. Yet, you pass the responsibility onto the next person or generation even when there are steps you can take. It is one of your people that I admire a great deal who perhaps said it most succinctly: Science may have found a cure for most evils; but it has found no remedy for the worst of them all—the apathy of human beings.

Norah frowned, not able to place the quote. "Who said that?"

Helen Keller, quite a remarkable woman.

Norah looked at the large grey. He knew so much about humanity. The sense of sitting next to a being of incredible knowledge and age was undeniable. It was as if Agaren had the answers and was waiting for the rest of them to figure it out.

"Why did you seek me out tonight? We've never spoken like this before."

Agaren's gaze drifted to Iggy before turning back to Norah. *I have watched you and Iggy. He means a great deal to you.*

"He does."

That gives me hope for your kind—your ability to care deeply for a species so different from your own.

"How could I not care about Iggy? He is easy to love."

Easy for you. But some will not be able to see beyond his otherness. Agaren lapsed into silence.

Norah let it stretch between them. She knew he was right. People didn't like what was different, humans especially. Humans seemed to break people into categories, creating artificial distinctions of *us* versus *them*. And the categories always changed: ethnicity, skin color, religion. There always seemed to be a reason to distrust.

And when talking about people as different as Iggy, Alvie, or Agaren, well the chances were people would have a great deal of trouble seeing beyond their otherness.

Norah sighed. *God, when did I start thinking like this about humans?* She'd like to say it was today. But it was her work with the D.E.A.D. that had started her down this path. She had tracked down aliens and killed them, no thought given to what they were. Because the U.S. government determined they were dangerous. That had been good enough for her. And she had gone along like a good little soldier. After all, she was tracking down literal aliens. How could they be anything but evil? She had let the U.S. government be her conscience. And that government had failed her. But giving over that control was the greater failure.

Aren't I doing the same by ignoring what's happening to the oceans, to all of the planet? She glanced over at Agaren who sat unmoving, looking up at the night sky. "Do you know about what is happening to our planet, to our environment?"

Agaren turned his opaque eyes toward Norah and nodded.

"What do you think?"

I think you are a species of great possibility. That you should be given a chance to prove that you are capable of being the stewards your planet deserves.

Norah frowned, not sure why his words sounded so ominous to her. "Are there those who think we *don't* deserve to be stewards?"

Agaren looked into her eyes. *This planet is a gift, one that others have argued you have squandered, defiled.*

The hair on the back of Norah's neck stood straight up. *Others?* It took her a few seconds to find her voice. "And what happens then? If the gift is abused?"

Then some argue you should not be allowed to keep it. Agaren stood. *Good night Norah.*

Norah watched him walk away, his footsteps once again not making any sound. Iggy shifted in his sleep, a frown crossing his face. Norah hugged him tight, but kept her eyes on Agaren's retreating form. And she watched long after he had disappeared from view.

No one knew why exactly Agaren's race had come to this planet. But they did know he was part of some sort of intergalactic peacekeeping force. So perhaps his presence here was to help humans prevent a worse danger from arriving.

But the fact that there was a peacekeeping force at all suggested there were some groups who did not agree with keeping the peace.

A tremor worked its way through her body as Agaren's words drifted through her mind again, this time from memory. *Then some argue you should not be allowed to keep it.*

She swallowed hard. *So what happens when those against us keeping the planet decide to act?* She stared around at the base and realized that perhaps she had just figured out why the base existed.

And if I'm right, God help us all.

~*~

A Word from R.D. Brady

FACT OR FICTION

As with all my books, they draw on real life to create. So here's a few things that you might want to know. Thanks for reading!

Diego Island Chain. This island chain is fictitious.

Extinction Event. The information on the extinction of animals over the last century is accurate. The forecasted extinction rates are scientist's predictions based on where we are now.

Unlivable Regions by 2100. Also true is the information on the heat surges that will occur in certain parts of the world such as the Middle East. By 2100, it is expected that temperatures will be too hot for humans to live there. The daily summer temperature in some of those areas is expected to exceed 135 degrees Fahrenheit.

Ocean Dead Zones. There are areas of the ocean that are have such low levels of oxygen that they are in essence, no longer a source of oxygen for living things. Animals and plants caught in these areas suffocate. Most avoid them all together. Like Norah, I did not realize this was possible.

Plastic in the oceans. The amount of plastic and garbage in the ocean and its impact on the ocean was truly terrifying. The Great Pacific Garbage Patch is also real. There are areas of the Pacific Ocean where garbage covers miles of ocean. And all of the information on the role of plastic in ocean life destruction is also true.

Overall, all of the horrible information about pollution, global warming, and our effect on the planet is sadly true. So, for those interested, here's another site to look at that has some ideas about what we can individually do to cut down on impact on the planet: global steward.

About the Author

RD Brady is a former criminologist who began writing full-time in 2013. *Turtle* is a short story companion to the popular *A.L.I.V.E.* series. You can sign up to be notified about her new releases on her website, rdbradybooks.com and receive a free copy of *The Belial Stone*.

~*~

Girt by Sea

S. Elliot Brandis

~*~

I SHOULD HATE THE OCEAN. My parents certainly did. My grandparents, too. Or so I assume. I never met them. Instead, I'm entranced by it. It's mysterious and powerful. It's the reason I'm alive.

There are no mysteries as to why my grandparents hated the sea. They were born on it. Yet, unlike the many generations before them, they died on land. So they saw both worlds. They were the first group of people in hundreds of years to be able to claim that. So they've seen the contrast—between cramped quarters, teeming with rats and disease and malnutrition, and the wide open lands of this country.

I don't know when my words will be read, or by whom, so I'll tell you what little I know. Many generations ago—nobody can quite agree when—there was a plague across the earth. A virus that attacked the very core of our beings—the head, the heart, the soul. It turned men into raving lunatics, hungry for flesh. It spread like a wildfire. It burned through the world.

The first to fall were the great nations, whose names we don't remember. My country, though, saw it coming. Not because we were any smarter than the rest. Simply because we

197

were far away. Australia is an island, some say the largest one there is. They shut down the ports. Not those for boats, but great ships of the sky. They closed the borders.

Still, the outbreak came.

Some stayed to fight, with the knowledge of learned men. But there was no fighting a plague like that. It wanted to destroy the world, so it did. There could be no other outcome. That is, except, for ours.

We are an error.

Eleven ships sought refuge on the ocean. Not large ones, like the bones of the vessels we've found rusting on the shore. These were little more than ferries, bouncing away on the waves. 1,500 scared people were spread across the fleet. They had little food, meagre supplies, and no hope. They merely wished to draw their deaths out, as men tend to want to do. Soon, the reports from land faded out. There was nothing left but silence.

For all the fleet knew, they were the last people alive on earth. Utterly alone.

Sometimes God makes mistakes.

That fleet of boats was his greatest.

My teachers used to press this point—the sheer hopelessness of their situation. The only water they had, once supplies ran out, was collected from the sky. The only food, from the ocean. But the biggest anomaly of all was the fact that the virus never reached them. They say—and we have evidence now—that many others tried the same thing. Many other ships left the shore, both from Australia and across the seas. They perished. For it took but one soul carrying the sickness to wipe out a crew. One. Bobbing on the ocean, an infected ship was a floating island of slaughter.

But our fleet survived.

One generation after the next, they lived on the water. The fear of land was so ingrained that they sailed beyond its view and lived as though they would never return. For generations, they didn't. Illness struck many times. Teeth fell out of sockets. Muscles withered and hearts failed. Madness came over whole groups, causing uprisings, murders, and executions. Still, people lived. They birthed children to replace those they'd lost. They maintained a sort of order.

Finally, one day, they landed. The population was 1,200 strong. Not many, but enough. Two of those were my grandparents.

I was born on land. A second-colonisation, second-generation Australian. Part of a new era.

An era of excitement and recklessness.

~*~

My story starts at a beach on the bay. I lived on the southern edge of the continent, so sunsets were never spectacular, but at that time of year there was something special about the place. All I needed were my thoughts, a jar of rum, and the view. I could be content for hours. Albeit, today was not one of those days.

"You're not so good at hiding, Johnny Boy," a voice called out from the edge of the sand.

The voice belonged to an acquaintance of mine named William, or Billy to most. We'd gone to school together, in one of the first buildings established in the new colony. I finished without him. His taste for education was exceeded by that for liquor. I cupped my hands tightly around my jar as he approached. A well-honed instinct.

"Apparently not," I replied.

Billy dropped down beside me on the sand. He dug two grooves with his bare feet, threw back his hands to act as supports, and offered me a wry smile.

"Have you heard the news?"

"Mavis finally find out about Scott's cheating?"

He laughed. "No, you idiot. About the expedition."

I feigned a smile, mixing it in with a genuine shrug. I'd been on my own for most of the day. I had heard little but the birds and the ocean.

"Burke is leading an expedition up north, on order of the Exploration Committee. A group of twenty, or there about."

"There's nothing up north."

"Sure there is."

I took a sip of my rum while I gathered my thoughts. I could feel Billy's eyes home in on it, like a moth seeking out a flame in the night.

There *was* nothing up north. I was sure of it. Once you travelled beyond the colony, the landscape turned from green to brown to red. The inland of this great island was a sunburned mess, the same in each direction for thousands of kilometres. The earliest expeditions had found little to declare. Many men were lost. Their bones baked in the interior with those of our distant ancestors—those from before the fleet. It was a shared graveyard.

"Let me put it this way," I said. "The land can't be farmed. And the animals out there are too quick to catch and no good to eat. The ones that won't kill you, that is. And that's if you're doing the hunting."

"Fair call," he said. "But that's not what the expedition is for."

"What is it, then? An exercise in human sacrifice?"

"It's coast to coast. They're going all the way to the top." He pointed out to the bay. "There's another ocean up there, just like this one. Another spot for you to park your balls in the sand. Except, y'know, flipped around."

He swirled his fingers, and my stomach turned with them.

Our early settlement had been adventurous but misguided. Men perished at a time in which there were few to waste. Still, other colonies had been established. One to the east, where they'd found the husk of a great city on a bay, and one to the west. Efforts to the north had proven pointless. It was a wasteland.

But the coast? The northern ocean? Even if they found the ruins of an old city, it hardly seemed worth the distance. Or the danger.

"What do they hope to achieve?" I asked.

"You know details aren't my strong point."

I sighed. I'd find out, soon enough.

I offered out my jar of rum. Billy knocked it away with a

jerky motion.

"I don't touch that stuff anymore," he said.

"Good for you."

We stared out together at the ocean.

Maybe some things do change.

~*~

Not to speak poorly of him, but I didn't entirely believe Billy at first. As I've said, he handled his spirits harder than most men, which was saying something. On that occasion, he was spot on. And, from what I observed in the following days, he really had given up the drink. He'd taken on an apprenticeship at the powderhouse. The powder in this instance being an explosive used to fire pellets from weapons called muskets. I believe this was the old term, too.

It's funny what knowledge had survived.

Our history was entirely oral, passed down at sea from members of the original fleet. Names changed and stories evolved. One of the ships, however, had a store of paper stock. Not only that, but a historian, too. I often pondered this next bit. He recorded nothing of our ancestors. There were no politics, no stories, no clues as to how they thought and fought. Instead, he wrote instructions. About metalworking and carpentry, agriculture and husbandry. It was all very practical stuff.

People debated, but I believe he knew exactly how bad things were about to get on the mainland. I think he saw how numerous the years before we could settle again. He, of course, never lived to see those days. But his writings lived on. My grandparents learned of his lessons on board, long before they had any real concept of the things he discussed.

His name was Melbourne. Or, that's what we called him, for the volume was called 'Instructions for a New Melbourne'. Our colony was named after that. His name was forgotten, so we called him that, too.

I think, without him, we would be in shambles. Our colony would be little more than another species of animal.

Speaking of animals, that was my labour. I managed

camels—two humped creatures named in his very volumes. Somehow, he knew they would survive. And they did. Along with cattle and horses. They roamed the lusher areas of the continent, unaffected by the virus that had wiped out their masters. As Melbourne had predicted, they were predisposed toward domestication. His papers taught us how.

He was wrong about the sheep, though. For all we know, he could have made them up.

That day, there was a buzz about town.

"You wouldn't believe it, but they've got us doubling our volume at the powderhouse," Billy said, settling into a chair opposite me at the eatery.

"For what?"

"The expedition." There was excitement in his voice.

"Yeah, but what do they plan to shoot? Night-stalkers?"

"You're obsessed with them. I'd say it's mostly for hunting. You hear they've been drying meat at the farms now? Rather than herding cattle up north, where most say they'll die. Dried meat. What an age we live in."

"That sounds disgusting."

I slurped on a spoonful of my stew, which probably wasn't much better. It was potato heavy, on account that was one of the more successful crops they'd managed to rediscover and harvest. Still, it got old. And the cooks of the colony heated it to a near-mush consistency.

"Are you going to apply?"

"To go north?"

"Yeah. There's a meeting in the square tomorrow. They're calling for volunteers. Able bodied men from twenty to thirty-five."

"You think they'd want a camel handler?"

"Think? I know it, Johnny Boy. From the sounds of it, Burke is a bit of a pompous bastard. I heard—no, seriously, get this—that he plans to bring a *desk*. So he can write his tour journal in comfort. You can't tell me they won't need at least a few camels to carry his guff, not even mentioning the sacks of dried meat."

I ladled another mouthful of stew. I'd intentionally not brought rum, to be kind to Billy when he showed up. It was hard to see that pained desire in his eyes.

North. I really did want to see the other ocean. It sounds stupid, but it was *progress*. I could be amongst the first in the new colonies to go coast to coast. To see what the world looked like from another perspective. To find clues of other survivors.

"I'm in if you are," I said.

"You bet your arse I am," he replied.

His toothy grin offset my nerves.

~*~

Burke stood in front of the colony with a pomp and grandeur that one usually didn't see. And when I say colony, I mean it. All of New Melbourne was there, or so it seemed. Certainly everyone within the designated age bracket. There were women, too. Which gave it all a very proper air.

How do I put this delicately? Women held a special place in society. I'm not sure whether you'd call it a burden or a privilege. You see, of the 1,200 people who landed aboard the original fleet, only 300 of them were female. I don't know why. But suffice to say, the balance between the sexes was delicate. They were crucial to the success of the colony but, in a way, their control over their own destinies was limited.

No women would be invited to take part in the expedition. I don't agree, but that's the truth of the matter. Please don't judge me for the rules of my colony.

Burke spoke loudly and clearly. "The party will be limited to myself and twenty men," he said. "As per the requirements detailed in the Exploratory Committee's notice. Those wishing to apply shall form a single line behind that desk. You will have but a moment to convey your name, and impress onto me your suitability for such a journey. Your applications will be assessed by Mr. Landells and myself."

The crowd began to move, no further direction required. As for myself, my shoes were planted to the dusty earth for a moment too long. I found myself toward the end of the line, which wound out of the main square, passing by the bakery and the butcher. The smell of fresh bread assaulted my nostrils. My stomach turned. I had wasted too many of my credits on rum. It was something I did when feeling restless. A bad habit.

I leant out of the line, looking again for Billy. I suppose the tables had turned. He was the responsible one now. Somehow.

"Oi, Billy," I called ahead.

He looked back from his spot, at least fifty men before me. "I thought you were going to be a no show!" he exclaimed.

"Wouldn't miss it for the world."

A sharp elbow dug into my ribcage. It belonged to the man in front of me, a brute of a creature. The top of my head was level with his shoulders.

"Don't you even think about skipping ahead," he rasped.

I could only offer a mumbled assurance.

The line moved slowly. To their credit, Burke and Landells worked quickly, but the sheer volume of applicants consumed their time. I retired to my thoughts.

There was a prod in my ribs, this time much friendlier. Billy stood beside me with a grin on his soot-blackened face.

"How'd you go?" I asked.

"Good, I think. I'm not sure. They're hard bastards to read. Blunt as an old knife."

"Any tips?"

He shook his head. "None from me. They'll ask about your trade. Your family history. Think of it this way—Burke is a copper, so it's like being interviewed at the station."

"I can't say I've ever done that."

"Of course not. Squeaky clean, aren't you?" He winked. "You'll be right, mate. I'll catch you later?"

"I'll shout you a bowl of soup."

"Good man."

A short while later, I was regretting my offer of soup—I could barely afford it—when I realised I'd reached the front of the line.

"Come forward, lad," Burke said.

His companion, Landells, said nothing. He assessed me

with beady eyes.

Both gentlemen had the most impressive beards. Before them, I felt like a boy. My face was smooth, my hours in the sun doing little to supress my youthfulness. Flutters of nerves wafted into my stomach. Both men looked tired and ready to finish.

"What's your employ?" Landells asked.

"I'm a camel handler, sir."

"Any experience breaking them in?"

"No, sir."

There was a pause. It stretched a moment too long. I filled it hastily, tripping over my words.

"I-I-I have experience, though. Travelling."

Burke smiled in encouragement. "Relax, son. Tell us."

I took a deep breath. "I was part of the party that travelled west, to the township on the bight. Not to the town, we received them halfway. I supervised the convoy of twenty-four camels, domesticated out west. Or, re-domesticated, for the animals were found to be rather docile. Now I work on the Hutcherson farm."

"And would you say your work is in management or more hands on?"

"Hands on, sir. I prefer to work outdoors. With the animals."

Burke stopped to write a few notes. Landells' eyes didn't leave me. He made no attempt to lighten the mood—not a smile or nod or any indication.

"And Hutchinson will speak highly of you?"

"Yes, sir. I'm sure of it. He trusted me to shepherd the caravan home, after all. That was his decision."

He readied his pen. "And your name?"

"King. John King."

Finally, Burke's face brightened. "Any relation to Ellen Orn?"

"Her youngest son."

He nodded, satisfied. "Carry on, boy. We'll let you know."

~*~

The expedition departed two months later. Burke, Landells, nineteen men, twenty-six horses, six wagons, and twenty-six camels. I was one of the nineteen men. An assistant camel driver. With the help of three others, thankfully. And Landells himself in charge of us four.

The fanfare was considerable. People lined the streets of New Melbourne. For the first time in my life, women looked at me. That was reason enough to return safely.

New Melbourne is the most prosperous colony of this new world. I think this is because it was founded from scratch. Far to the east, on a separate bay, lies the colony of Albion-Sydney. There they found the remnants of a once great civilization, proof of the validity of our oral history. Metallic buildings reach to the sky, taller than any structure a man can dream of. Their insides are burned and gutted, yet they remain. The skeletons of a past world. New Melbourne, however, is different. There are remains, true, but they pale in their significance. Time had not been kind.

My parents used to tell me myths, passed on from their parents, and those before them. They say that even when the fleet lost sight of land, the cloud bellowed with smoke for months and years. The outbreak was cruel. The old city, it is said, burned to the ground. Time and nature did the rest.

I didn't doubt it. Even in the lushest of plains I sometimes found ashes.

"Enjoy it," Landells said from atop a horse beside me. "This will be the last of society you see."

"Until we return," I replied.

"If you return."

He rode his horse to the front of the group, ignoring the crowds around him. I couldn't help but grind my teeth.

"Smile for the nice folks," chimed a familiar voice. Good ol' Billy, along for the ride, an expedition assistant in charge of the armaments. By which I mean he did all the dirty work—cleaning and oiling and preparing the powder.

"I'm afraid my boss is a bastard."

"Aren't they all?"

"Burke seems nice."

"Burke has no clue."

"I'm trying to calm my nerves."

He waved to a group of children. They giggled and ran along.

"We'll be fine," he said.

"I hope so," I replied.

~*~

My hope didn't last long. Of the five appointed officers, two of them were self-proclaimed doctors, confusingly named Becker and Beckler. One had been a surgeon at the colony, the other…I was never quite sure. He seemed more academic, turning his nose up at the mere sight of a blister or welt. Neither had travelled beyond the outskirts of our fledgling society.

Of the officers, I got along best with a man named Wills. He was quiet and astute, with a narrow face and a dignified beard. On top of that, he was the most competent of all men to lead this type of expedition. He'd worked in hard labour as a farmhand before studying as a surveyor. In fact, the duty of charting the voyage fell entirely in his hands. At night, he'd scour over scavenged maps from the old world, plotting a path through the nothingness. Each day he guided Burke with a gentle touch.

Then, of course, there was Burke. I stand by my first impression that Burke was a fine man. He'd spent his life policing. In the colony, this was no mean feat. He had to keep drunks in line, and his own men, too. He was respected and commanded the attention of those beneath him or against him. But he was unsteady atop a horse and clearly outmatched by the natural elements. He departed town wearing formal attire. I'd thought it was for show, but it proved to be otherwise. He brought four suits, a desk, and a hardwood chair. That was only the start of it.

Finally, there was Landells. There never was a more miserable bastard.

The first part of the voyage was supposed to take two

weeks, to a point that Wills called Menindee. Those two weeks came and went, and then another two after them. That was when tempers started to flare, the day before we left the road.

These roads, unlike the ones in our colony, were artefacts of the old world. Rather than packed dirt and stone, they were capped with a heavy black tar. Unfortunately, the years had worn them away. The easy riding the wagons enjoyed heading out of New Melbourne came to an end. Soon, we had no choice but to cross the naked desert.

"Hurry the hell up," Landells barked at the wagoners.

"We can't go faster," replied the biggest of them.

"Then whip the horses harder."

"It ain't their bloody fault." He wiped sweat from his brow. "You think these wagons are made for sand? The wheels are sinking down to the axle."

"I'll take none of that rubbish. You whip the horses or I'll whip you twice as hard. Right across your lazy arse. You got me?"

"Sure."

Some days, we seemed to crawl but a couple of hundred metres. The slower our progress, the redder Landells' face grew.

One night I was unloading the camels when Burke called my name. He was sitting by the fire with a man named Charley—not an officer, but one of the ostlers responsible for taking care of the horses at the end of each day. What I did for the camels, he did for them. His face was grim from the situation.

"Sit with us," Burke said.

I did as he wished, but I won't say I didn't feel strange about it. Early in the journey, Landells had tried to maintain separation between the officers and assistants. Separate fires, different rations, and wildly variant rules.

"Charley says his horses are about worked to death," Burke said. "How are the camels?"

I hesitated. "Shouldn't you ask Landells, Sir?"

"Forget him. I want to hear it from you. You do all of the

work anyway, right?"

"Some of it. But the others—"

"You're the first to unload them and the last to supper. Don't be humble. There's no time for that." He reached down behind him and pulled out a jar. I could smell that it was rum before he handed it to me. My mouth watered. "Loosen your lips."

I took a sip. The pain in my shoulder, carried with me for three days, seemed to vanish at the first drop. Maybe my yearning for spirits was as bad as Billy's?

"The camels…" I started. I took another sip for confidence. "Their loads are too great, sir. They're built for this terrain, but not for the weight bearing down on them. It's too much. It's only so long before one of them collapses."

"Wills says we should reach water soon. A river up the way."

"That won't matter if they're dead."

He sighed heavily and reached for the jar. I was reluctant to give it up. After a long sip, he leant back and looked at the stars.

"Why are you doing this, son?"

"I want to travel ocean to ocean. I think my parents would be proud. My grandparents, too, could they conceive of doing such a thing."

He looked back at me, the stars now in his eyes. "Your mother was Ellen Orn, yes?"

I nodded.

"She was my nurse as a boy. A sweet lady. She recounted folk tales of the sea. They've stuck with me, all these years."

"How so?"

"This land here…" He pointed toward the earth. "She's untameable as the wildest brumby. But the ocean is a monster. The good Lord's given us one more shot at settling. Only he knows why. So, we push on. The next time we're driven back to sea shall be our last. We have to grip this chance with both hands, even as they grow bloody. Do you understand?"

"I do, sir."

"Get some rest tonight. Tomorrow will be painful."

I couldn't guess at just how right he was.

~*~

The next morning, I went about my usual duties tending to the camels and preparing them for the day's travels. Billy was keeping me company—ever since giving up liquor, he'd become somewhat of a morning person. We'd chat and he'd stoke the coals of the previous night's fire, eking out enough heat to boil a billy of bush tea.

"What was that about last night? With ol' man Burkey."

"I think," I said, choosing my words carefully, "that he's finally realising what we did weeks ago."

"That we're muddling our way through to a long death in the middle of bloody nowhere?"

"Something like that."

Before long, the man himself appeared. It was unusual, as the officers tended to sleep until dawn, savouring every last second of night before the overpowering sun bore down on us. He had now foregone his formal attire, instead wearing a thin shirt, the white fabric stained brown from dirt and sweat.

"Morning, gents," Burke greeted us.

"Morning," we echoed, a little unsure.

"William, do you mind waking the men? The officers, too."

"That sounds like a good way to get shot at."

"Well, then good thing you tend to the muskets. Hurry on."

Billy scampered off, leaving Burke and I alone for a moment. I won't lie, I'd grown quite fond of the man, but I wasn't comfortable being alone with him. I don't mean that in a bad way. His position and past as a copper gave him an air of authority. It was like being alone with a teacher at school.

"Do me a favour and hold off on loading the camels," he said.

"But, sir," I protested, before biting my tongue.

"Yes?"

"Well, no disrespect. But if I don't load them up before the men take breakfast, we'll be late in leaving. And I need to get the beasts to water sooner, not later."

He nodded. "That is my intention. Trust me."

A short time later, he gathered the entire party into a makeshift circle. The officers looked slighted. Even behind weary eyes, Landells seemed full of fury.

"Last night we lost two horses," Burke said.

"You can't blame me for that," said Charley's boss, a wagoner, "I told you they're not cut out for this terrain."

"I'm not blaming anybody," Burke replied confidently. "I merely wish to right the ship."

There was a moment of silence. The wind picked up, dusting us all with a fine pepper of sand and soil. The sun was peaking over the horizon, orange and warm.

"Our expedition is bloated," he continued. "For this, I take responsibility. We did not accurately prepare for the trials of this land. I stayed up last night, considering our present situation. It appears to me that the only course of action is to shed load drastically. I am cutting our supplies, abandoning non-essentials in this very desert."

"Says the man that brought a goddamn desk," Landells muttered.

If Burke heard him, then he chose to ignore it. "Becker and Beckler, this means your scientific equipment must be abandoned."

"Under whose authority?" Beckler rebutted. "We are commissioned directly by the Committee. You have no right to stall our work."

"Under the authority of this here land. A telescope is worth as little as our bones, should we perish out here."

Becker joined the protest, but his words were choppy and incoherent. He was a man of science, not used to having his opinion disregarded. Burke waited for his spluttering to cease.

"Furthermore, each man shall be limited to thirteen kilos of personal effects. And, at least until our plight improves, all men shall walk the journey alongside the beasts."

"Officers excepted," Landells said.

Burke looked at him gravely. "No men are to be excepted. The lines between officers and men mean nothing out here. It is time to accept the gravity of our situation."

"Not on my watch. I'm second in command."

"Then you shall be relieved of your duties."

"Then I quit. You utter bastard."

"So be it."

The silence was complete this time. Even the wind dared not to lurch forward. Dust hung in the air, not wanting to move. My stomach began to flutter.

"I challenge you to a duel. For control of this expedition."

"Don't be foolish. There will be no challenges."

Landells slipped a hand into his vest, withdrawing a revolver. It was ancient, something salvaged from the past world rather than forged within our colony. He levelled it at Burke, his face reddening by the minute.

"A duel, you coward!" he barked.

I glanced at Billy. His face told the story—he'd never seen that piece before. Landells had brought it with him.

"Stand down," Burke said firmly.

"I will do nothing until the leadership of this party is resolved."

"I said stand down!"

Landells cocked the hammer. "Give the fool a musket. We'll settle this here and now."

Burke moved toward him in confident strides. Time slowed. I watched as contempt boiled to the surface of Landells' entire being. He had broken, and there was no going back. Still, Burke strode.

Landells squeezed the trigger. My heart rose up into my throat.

There was no bang.

The gun had jammed.

Burke clenched his meaty fist and punched Landells in the jaw. He dropped like a sack of potatoes. No one dared to come to his aid.

"Then that settles it. We do as I say."

Nobody spoke for the rest of the day.

~*~

The expedition changed drastically after that morning. Thankfully, we reached water two days later. Two more horses died on the way. The rest, and my camels, recovered on the banks of the river. They fed on grasses, saving our thinning supplies.

The biggest change was to our party. Landells left, as did Beckler and Becker shortly after. A number of men joined them, either travelling with the former officers or in groups of their own. Burke gifted them wagons and horses. He didn't wish them to die in the desert. He was stern but not unreasonable.

I don't doubt that more men would have quit had it not been for the stabilising influence of Wills, the surveyor of the party. Burke promoted him to second in command, filling the void left by Landells' resignation. He was a quiet man, but astute and level-headed. He offered the remaining men a sense of purpose. At night, he'd quietly work on his maps and notes, marking the many changes he observed in the land since the days of old. In the mornings, at the request of Burke, he briefed us on what lay ahead. At first he was shy, but he later grew confident. He saw how our hungry minds sought something to hold onto—news of a creek ahead or an easing of the terrain.

That's not to say it was easy going.

Halfway between the river and a place Wills called Cooper Creek, illness struck me. I shall spare you the details, but my stool was so bloody that not even Satan himself would have wished that upon me. I grew feverish and dehydrated, but still we had to push on.

One night I rose from my bedding under the stars. I needed to relieve myself. It is a cruel fact that even the most dehydrated body will flush itself of water it can't afford to lose. I wandered out into the barren darkness. I could not find a single bush. So I unbuckled my trousers and urinated into the sand. It sopped it up, as thirsty as I was.

As I tidied myself up, I heard a sound. I looked around only to see white eyes staring out at me, illuminated by the moonlight. My heart stopped.

I wanted to scream, but could find no sound. I dropped to my knees. I am embarrassed to say that my own fluids muddied my breeches. I saw the glint of cold metal, what I can only imagine was the sharp of a spear.

This was surely how I was to die. Murdered by apparitions in the night.

Instead, they retreated. Their footsteps were light, as if muffled by feathers.

I don't remember returning to my bed.

I was shaken awake the next morning, the sun already risen. Billy was kneeling over me.

"Johnny Boy, are you all right?"

"They've come for me," I muttered.

"Who?"

"Them. The ones that stalk the land. The people before people. Night-stalkers."

He paused for a moment, then offered me water.

"You mean from the nursery rhymes? Matey, they're just stories to stop kids from wandering away from the colony."

"No." I tried to sit up, but my stomach pained. "I saw them. They've retreated to this—the land of nothing. They wish for us to die. All of us. You and I."

He pressed his palm to my forehead. "Jesus, you're burning up. I'll talk to Burke. I'm sure he'll let you ride today."

They were real. I knew it.

The night-stalkers were...well, it's complicated. We liked to think that when the fleet landed, this continent was void. It did appear barren. But something still roamed the land. There were things the first generation chose not to tell us, other than in rhymes and song. We had disturbed the spirits of the land. They wished to drive us back to the sea.

"We're all going to die," I said

Billy hugged me. "You'll be fine. I promise."

I was carried to Cooper Creek on the back of a horse. I remember very little.

~*~

As fate would have it, it was not yet my time to die. We reached Cooper Creek and I bathed in its waters. I was weak but I recovered. Billy took care of me as though I were a babe. Back in the colony we would have found it embarrassing, but we'd grown up a lot on that tour. Death felt close. He watched over us in our sleep. So, if a grown man was too sick to wipe his behind or chew his food, then somebody did it for him. We were in this together.

Thankfully, Burke decided to stay at Cooper Creek for a spell. There were rumours of all sorts—that we may turn around and return to New Melbourne, or sit and wait for reinforcements. Burke himself dispelled this one morning as we sipped bush tea and evaluated our sores.

"I have decided to divide the party," he said.

"We can't fracture anymore," Charley replied.

It was what we were all thinking, or at least what I was. By the look of Billy's scrunched up nose, similar thoughts were running through his mind.

"Not like before," Burke continued. "These past few days, I have been assessing the situation with Wills. Nothing about this journey has been easy, but travel from here to the north coast will be harder still. I can no longer, within reasonable morals, compel you forward. Alas, it is safest for the majority to remain here, where there is water and perhaps even food. The wagons shall remain, too. You men shall settle and form a depot. Wills and myself will travel onwards."

"For how long?"

Wills said, "For three months."

"That is the fairest estimate," Burke clarified, "based on the travel still ahead, and the food supplies that remain. If we're not back by then, you have orders to leave."

A silence fell over us all. Their point was clear—we, as volunteering men, were owed the right to return home alive. Or, at least, to have a chance at it. Burke and Wills had given their lives away for the good of the mission. They would head north, not knowing if they would return. Not knowing if they would survive.

They were sacrificing themselves for the good of the colony.

I raised my hand, my fingers shaking.

"Yes, King?"

"I'll come with you. You'll need camels."

"I won't order you to do that."

"You don't need to, sir. I'm coming."

"Me too," said Billy, not skipping a beat.

Burke shook his head. "King, you're welcome. I wished it but could not request it. But you, William, are needed here. A small party is a small target, quiet and agile. But here, with the wagons, you're a plump calf. We shall take muskets, but the depot must be able to defend itself. From anything that may arise."

The image of eyes floating in the dark returned to me. Did Burke know about the night-stalkers? I wanted to ask, but acid rose in my throat. I felt sick, once again.

Billy ground his teeth. He looked at me with wide eyes, as if to say he was sorry.

He needn't apologise.

At last, I was going to see the northern ocean. If I could only make it there alive.

~*~

We left three days later. Charley had volunteered after a night of thought, insisting that he should ride along to act as a scout for the party. We had been reduced to four men, six camels, one horse, and a three-month supply of food.

"We'll be here when you get back," Billy said the morning of our departure.

"You heard Burke. Give it three months. Any longer and we're dead."

"I'll wait what it takes."

"Billy…" I paused, trying to gather the words. "You can't do that."

He shrugged.

"Promise me you won't."

"We'll see. If the time comes, I'll leave you a sign. Okay?"

"Sure."

"I love you, Johnny Boy."

"I love you, too, you daft bastard."

We embraced. I patted his back hard. Both of us shed tears.

Those were the only words we spoke that morning. They were enough.

~*~

Two months later, I wished I'd stayed at the depot. It wasn't all bad—the terrain was more forgiving and the rains more frequent—but Wills had again underestimated the journey. He knew maps, but I'd be damned if he knew much about time.

I stood beside my camels, two of them trembling in pain. There were grasses throughout the land as sharp as knives, which ate at the animals' ankles. These two had wounds that had grown infected. My heart sank as I looked at their flesh, putrid with maggots.

"Shoot them both," Burke said. "Salvage them for meat."

"But sir—"

"No buts. These animals are suffering. Our food supplies are low."

He handed me a musket, packed and ready to fire. I pressed it to the first camel's skull. I felt ill to the depths of my stomach. I'd already lost two camels, weeks earlier. One to exhaustion and the other to sickness.

I pulled the trigger.

Another life lost.

I will spare you the gruesome details. I wish not to recount them.

I cried myself to sleep that night. We were two months into a three-month round journey, yet had not reached sight of the coast. Wills had told us it was near. I'd believe that when I saw it.

"What do you hope to find?" I asked Wills the next morning.

"Where?"

"At the north coast. The ocean."

He smiled sadly. "We shall see."

"I need to know," I said. "My bones are weak. My soul feels sick. Give me a reason to keep going."

Wills sighed. He looked into the middle distance. His face had grown gaunt, his skin thin and paperlike. Maybe time *was* different for him; each week he aged a year.

"We know from salvaged maps that the bulk of humanity lived above us, spread across continents great and sprawling. If others survived the great purge, then they lived north of here. Whether they be on land or still at sea, the clues will be found on the shores. The Committee's instructions are to scout a site for a future colony. An outpost to the rest of the world. Should there still be a rest of the world. Whatever scraps remain."

"And why didn't you tell us before?"

"I wasn't allowed. They said there would be deserters, and there were. But now…" He sighed again. "Who is there left for you to tell?"

I swallowed what little moisture I had left in my mouth.

Who, indeed?

~*~

Two days later, we reached a creek. It should have been a respite, but there was no time for us to waste. Before we could so much as fill our water tins, a bloody row broke out.

"Get to your feet," Burke snarled at Charley.

"My stomach is as hard as a stone, my urine as orange as the sun. If I don't rest, I'll die tomorrow."

"If you so much as try, you'll die today."

"What's the difference?"

Burke's face turned bright red. I could see the heat rising off of it, as it did from the baking earth. He was half-starved, half-mad, and completely serious.

"What did you say?"

"I said what's the bloody difference? I'll die today, or tomorrow, or sometime thereafter. We're all dead within a month. The depot will desert us, our food will dry up, and we'll die in the goddamn desert."

"I am your superior officer."

"You're a fool and you've led us to our deaths. Landells

was right from the start."

Burke grabbed Charley by the collar, hoisting him up like a child's sack doll. With a mighty fist, he knocked him back down. A bloody tooth escaped Charley's mouth, spiralling in the air and landing soundlessly in the dust. Burke struck him again.

Then again.

And again.

"Enough!" I shouted.

"Stay out of it, King."

"If he wasn't sick before, then he sure is now."

Burke's bloody fist was still clenched tight. As was his jaw, which bulged at the sides. There were signs before, I should have seen them, but now he had finally broken. We all had. The land had broken us all.

"Fine," he said at last. "We'll camp the night. Wills and I will continue in the morning. You can stay here with the camels. Try not to let these ones die, too."

My spirit sunk down into the earth. For the first time, I wished with every fibre of my being that I had never left the colony.

Had I a musket in my hands, I don't doubt that I would have shot Burke dead.

~*~

That was it.

I never saw the other ocean. I waited by the creek, tending to Charley's wounds. He had a mouth like a broken jar. Shards of teeth, festering gums. I fed him what was left of our food, ground to a pulp and mixed with water, but it did little to revive his spirits. He died in my arms on a rainy night.

It rained on and on.

I spent one morning digging a grave, but the ground was too soft. Beaten, I laid Charley's body in a muddy groove.

I said a few words.

"I've travelled this land, from south to north, hoping to see the ocean. I failed. My parents said our ancestors dumped their dead at sea, letting the waters swallow up their bones. Now, it's the land that consumes us. We sink into the mud, letting the maggots consume our flesh. We turn to earth, not water. Our master has changed. The results are the same."

I stayed up, wet and shivering, looking for eyes in the darkness.

~*~

One more camel died. The other wandered away. I was too weak to try and find it. I expected to die there, my body beside Charley's.

Somehow, Burke and Wills returned. They had reached the coast. Only they hadn't.

"There were swamps, the mud as thick as the seas themselves," Wills told me in a whisper. "We glimpsed the ocean through the mangroves. But that is all. It is a land fit for no man."

And at that stage, they were barely men. They were closer to skeletons. Their limbs were gangly, like misshapen spider's legs, and their skin festered with sores and blisters. Burke ordered that I burn fifteen trees, as a marker of our journey. He was unwilling to admit it had all been for nothing. I was too weak to argue.

We left the creek, the trees still alight behind us. I took one last look. It was as though hell itself had risen up to greet us. I suppose, in a way, it had.

We wandered back to the depot.

The others had abandoned us. When we returned, it had been four months. I didn't begrudge them. They were following orders.

In desperation, I scouted the site for signs. Billy had promised me that much. On the other side of the river, I found a scarred tree. It told me to dig, so I did.

Buried in the earth was a tin container. Inside it were rations and a note. It had been written by Billy himself. It told me that four men were left alive, one severely injured. They had left, heading south, with what remained of the horses and camels. They were in poor spirits, but wished us good health.

"What day is it?" I called to Burke, my voice weak and

crackled.

"What does it matter, now?"

"I think they left today."

Between the three of us, we couldn't confirm that fact. Our minds were weak and wandering. We shared the food in equal portions, too tired to fight.

We slept uncovered on the dusty earth. The sun had not yet set. Our futures had long faded.

~*~

For a while, Burke and I tried to survive by the creek. We scavenged seeds from bushes, grinding them into an edible paste. It only made us weaker. Each passing day, death grew closer. Wills travelled south alone, hoping to find signs of the departed group. He returned a week later, his pulse barely a quiver.

We left together. Three men, no animals, and no food.

"There should be a waterhole," Wills said, some days later. "If the maps are correct."

They rarely are, I wanted to add, but I held my tongue, too weak to bicker. Our bones showed through our skin and our blood had retreated deep within our bodies.

We lay Wills down, propped beside a tree. Burke and I continued.

Then Burke himself collapsed.

"You've been a fine companion," he said without sarcasm. "I hope that you will be rewarded."

I would have laughed, for we both knew no reward waited for me, but I knew those were amongst his final words. At his request, I left him splayed on the ground with a gun across his chest. I don't know how he died—whether through starvation or a bullet through the skull. I don't wish to know. I doubt they'll ever find his body.

I had nowhere to go. There were no signs of a waterhole. There were no signs of life at all. It was a barren wasteland, as featureless as the widest ocean. I had accepted my fate. I was a dead man, barely walking. Resigned to that fact, I returned to Wills.

He had beaten me to death. Flies encircled his sitting corpse.

I wandered into the nothingness. Night descended. I stumbled forwards.

Finally, I collapsed.

Somehow, I didn't die.

I was woken by eyes, floating in the night. They carried me away.

That was the end of my journey.

~*~

You may wonder, how did I live to tell this story?

I was rescued that night by those eyes, or more rightly, by the people they belonged to. I had failed my mission to see the northern ocean, but I had found something else instead. Something miraculous. Or, correctly, something had found me.

Night-stalkers.

You see, we are not the only people, us children of the fleet. There are others that live on the land, in the remotest places, by the most cunning of means. I don't speak their language, but I am trying to learn. Until then, we speak in gestures and vivid expressions.

They are survivors of the great purge. They are the ancestors of our ancestors, the few people who lived through the outbreak. It appears, and this is my judgement, that they have descended from the fraction of people who were somehow immune. The smallest of fractions. Infinitesimal. But they have repopulated pockets of this land, like saplings emerging from the ashes after the greatest of bushfires. They are different, so very different, in appearance and culture, but in a way we are the same. We survived on the seas, against all odds. They survived on the land, where their odds were even slimmer.

I can only say this: the land is as harsh as the ocean, perhaps even harsher, but a spark of life remains.

We must cup our hands over it and hope we can reignite our species.

If I see my people again, I hope our kinds can find peace

together.

Or we may all perish again.

God may make one mistake, but he doesn't make two.

This is our final chance.

Together, girt by sea.

~*~

A Word from S. Elliot Brandis

People like to joke about Australia. They say that everything in this country wants to kill you. Snakes, jellyfish, spiders, currents, bushfires, floods—take your pick. The truth, as is often the case, is far milder. Almost 90% of the population lives in urbanised areas. Safe, protected, and happy.

It wasn't always this way.

My story, *Girt by Sea*, mirrors the early days of Australia. It takes a real chapter of our history—the Burke and Wills expedition of 1860—and reinvents it for a future time. I wanted this sense of danger, the soul-crushing feeling brought on by the magnitudes of distance, of trying to conquer what can't be tamed. It isn't a story about heroes. It is a tale of error, survival, and death.

The title comes from our national anthem. *Our home is girt by sea.* Nowadays we cling to those seas. The interior, in a way, has beaten us. We have accepted defeat.

Stories like this remind us of why.

About the Author

S. Elliot Brandis is an engineer and author from Brisbane, Australia. He writes post-apocalyptic and dystopian fiction, often infused with a variety of outside elements. He is a lover of beer, baseball, and science fiction.

His novels are about outlaws, outcasts, and outsiders.

For more information visit selliotbrandis.com

~*~

Full Circle:
A CHRONOS Story

Rysa Walker

~*~

THE GARDEN FORK VIBRATES in my hand as it hits another bone.

I kneel down and tug away the stray roots that have crept into the garden bed over the years. There's no telling when it was last used to plant anything, but it's increasingly clear that someone's pup decided this was the perfect spot for hiding treasure.

Like the other three I've found, this object isn't an *actual* bone, just a bone-shaped piece of plastic or maybe rubber. Unlike the other three, however, there are letters carved into the side of this one: *NYLABONE.*

I've never heard of the brand, so I record the image to my lens and tell Jarvis, my digital assistant, to run a search.

"This is a synthetic dog bone."

"No kidding. Just search the company. I'm trying to figure out how old the thing is."

He's back momentarily. Several pictures pop onto my lens as he gives me a brief history of the Nylabone company. They produced dog toys from the mid-20th century until the late 21st, which gives me no clue at all as to which of my forebears owned the pup who liked to dig in the garden.

I toss the chew toy toward the large oak tree behind me, startling a squirrel perched on the bottom branch. It scurries up into the tree, one of the tallest in the neighborhood, and then chatters down at me, clearly annoyed. It's odd that none of the squirrels here are red, and they have shorter ears than the ones I remember from my summer hikes with my father near Glendalough. This grey variety is far bolder, too—as I learned the hard way when I left an open pack of crackers on the patio table last week and came back to an empty wrapper.

"Jarvis, display garden diagram from my files."

The sketch I made last night pops up. Once I've confirmed the spacing and location for the three tomato seedlings, I grab the edge of the box and scoot back over to the freshly-turned soil to dig a small hole for the first plant. I scoop the soil out with my hands, enjoying the feel of the earth against my skin.

Once all three are planted, I move on to the herbs. That's when I notice a pale orange light shining up through the clumps of dirt.

The sun, maybe, glinting off a piece of glass?

A quick glance at the sky dispels that notion. The day is too overcast for me to even *see* the sun, let alone for it to reflect this brightly.

I brush away the soil and pull out a round, flat disk. Seven, maybe eight, centimeters across, with spokes that meet at an hourglass positioned in the center. Bright flecks of light, which look like grains of sand, flow from one side to the other in a repeating pattern.

A beep in my ear signals an incoming call and my grandmother's name pops up.

"Shall I hold the call, mistress?" Jarvis asks.

It's tempting, but I've ignored her for two days. That's probably as much as I'll be able to get away with before she notifies the police or dredges up some distant relative who still lives in the area to come check on me. Or, worse yet, calls my department at the university to inquire whether I'm doing well. Making friends.

"No." I sigh, dropping the weird circle onto the grass. "I'll take it."

A second later, Nora's face appears on my lens. She's in her late seventies, impeccably dressed as always. Her completely modern apartment has all of the amenities, but the teacup that sits on the table next to her would have been more at home in the Edwardian era than the mid-twenty-second century.

"Madi! I was beginning to worry. Why didn't you answer my calls?"

"I'm sorry, Nora. I've been meaning to call you back. I've just been busy with classes and getting the house set up and—"

"Well, it's good to hear your voice. But why can't I *see* you?"

"Probably because I'm outside."

"Oh, dear God. He didn't even bother to set up outdoor transmitters?"

She has a point. Most people have remote cameras, even outside, to send visuals. But Grandpa James—who is Nora's father and the previous owner of this house—doesn't seem to have bothered with equipping the backyard. The transmitter on my comm-band would normally kick in when I'm outside the range of a transmitter, but the band is currently in my pocket, in deference to my arms being elbow-deep in soil.

"Hold on." I tug the comm-band from my pocket, brush the stray dirt off of my arm, and strap it onto my wrist.

"Better?"

"Actually, no. You look…terrible. Why are you sweaty and what *is* that on your cheek?"

"Dirt, maybe? I told you I was going to plant a garden."

"Yes, but I thought you'd at least have the good sense to plant it inside. Don't you have enough to keep you busy with school? I thought you said you made some friends?"

I sigh. "Yes. I have made friends."

This is true, although I can count them on one hand with several fingers left. Okay, *technically*, with four fingers left. The truth is I made a single friend, Jack, who is in my program at Georgetown. But Jack has a much larger cast of friends who hang out with us on occasion. Two roommates, as well. I think *some* of those people might even know my name, so *friends*, plural, isn't quite a lie.

And Jack has become a very *good* friend. We lunch together most days, and we've been to a couple of shows. Out to dinner, twice. I think he considered the second dinner, which was last night, to be a date, because he gave me a quick kiss when he dropped me off.

It startled me, that kiss. I'm usually pretty good at reading romantic signals, but Jack caught me totally unprepared.

I don't share these facts with Nora, and she still looks skeptical. She's all too familiar with my introverted nature.

"Well, if you insist on cataloguing his papers, you should stop digging in the dirt and get started. I've seen that library recently. You have your work cut out for you. The house is a bloody mess."

My grandmother has already told me that she thinks this entire enterprise is insane. Not just the garden, but my decision to come to the States for graduate school. My decision to move into this huge, empty house and sort through the chaos in my great-grandfather's library. It may, in fact, be the only thing that she and my mother agree upon.

"I *have* started," I tell her. "And I like the house. Most of the stuff in the office is just clutter that accumulates over time. I've trashed half of it already."

"You could hire someone, you know."

"A few days of cleanup duty is a small price to pay for direct access to the papers of the greatest writer of the 21st century."

As I fully expected, the praise generates a string of colorful language, the type you'd expect to hear from a drunken sailor when his favorite pub has run out of bitter, not from the mouth of a proper-looking gran. Suffice it to say, Nora Coleman Grace was not her father's greatest fan.

When Nora's stream of profanities slows, she pauses to

take a sip of her tea and regain her composure. "James Coleman was a hack with a skill for marketing. Nothing more. I'll grant that he was prolific, but that's it."

This is pretty much the standard critical assessment of the literary oeuvre of James Lawrence Coleman. He wrote *everything*. Not just every literary genre, but a wide-ranging collection of nonfiction as well. I've read most of his works. Some are brilliant. There's a short story called "The Lottery" that was breathtakingly good. I also enjoyed his novels, *The Fixer* and *The Exorcist*, and most of his crime series featuring a detective named Philip Marlowe.

Some of the others, however, are quite awful. There was a historical romance series that made me cringe, and several works of alternative history that were downright boring, even though I like the genre. Those books were barely even fiction, just dry recitations of some slightly different history that he cooked up in his overly fertile—and, as Nora noted, unbelievably prolific—imagination.

I'll be re-reading those books, along with the others, plus his notes and diaries, over the next two years. The goal of my thesis is to find some coherent thread, some tiny bit of logic that connects Coleman's works, either to his life and times or to each other. Biographers have tried and failed in that regard, but I have the advantage of unfettered access to his notes and diaries—assuming I can sort through them.

But I'm not going to get into this with Nora. I've been hearing her bitter recollections of life in her father's shadow for years, so I doubt she has anything new to add.

"Okay," I say with a teasing smile. "I'll mark you down as *undecided* on the literary genius of James Coleman."

She sniffs, as expected, and I change the subject slightly. "Did you know your grandmother's papers are in the library as well? I didn't realize she was also an author."

"Well, I wouldn't exactly call her an author. She was more of a professional activist—said she had an obligation to make this world the best it could possibly be. Which was admirable and all, but..." Nora shrugs. "I think my grandfather would have preferred to lead a quieter life."

I don't argue the point about her grandmother being an author. I never met her, so I'll defer to Nora's recollections. But there are several works in the files with the name Kate Pierce-Keller listed as author, even though they were never published. Most of them even had covers, one of which I remember clearly. Tall buildings rising out of a red sea. It was titled *Odds Against Tomorrow.*

"She continually butted heads with politicians on the environment, foreign policy, human rights," Nora continues. "Pretty much everything. And then a few years before she died, the scandal hit. She defended him, though. Through it all."

The plagiarism trial was the one dark episode in an otherwise illustrious career. In late 2069, three plaintiffs claimed that James Coleman had stolen several of the books published under his name. Two of the works were challenged by relatives of deceased writers, and another was challenged by an elderly man named Cale Madewell. The manuscript of *The Bleak Season* the old man presented as evidence was printed on paper with crumbling edges, yellowed with age.

Grandpa James settled out of court, maintaining his innocence until the end. Most of his loyal readers believed him, but several literary critics said that the plagiarism charges made a lot of sense, given his bizarre variation of style and proclivity for genre-hopping.

I've read a few of the letters my great-great-grandmother wrote in defense of her son. She never explicitly stated whether he was innocent or guilty, just stressed again and again that those works needed to be published. That it would have been a tragedy if a book like *The Memory of Water*—one of the challenged books, and one of the few for which Coleman won a literary award—had never reached readers.

I haven't formed an opinion yet, but the unpublished books up there with *Kate Pierce-Keller* on the cover seem to point toward him being innocent. If he was okay with swiping other writers' work, wouldn't unpublished books by his mother have been prime candidates? She'd probably have given him permission, but if not, he published dozens of books after she died.

Any questions I have concerning the trial, however, are more likely to be answered by further research into the documents inside the house than by further conversation with my grandmother while I sit here in the garden. The impact that her father's plagiarism trial had on her as a teenager is well-traveled ground and I know better than to encourage her.

So, again, I shift the subject. "Why didn't you tell me about the pool?"

"The...pool? Oh, *that*. He put it in for his second wife. She had some sort of health...thing, and claimed she needed to swim for therapy, but I think she really just wanted him to spend an ungodly amount of money renovating the basement."

"Well, I'm delighted that she did." I give my grandmother a wide smile. "It's wonderful. Like swimming in a cave."

"I'd suggest you hide the existence of that pool from your mother," Nora says. "If she learns you're swimming alone, she'll have nightmares and I'll never hear the end of it."

I *haven't* mentioned the pool to my mother, and I won't. She claims to have psychic flashes, and she's terrified of the water. It's so bad that she won't even travel by air if the route crosses over the ocean for fear the plane will crash and she'll be trapped, unable to breathe, unable to swim. That's one reason she registered me for swimming lessons before I could even walk...and made my father take me to those lessons and, later, to swim meets. Even once she knew I was the top swimmer on our team, even once she saw the medals and trophies I won, she couldn't watch without triggering a panic attack. When my father died two years ago, I think Mum was less surprised by his sudden death than by the fact that he didn't drown.

"I absolutely agree that we should hide this from her. And speaking of hiding things...did Grandpa James have a dog at some point?"

She frowns in concentration for a moment. "Not to my knowledge, although I believe my grandmother did. Why? Are you thinking of getting one?"

"I am, actually. A real one, not like the Drog I had as a kid."

"Where did this come from? If you're lonely, you should find a roommate. There's a very good reason people prefer Drogs, dear. I think you'll figure that out rather quickly."

"My hands have been in fertilized soil all morning. I think I can handle scooping dog poop. Droid dogs are too predictable to be good company. They don't bury bones in the backyard, for example."

"I'm sure you could program that behavior."

"Well, maybe," I admit, "but that takes all of the fun out of it. The reason I asked whether he had a dog, however, is that I found these."

When I hold up two of the bones, Nora's nose wrinkles in disgust.

I laugh. "They're not real, silly. Some sort of plastic. But wait…I found something else."

The strange orange circle is on the grass next to me, and I pick it up so that she can see. "Does this look familiar to you? I thought it might have been one of your toys when you were a child."

She squints at the object for a moment. "Not a toy. A religious token of some sort. Grandma Kate had one, although I'm quite certain Grandpa Trey had it buried with her ashes. My father said it had something to do with the Cyrists, but she detested that so-called religion. I never really understood why she wore it."

There are still plenty of Cyrist churches around, although nothing like their heyday when Cyrist International was one of the largest organized religions. A scandal rocked the church in the early 21st century, when a group of Cyrist extremists plotted a bioterrorist attack. It was mostly aimed at other, more moderate church leaders, but rumors circulated about one of their prophets being a fraud and membership dwindled over time. Plus, the first and only president to be a member of the Cyrist church was responsible for pulling the country out of a number of environmental agreements that she felt were too restrictive. History did not view her favorably in the decades that followed. But I think the real reason for the Cyrists' decline was that they forbade any sort of sexual contact for teens, aside from supervised hand-holding. That made it rather difficult to attract younger followers.

This medallion doesn't look like anything I've ever seen in Cyrist histories, however.

"I thought the Cyrists' symbol was that odd-looking cross. With the curved top and arms? I've never seen anyone wearing something like this."

Nora shrugs. "I'm just telling you what my father said. The fact that he said it is no indication of its veracity in my book. Where did you find the thing?"

"Buried with the fake bones. Should I send it to you?"

"Dear God no. Toss it with the rest of the trash in that house. I have plenty of other things to remember her by. Why would I want that drab looking thing?"

I don't respond, but I do take another look at the circle, now in the palm of my hand. Nora's comment is baffling. Given her relatively subdued style and the fact that the medallion is shooting out beams of orange light, I could understand her calling it *gaudy*. But *drab*?

As I stare down at the medallion I notice something new. It's no longer two-dimensional. A holographic menu now hovers above my hand. Nine squares, each with a moving image. It's a mix of outdoor and indoor shots except for the very first square, which is just black with white dots floating past.

I swipe left with my gaze and a new set of nine images appears. I'm now starting to question my theory about this thing being buried here by some 21st century dog. The interface is modern, maybe even newer than some of the VR games I used to play a few years back.

One image near the bottom of the display draws my attention. It's an underwater scene, obviously filmed on a sunny day because everything seems to shimmer. In the center, however, is an oddly out-of-place white rectangular box—a container of some sort. It's wedged into the sand and the lid is slightly askew.

"Madison Grace!"

I blink, startled. The full name, combined with Nora's tone, makes it clear that this isn't the first time she's spoken. I was so wrapped up in the weird medallion that I forgot we were talking.

I don't have time to reflect on this fact, however.

Something is wrong. Very, very wrong.

The sensation of water on my skin triggers a response that's now second nature after years of swimming—*don't breathe in.*

When I open my eyes, it's as though I've stepped—*swum?*—into the scene I was viewing in the holographic menu. I feel sand beneath my bare knees. I'm still in the shorts and tank top I was wearing, and the medallion is still in my hand, although the holographic menu has vanished.

The container, which is made of marble or some other sort of stone, is directly in front of me. It's huge—roughly ten meters long and three or four meters wide.

The name *Cyrus Reed Teed* is engraved into the stone, followed by:

October 18, 1839 – December 22, 1901
Seventh Messiah

A long, silvery-gray fish squeezes through the gap between the edge of the crypt and the cover, then disappears behind the box. Sunlight flickers off the ripples in the water around me, and a school of smaller fish float by. They're closer to the surface, but I can't gauge the distance.

My first thought is that this is truly advanced virtual reality, far better than anything I've experienced before. That line of reasoning, sponsored by the logical part of my brain, tells me that I should go ahead and breathe normally. I mean, really—the game can't have actually immersed me in the ocean, right? It's at least eighty kilometers to the Chesapeake Bay, and probably twice that to the ocean itself.

The *il*ogical side of my brain, however, is fairly certain that I am indeed in the ocean, and I don't have time to worry about how or why that has occurred. I pull my feet beneath me and kick off hard against the sandy floor, tucking the medallion into my pocket for safekeeping. As I swim upward, I dart my tongue out and taste the salt, trying to remember if I've ever been in a VR adventure that included taste.

It's soon painfully obvious that the surface is farther away that I thought. I wasted too much time at the bottom, and now my lungs are straining, screaming for air.

I wish I'd gotten up the nerve to tell Jack that I didn't mind the kiss. It was very nice, actually. He just caught me by surprise.

My very last thought before my body turns traitor and inhales is that maybe my mother really is psychic. Her nightmares weren't about my father drowning or drowning herself. They were about *me*.

~*~

Air rushes into my lungs and my eyes open to the face of a girl, maybe fifteen or sixteen, directly above me. She pulls her mouth away from mine and takes a deep breath, preparing to give it another go when I begin coughing. I turn to the side and expel the salt water into the sand next to me, along with the fruit and cheese I had for lunch. When I'm done, I lie motionless for a moment, focusing on pulling air into my aching lungs as I try to remember how in God's name I got here.

The girl is yelling now. I open my eyes, squinting at the bright sky and the blindingly white sand now that the girl's face is no longer shadowing my own. I start to answer, thinking she's yelling at me, but she's looking off to my right.

"You don't have to run, June. I did it! She's breathing."

I follow her gaze inland and see two people approaching. The first is a guy, a few years older than the girl. He's dressed in one of those one-piece retro bathing costumes that were trendy a few decades back. His reddish-blond hair sticks up in the back, and he's sporting a sunburn on his shoulders and face.

A woman runs behind him, although the sand isn't making her progress easy. She's dressed oddly, too, in a white blouse and dark skirt that seem too heavy for the beach. A large handbag of some sort is clutched in her right hand. Her hair is mostly gray with streaks of black. It's pulled up into a bun on the back of her head, but several stray curls frame her face.

The events of the past few minutes are starting to come back to me. Aside from the nearly drowning part, this still smacks more of an immersive game than of reality. I reach into my pocket and extract the medallion, flipping it over to see if there's anything written on the back—a brand-name or address. Because if this *is* a VRE, I plan to sue the hell out of them for nearly killing me.

When the woman reaches us, her eyes go immediately to the circle in my hand. Her lips press into a determined line, and then she turns back to face the girl.

"Good work, Lucille. I'll take it from here. You and Bert need to get the skiff back to the Unity right now—although I'd advise being a bit discreet about walking up from the landing at the same time. I will not report you for being here together without a chaperone. I'm not even going to ask what you were doing here, because I'm really not in the mood to hear whatever lie you're concocting right now."

The girl and boy exchange a nervous look, but remain silent.

"Of course, if either of you so much as hint that you found someone here on the island, I'll have to rethink that decision. *You were never here.* This"—she nods down at me—"*never happened.* There will be no bragging about how you saved a woman's life, because that will raise questions I'm certain you don't want to answer. And both of you—*separately*—will stop by my clinic tomorrow so that we can have a frank discussion about the celibacy rules you will follow if you wish to remain part of our community. Are we clear?"

They both nod, but their feet remain rooted in the sand.

She rolls her blue eyes—eyes that seem vaguely familiar,

although I'm not really sure why. "Then *go!*"

Once they're out of earshot, she leans toward me. "Let's get you into La Parita and check you out. Can you walk?"

I'm not entirely sure on that point, but I nod. As she helps me to my feet, I notice a light—the same pale orange as the circle in my hand—shining through the fabric of her blouse.

She hooks one arm beneath my shoulders for support and we begin walking up from the shore toward a group of buildings on our right, clustered at the point of this...island, I guess? The beach continues off to the left for as far as I can see, but aside from these buildings, the only thing manmade is maybe a hundred yards away. It's a white stone Cyrist symbol. The shape is a combination of a Christian cross and an Egyptian ankh, except the arms curve into an infinity symbol. A lotus flower is in the center. It's huge—at least forty feet tall—and sits on the highest peak on the island. I haven't seen one this large outside of historical photographs.

The woman looks at me from the corner of her eye. "I'm June," she says. "I'm the doctor here. When are you from?"

"I'm Madi," I respond. And since I've clearly misunderstood the beginning of her question, I give what I assume is the expected answer. "Usually Ireland, but I've lived near DC on and off. I'm living there now."

She huffs. "Not *where*. *When*. But on second thought, don't tell me. I can see from the clothing and that device on your wrist that you're from the future. The less I know, the safer you'll be. The safer we'll *both* be. Why in the name of Cyrus would you jump into the ocean without a breathing apparatus?"

The name *Cyrus* reminds me of the stone coffin I saw on the ocean floor.

"But that's just it," I say. "I didn't...*jump* into the ocean. I was in the garden and then..."

I stop just before we reach the steps and turn to the side, heaving up another gusher of water.

Or maybe I'm just imagining that I vomited? Maybe this is all in my head, every bit of it. The stupid circle is just the controller for a late twenty-first century game that was no doubt recalled by the manufacturer or banned by the courts for being *too* realistic.

"Sorry," I say, after the coughing subsides.

"Not a problem." June's tone is softer now. "Your body knows what it's doing. Let's get you inside so I can make certain you're okay and you can get back home."

We climb the steps to the porch, avoiding a wooden clipboard someone has abandoned on the bottom stair. June holds the door open with her shoulder so that I can enter and then asks, "You okay here for a sec?"

I nod and lean against the wall as she goes back outside to retrieve the clipboard. Once she returns, we go into the foyer and she hangs the board on a small hook near the grandfather clock. There are maybe ten lines scrawled on the page, each with a date, time, and brief message. I scan the list quickly. The dates range from 1901 to 1906, and the messages all seem to be about medical emergencies—*stitches*, *burnt hand*, *spider bite*, *broke a toe*.

At the very bottom:

10/12/1906. Girl drowned. 2 pm.?

I suck in a sharp breath, which triggers another bout of coughing, but I manage to avoid throwing up this time.

June is watching me as I stare at the message board, and she gives me an apologetic half-smile. "I'd have arrived earlier to spare you Lucille's efforts, but no one will listen to me about replacing this stupid clock. I figured for it being half-an-hour off, but it's more like an hour. Then once I was here and you were coughing up the seawater, it didn't seem to be worth the double memory for either of us if I went back to change it."

I don't respond, just nod in what I hope are the right places. My best chance for now seems to be playing along until I can figure out what's happened. If this is a game, I need to collect all of the clues I can to get out of it. And if it isn't a game, that still seems like the optimal strategy.

"My warnings to Lucille and Albert will only buy us a few hours, though. There's no way either of them will be able to resist telling someone. Rumors and gossip are a sort of currency when you live in an insular group like the Unity. Did they see the CHRONOS key?"

"The what?"

"The key. In your hand."

I glance down at my hand, still clutching the medallion. Streaks of orange light leak out between my fingers.

"No," I say. "At least, I don't think so." My voice is raspy, my throat feels like I've swallowed broken glass.

"You're probably right," she says. "I noticed it when we were a few yards down the beach, but they're not jumpers so they can't pick up the light. They do know what the keys look like, though, so let's hope they didn't see it. That would just complicate matters. Although if word had gotten back to Simon or Pru, they'd be here already."

She seems to be talking to herself as much as to me. But her last comment confuses me to the point that I risk a question.

"But…the two of them just left. They weren't even wearing comm-bands. How would you know whether they'd gotten word to anyone yet?"

Raising her eyebrows slightly, June taps the area beneath her blouse that's glowing orange. She seems to think this is an adequate explanation, but it sails clear over my head.

My bewilderment must be written on my face because, after a moment, she continues—slowly and in a tone that suggests I'm not very bright. "Simon and Pru both have keys. If they'd caught word of a stranger on the island—a stranger with a CHRONOS key—they'd have been here when Lucille was dragging you from the water to suss out whether you are a threat or a potential recruit."

That makes no more sense than anything else she's said, but this time I go with my original instinct to just nod. Asking questions isn't helping anyway. Her answers just confuse me more.

She leads me into a small room with a twin bed shoved against the far wall. "Pull off those wet things and get under the blanket. But don't lie down...your lungs will probably fare better sitting up for the time being. I'll be back in just a sec."

As loathe as I am to strip down to nothing in this strange place, there doesn't seem to be another option for getting warm. Once the wet clothes are off, I sit on the bed and pull the flowered quilt around my shoulders like a serape as I survey my surroundings.

No overhead lights or electrical outlets. No climate controls. No communications devices.

Which reminds me to check my comm-band. And...there's no signal.

I reach for the orange medallion, now on the nightstand, but June is back with her bag in one hand and a glass in the other. A white robe, or maybe it's a dress, is folded across her arm.

"Take these," she says, handing me the glass and several capsules that were hidden in the palm of her hand.

"What are they?"

"An antifungal. The water out there isn't especially brackish, but we're right next to an estuary. Better safe than sorry."

I'm even more reluctant to swallow the pills than I was to take off my clothing. But again, my options seem limited, so I toss them back. The lemonade is cool and feels good against my throat, which is raw from expelling the ocean water.

June puts her medical bag and the garment, which I can now see is a dress, on the bed next to me. Both the dress and her bag—a brown leather satchel with handles—are very nineteenth century, so I'm surprised when she pulls out a tricorder much like one the doctor used at my last checkup.

If this is a game, there are a lot of inconsistencies. Not just the tricorder, but also some aspects of June's character. If this is supposed to be 1906, would she have used slang like *okay* and *just a sec*? The writers need to hire a few historians as consultants. Maybe I'll apply for the job after I finish suing their asses for drowning me.

June tells me to breathe in and hold it, then runs the

scanner across my chest.

"Release," she says.

We go through this several times. Then she looks down my throat and up my nose. Finally, she steps back.

"I think you'll live," she says, with a quick smile. "And since that concludes my duties under the physician's oath, you're free to get dressed and jump back as soon as you're up to it."

When I don't immediately respond, she says, "How much time does it usually take before you can use the key again?"

I open my mouth, planning to bluff my way through again. My brain isn't cooperating, though. Maybe it's from the lack of oxygen earlier. Or maybe it's the fact that she seems genuinely nice. Whatever the reason, I decide it's time to drop the pretense.

"This is the first time I've used it. I don't even know what you mean by *jump back*. The stupid thing was buried in my garden, and I made the mistake of digging it up. The next thing I know I'm underwater, staring at someone's crypt."

That gets a laugh, for some reason, but then her brow furrows. "Either you're an extraordinarily good swimmer or someone lied about exactly how far out they towed that old fraud's tomb. Are you seriously telling me that this is the first time you've used a CHRONOS key?"

"It's the first time I've ever even heard of a CHRONOS key."

"So I guess that means you don't have a stable point set for the return trip." June shakes her head. "Can you pull up the interface yet?"

I take the medallion from the nightstand, holding it gingerly by the edges, and look down into the circle. Nothing happens.

"Not like that," she says. "It has to sit flat in your palm to read your genetic data."

Once the medallion is repositioned, the menu pops up.

"Good!" June says just before the display flickers out. "Your hand is shaking. Hold it steady."

That's easier said than done. I'm exhausted. Also, the idea that this was a game—a game for which I'm woefully unprepared—was frightening enough. Now I'm increasingly worried that this is a *reality* for which I'm woefully unprepared, and that is utterly terrifying.

But I close my eyes and take a few deep breaths. Then I try again. This time, the display sticks.

"Okay," June says. "I can see that you've pulled up the interface from the change in the light's intensity, but I'm not able to see what you see. So you need to listen carefully. First, that black square with the ashes floating about? Don't look at it. If your eyes pass near it, look away. Whatever you do, *don't blink.*"

The white specks really don't look like ashes to me. And now I'm looking at the very square she said to avoid. I quickly focus on the one next to it.

"Second," she says. "Do you see numbers, in a date format, near the top?"

I nod.

"The current string of numbers is today's date and time: 10121906…"

"1356," I finish for her. "So you're saying that it's October 12, 1906?"

"At 1:56 in the afternoon. Yes."

"What about the numbers below that?" I ask.

"Those represent our geographic location—the southern tip of Estero Island, Florida. If you'd blinked on that little button next to the geographic string *before* you jumped into the ocean, that would have set a stable point, which would have made getting you back home much, much easier. But since you didn't, you'll need to change the first set of numbers to the date and time you want to return to, and then we'll look for a location reasonably close to DC." She stops and looks at me. "What's the matter?"

My hand is shaking again, and the interface flickers out. I curse under my breath and then ask her the question I've been avoiding. Even though I try really hard to keep my voice level, to keep the hysteria at bay, I fail miserably.

"Is this real?"

It's not that I've never contemplated the possibility of time travel. Every historian has wished there was a way to go back in time. But even the experts say that's not possible. One of Jack's roommates, Alex, is in the Temporal Physics graduate program at Georgetown, and we've had this discussion. He gets asked the time-travel question a lot, often enough that he has a standard answer. *Maybe to the future*, he says whenever someone asks, *in twenty years or so. But not to the past. It's impossible to bend time or space that far.*

And this isn't a matter of simply bending time *or* space. This device bent *both*. If I accept what June is saying, I'm hundreds of years *and* hundreds of miles from my point of origin.

"Is this *real?*" I repeat. "Because it can't be. It's a VRE, right? A virtual—"

"Virtual reality environment," she says. "Yes. I know. A good deal of my medical training was done in VR environments. And Brother Cyrus has a decent gaming setup that I tried a few times, although truthfully, I prefer to read a book."

There's that name again. "Cyrus. Cyrus Reed? That was his crypt I saw, buried in the ocean."

June laughs. "No. Cyrus *Teed* was a con-artist. A snake-oil salesman who tricked a good number of people out of their life savings. The reason his crypt, as you put it, is underwater is that it was the only way to keep the Hollow Earth crowd from keeping vigil, waiting for him to rise from the dead. I was talking about the *actual* Brother Cyrus."

"How does anyone have a VRE system in 1906?"

"He's not *in* 1906. But, to get back to your question, this isn't a simulation."

"You'd probably say that if this was a simulation, though. Right?"

She rolls her eyes. "Maybe. I guess it depends on who wrote it. My philosophy professor once made a decent argument that we're all part of a simulation, so who knows? But to the best of my knowledge, this isn't VR. I'm not sure why the key was buried in your garden or why you're able to operate it...."

A twinge of guilt crosses her face as she trails off. "I should probably be asking you a lot of questions along those lines. And I should probably consult with Brother Cyrus about this. He likes to keep tabs on the CHRONOS keys, to make sure that no one is out there working against our goals."

I shake my head emphatically, gripping the key so tightly that it cuts into my palm. "No. I'm not working against anyone. I just want to plant my garden, go to classes. Maybe get a dog." I'm babbling, but I can't seem to stop. "I don't want to stay here, and I need this key to get home."

"Okay," she says. "Calm down. I'm not planning to force you into anything. I was just thinking that if you heard about our goals, about the community that we've built here at Nuevo Reino, you might consider joining. We will change the world. We *are* changing the world. Only through The Way can we—"

"No. I want to go home."

She sighs. "Then let's get started teaching you how to use that key."

A few minutes later, I've managed to set the return date, and now we're working on the time.

"It needs to be as close as possible to when I left," I say. "I'm worried about Nora, my grandmother. She was watching when I blinked away. It has to have frightened her to see me suddenly vanish like that."

"Understood," she says. "Just be careful not to set it *too* early. You don't want to cross your own path. Believe me it's not worth the headache, and if you do it too often, it can take a toll on your san...ity."

A slamming noise echoes on the far side of the house and a male voice calls out, "June? Are you in here?"

"Simon." She curses softly, then scoops my wet clothes off the floor and hands them to me. "You need to go," she says. "You can find a spot closer to home once you get back to your time. I'll try to hold him off for a minute, but...you won't have long."

"I thought you said he couldn't have—"

"They may not have seen the key. The fact that you're pretty and possibly vulnerable might be enough to get that weasel to pop in, but he'd have wanted to wait until you were done throwing up." She gives me a grim smile as she crosses to the window and slides it open. At first, I'm confused, but then I realize why. That's a viable escape route that won't immediately tip this guy off to the fact that I have a key.

I don't know who this Simon is, but June sounded wary of him, so I have no desire to meet him. What if he decides to confiscate the key? I toss aside the quilt and quickly tug the dress over my head. It's too big, but at least it's dry and covers me.

"Now I just have to convince him you're not interesting enough to blink back and investigate himself," June says.

"But...I'll already be gone, so...?"

June sighs, closing the door behind her.

I follow her, hoping to lock it and gain a bit more time. But there's no lock.

June is talking to someone, a man, but I can't make out what they're saying. I tuck my wet clothes under my arm, and sit down on the bed. Holding my hand as steady as possible, I center the key in my palm again and pull up the holographic menu.

"Or maybe," June says, "you could go outside and see if you can spot a fishing boat? I'm sure her husband is looking for her by now."

My eye is drawn immediately to that odd black square, but I look away toward the button June said would set a...*stable* something. Stable point?

Because she's right. My priority is getting back to the correct time. I can worry about getting back to Maryland once I'm back in 2136. My comm-band will work then. I can rent a Dryft and fly home. Hell, if all else fails, it's physically possible to *walk* home from Florida even though it might take me a few months.

But I can't walk home from 1906.

"…must not be looking for her very hard." His footsteps are coming toward the door now.

A new square pops up once I set the stable point.

"Poor thing is pregnant, too," June adds as the door handle turns. "I hope the baby wasn't—"

Time's up. I don't have the luxury of examining this new stable point. I simply blink and hope for the best.

For the second time in maybe thirty minutes, I find myself underwater. I'm certain that I was looking at the new stable point. How did I manage to blink back to the other location?

I push upward, toward the surface, before my eyes even open. But when I glance down, I see that there's no crypt in front of me. And the water is barely above my head this time.

Off to my left is a sandbar. A concrete pillar, maybe ten feet tall, juts up from the ground. It's almost the same shade as the sand. Next to it is another concrete structure, about one-third the height, which looks like an upside-down letter U.

I swim toward the pillar, still clutching the key. Once my feet can touch, I trudge through the water. The white dress is now as wet as the clothes I'm carrying beneath my arm. It clings to my body, weighing me down. If I'd been wearing this the first time this damned key tossed me into the ocean, there's no chance they'd have been able to resuscitate me.

"Jarvis, where the hell am I?"

I mutter the words out of habit more than really expecting an answer. But a few seconds later, the familiar voice chimes in.

"You are in the ocean near Estero, Florida, mistress."

"What year is this?"

"2136."

That's the thing I love about virtual assistants. There's no judgment when you ask a question that would cause pretty much any human to classify you as completely insane.

As I draw closer to the pillar I'm hit by two realizations at the same moment. The first realization is that this scene reminds me of the book I saw in the library files a few days ago, one of the volumes with Great-Great-Grandma Kate's name on the cover, entitled *Odds Against Tomorrow*. The surrounding water is blue, not red, but there's the same sense of man-made structures rising out of flood waters.

My second realization is that the structure in front of me is the remains of the cross-like statue that I saw just down the beach in 1906. The curved section protruding from the sand is one side of the infinity symbol that formed the arms. I'm guessing the rest of it washed out to sea during a storm, joining Cyrus Reed Teed's crypt on the ocean floor.

This is what's left of the beach. The statue was on the highest point on the island, or at least the highest point I could see. Admittedly, it wasn't exactly a hill, just a gentle rise. But now, the base sits in a good eighteen inches of ocean. Two hundred and thirty years later, the island is gone.

Off in the distance, I see buildings. A hotel, I think, because there's a beach out front. I spread my wet clothes over the concrete U and then hike myself up to sit next to them.

"Jarvis, call Nora. Audio only."

Nora is, as I expected, in a mild state of panic, even though it has only been—at least from her perspective—a couple of minutes since we last spoke. I tell her that we seem to have been disconnected, and that something is wrong with my comm-band. Probably some dirt from digging in the garden. She makes a few disparaging statements about the primitive state of American technology, conveniently forgetting that she bought this comm-band for me just before I left for the States.

"You sound hoarse, dear. Are you sure you aren't coming down with something?"

"No, I'm fine. Maybe something's wrong with the audio, too. Love you—I'll call you in a few days!"

Love you—I'll call you in a few days is Jarvis's standing signal to cut the transmission.

I look out toward the shore and then down at the orange circle in my hand, debating my options. The menu doesn't pop up at first, and then I remember what June said earlier. *It has to sit flat in your palm to read your genetic data.*

She also said that the couple who pulled me out of the

water couldn't see the light.

So…something in my genetic makeup powers this device. And given that I found the circle in the garden of the house once owned by my paternal great-great-grandmother, I'm pretty sure I know the side from which I inherited that ability.

I seat the medallion—the CHRONOS key—in my palm and the menu pops up. Swiping with my eyes, I scan through the pages. Only twenty-two squares, twenty-two stable points, total. That includes the black one June told me never to use, the watery grave of Cyrus Teed, and at the very end, the stable point that I just set in the two-story house that is long gone.

Curiosity kicks in, and I roll the time back, back, back. 10121906_1400.

I see my own bare feet, sticking out from beneath the long white skirt. June is in front of me. She's talking. There's no audio, but this is where she was telling me to be careful about crossing my own path. That it would scramble my mind.

And then she's looking over her shoulder. Scooping up my wet clothes. Opening the window.

When the door bursts open a moment later, I'm so startled that I very nearly blink.

A stocky man in his late teens or early twenties enters. Simon, I guess. He's wearing a t-shirt with a cartoon mouse on it and jeans, and takes a few steps before crossing out of my view. June stands in the doorway, talking, but I can't make out the words.

When Simon comes back into view, he's laughing about something. June laughs along with him, and then steps to the side to let him pass. Once he's out of the room, she glances back briefly, a look of relief on her face. For a split second, it's like she's looking straight at me, and then she closes the door.

It's hard to imagine the house I was in minutes ago now being six feet underwater. I mean, we've covered the steady rise of the oceans in school and talked about the displacement that followed. The refugee crises, the finger-pointing and laments of how it could have been prevented if people would have listened.

But this is almost like watching it happen in real time. I follow the instructions June gave me and set a new stable point for the exact spot where I'm sitting, facing the ruined pillar, and roll the time forward by increments of a decade. The water slowly creeps up the pillar. By the time I reach the year 2336, the "camera" or whatever this is, is fully submerged. Barnacles cover the lower half of the pillar and I watch, mesmerized, as a small school of fish swims past.

I try rolling the time back before today's date, to see if I can find out when the storm that knocked the top off this Cyrist cross happened. No luck. I can only roll it back about a minute, to the precise moment I set the stable point.

The historian in me is both staggered at the possibility of this device and frustrated at its limitations. There are so few stable points! One is inside a cabin in rural New York in 1968. Another is an alley outside a Harlem nightclub in 1929. Liverpool in 1957. Memphis, Tennessee in 1952. The only commonality that I can see is that they're sheltered areas, off the beaten path where it's unlikely anyone would notice if you just popped into view.

Only one is in DC. The date is April 9, 1939 and shows a shadowy area near the side of the Lincoln Memorial. I roll the time forward nearly two centuries to the current date. This is one monument that I know is still standing, one of the few that survived the terrorist attack in 2092 without any damage.

As eager as I was to dig into my great-grandfather's papers, I'm even more interested to find out more about his mother. Did Kate Pierce-Keller use this medallion—this CHRONOS key—to see the future? Or maybe even to *go* there? Is that why my great-great-grandmother was so passionate about environmental causes? Was the rise of the oceans not merely a likelihood for an unknown future, but a known reality in a future she had seen with her own eyes?

She lived in an era when the damage might have been contained. And if what I suspect is true, she had access to a device that allowed her to go back to a time when it was *reversible*.

But what evidence could you give to those in positions of power who didn't have the genetic ability to see that future? How would you make them believe you when they couldn't see the evidence firsthand?

June implied there were people who could use the key back in 1906. Are there still others with this genetic quirk today, bouncing around time? Maybe even *changing* the course of history?

So many questions are running through my head. And none of them will be answered on this sandbar.

I glance down at my comm-band. Jarvis could have a Dryft here in only a few minutes. It can't be more than a two-hour flight to DC. Even if I got one of the older models, that would obviously be the safer option. This medallion has dropped me into the ocean twice.

Only because you didn't know how to operate it, Madi. And you know you're going to use it again eventually.

The voice in my head is right. Who am I kidding? The possibilities are endless here. There's no way I'm sticking this thing in a drawer until I've visited every stable point available to me. Might as well start now.

I strip out of the white dress and pull my gardening clothes back on. They're still wet, but I'll attract far less attention popping in at the Lincoln Memorial in those than I would in an equally wet ankle-length, high-necked dress. After a moment's hesitation, I fold the dress and tuck it under my arm. It would just blow away into the ocean, and it doesn't belong here. It doesn't even belong *now*.

Then I activate the key. The interface wavers, so I lean against the pillar and focus on steadying my hand. Eventually, I locate the Lincoln Memorial stable point and set it for today's date. Then I scan for a time when the crowd thins out. At 18:27, a rainstorm hits, scattering most of the tourists. A person in wet clothes couldn't ask for better cover.

Traffic noise is the first sign that I've made it. My bum hitting the ground is the second. Note to self: do not lean against anything when attempting to time travel.

I brush off my bruised dignity and ask Jarvis to page me a car. Then I call Jack.

He picks up on the second ring, sounding a little nervous.

"Madi! What's up?"

"Hey, Jack. I just wanted to tell you that last night was…really…nice. All of it."

Silence, and then, "Oh. Good. I thought maybe I'd overstepped—"

"No. Not at all."

I glance down at the medallion in my hand. If I don't share this with someone I'm going to explode. It's not going to be family, because I'm pretty sure they'd tell me this device is much too dangerous to play around with. And I most definitely want to play around with it.

"Why don't you come over tomorrow? I'll make dinner. And um…see if you can pull your friend Alex away from the Temporal Physics lab for a bit. I've got something that the two of you are going to find *very* interesting."

~*~

A Word from Rysa Walker

I grew up near the Florida coast. My happy place is still near the ocean. I sleep most soundly when I can hear the waves crashing against the shore—although most of the time, I have to settle for waves generated by a white noise machine.

The underlying idea for this story came about several years ago as I was researching the Koreshan Unity, one of the many historical cults that my fictional villain Saul Rand united to form his new religion, Cyrist International. The Koreshans came to Florida in the 1890s and settled near Fort Myers.

In real life, the Koreshans' numbers gradually shrunk (as celibate groups generally do) and they handed over their lands to the state for a historical park in the 1960s. In my CHRONOS Files series, however, the Cyrists were still using that land centuries later. And rising sea levels would likely mean that much of the Koreshan territory would be underwater long before the Cyrists were done with it.

To a time traveler, today's island is tomorrow's ocean floor. Those of us who must move through time in a single direction, one second at a time, however, are a bit like the (apocryphal) frog in a slowly heating pot. Incremental changes make it difficult for us to see the impact of climate change on these coastal areas, until we are faced with some sort of disaster. As I write this, one of the most powerful hurricanes ever recorded is barreling toward Florida, and the area where the Koreshan Unity Park is located is under a state of emergency. This is a mere week after the Texas coast was drenched by more than fifty inches of rain from Hurricane Harvey. Two more hurricanes are currently waiting in the wings, gaining strength from an ocean surface that gets a bit warmer each year. Despite the mounting evidence, our leaders continue postpone tough decisions, kicking the can to the next generation who may well find that it's too late to reverse the damage we've caused.

Thanks for reading "Full Circle." If you enjoyed this short story, you can learn more about the CHRONOS Files series at rysa.com. Readers who are curious as to how a CHRONOS medallion wound up in Katherine's garden may want to check out "The Circle That Whines," coming this November in the anthology, **Tails of Dystopia**. And if you'd like to read more about Madi's travels through time, keep an eye out for a new CHRONOS series beginning in 2019.

About the Author

RYSA WALKER is the author of the bestselling **CHRONOS Files** series. **Timebound**, the first book in the series, was the Young Adult and Grand Prize winner in the 2013 Amazon Breakthrough Novel Awards. The **CHRONOS Files** has sold nearly half a million copies since 2013 and has been translated into ten languages.

Rysa currently resides in North Carolina with her husband, two youngest sons, and a hyperactive golden retriever. When not working on the third book in **The Delphi Trilogy**, she watches shows where travelers boldly go to galaxies far away, or reads about magical creatures and superheroes from alternate timelines. She has neither the time nor the patience for reality TV.

~*~

Dispatches from the Cradle: The Hermit— Forty-Eight Hours in the Sea of Massachusetts

Ken Liu

~*~

BEFORE SHE BECAME A HERMIT, Asa <whale>-<tongue>-π had been a managing director with JP Morgan Credit Suisse on Valentina Station, Venus. She would, of course, find this description small-minded and obtuse. "Call a woman a financial engineer or a man an agricultural systems analyst, and the world thinks they know something about them," she wrote. "But what does the job a person has been channeled into have to do with who they are?"

Nonetheless, I will tell you that she was responsible for United Planet's public offering thirty years ago, at the time the biggest single pooling of resources by any individual or corporate entity in history. She was, in large measure, responsible for convincing a wearied humanity scattered across three planets, a moon, and a dozen asteroid habitats to continue to invest in the Grand Task—the terraforming of both Earth and Mars.

Does telling you what she has done explain who she is? I'm not sure. "From cradle to grave, everything we do is motivated by the need to answer one question: who am I?" she wrote. "But the answer to the question has always been obvious: stop striving; accept."

A few days after she became the youngest chief managing director for JPMCS, on Solar Epoch 22385200, she handed in her resignation, divorced her husbands and wives, liquidated all her assets, placed the bulk of the proceeds into trusts for her children, and then departed for the Old Blue on a one-way ticket.

Once she arrived on Earth, she made her way to the port town of Acton in the Federation of Maritime Provinces and States, where she purchased a survival habitat kit, one identical to the millions used by refugee communities all over the planet, and put the pieces together herself using only two common laborer automata, eschewing offers of aid from other inhabitants of the city. Then she set herself afloat like a piece of driftwood, alone on the seven seas, much to the consternation of her family, friends, and colleagues.

"Given how she was dressed, we thought she was here to buy a vacation villa," said Edgar Baker, the man who sold Asa her habitat. "Plenty of bankers and executives like to come here in winter to dive for treasure and enjoy the sun, but she didn't want me to show her any of the vacant houses, several of which have excellent private beaches."

(Despite the rather transparent ploy, I've decided to leave in Baker's little plug. I can attest that Acton is an excellent vacation spot, with several good restaurants in town serving traditional New England fare—though the lobsters are farmed, not wild. Conservationists are uncertain if the extinct wild lobster will ever make a comeback in the waters off New England as they have never adapted to the warmer seas. The crustaceans that survived global warming were generally smaller in size.)

A consortium of her former spouses sued to have Asa declared mentally incompetent and reverse her financial dispositions. For a while the case provided juicy gossip that filled the XP-stations, but Asa managed to make the case go away quickly with some undisclosed settlements. "They understand now that I just want to be left alone," she was quoted as saying after the case was dismissed—that was probably true, but I'm sure it didn't hurt that she could afford the best lawyers.

"Yesterday I came here to live." With this first entry in her journal, Asa began her seaborne life over the sunken metropolis of Boston on Solar Epoch 22385302, which, if you're familiar with the old Gregorian Calendar, was July 5, 2645.

The words were not original, of course. Henry David Thoreau wrote them first exactly eight hundred years earlier in a suburb of Boston.

But unlike Thoreau, who often sounded misanthropic in his declarations, Asa spent as much time alone as she did among crowds.

~*~

Excerpted from *Adrift*, by Asa <whale>-<tongue>-π:

The legendary island of Singapore is no more. But the idea of Singapore lives on.

The floating family habitats connect to each other in tight clan-strands that weave together into a massive raft-city. From above, the city looks like an algal mat composed of metal and plastic, studded with glistening pearls, dewdrops or air bubbles —the transparent domes and solar collectors for the habitats.

The Singapore Refugee Collective is so extensive that it is possible to walk the hundreds of kilometers from the site of sunken Kuala Lumpur to the surviving isles of Sumatra without ever touching water—though you would never want to do such thing, as the air outside is far too hot for human survival.

When typhoons—a near-constant presence at these latitudes—approach, entire clan-strands detach and sink beneath the waves to ride out the storm. The refugees sometimes speak not of days or nights, but of upside and downside.

The air inside the habitats is redolent with a thousand smells that would overwhelm an inhabitant of the sterile Venus stations and the climate-controlled domes of the upper latitudes. Char kway teow, diesel fumes, bak kut teh, human waste, raja, Katong laksa, mango-flavored perfume, kaya toast, ayam penyet, burnt electric insulation, mee goreng, roti prata, sea-salt-laced reclaimed air, nasi lemak, charsiew—the heady mixture is something the refugees grow up with and outsiders can never get used to.

Life in the Refugee Collective is noisy, cramped, and occasionally violent. Infectious diseases periodically sweep through the population, and life expectancy is short. The fact that the refugees remain stateless, so many generations after the wars that stripped their ancestors of homelands, seems to make it impossible for a solution to be envisioned by anyone from the Developed World—an ancient label whose meaning has evolved over the centuries, but has never been synonymous with moral rectitude. It was the Developed World that had polluted the world the earliest and the most, and yet it was also the Developed World that went to war with India and China for daring to follow in their footsteps.

I was saddened by what I saw. So many people clinging to life tenaciously on the thin interface between water and air. Even in a place like this, unsuitable for human habitation, people hang on, as stubborn as the barnacles on pilings revealed at every low tide. What of the refugees in the deserts of interior Asia, who live like moles in underground warrens? What of the other floating refugee collectives off the coasts of Africa and Central America? They have survived by pure strength of will, a miracle.

Humanity may have taken to the stars, but we have destroyed our home planet. Such has been the lament of the Naturalists for eons.

"But why do you think we're a problem that needs solving?" asked a child who bartered with me. (I gave him a box of antibiotics, and he served me chicken rice.) "Sunken Singapore was once a part of the Developed World; we're not. We don't call ourselves refugees; you do. This is our home. We live here."

I could not sleep that night.

This is our home. We live here.

~*~

The prolonged economic depression in much of North America has led to a decline of the region's once-famous pneumatic tube transportation networks that connected the climate-controlled domed cities, so the easiest way to get to the Sea of Massachusetts these days is by water.

I embarked in balmy Iceland on a cruise ship bound for the coast of the Federation of Maritime Provinces and States—November is an excellent time to visit the region, as the summer months are far too hot—and then, once in Acton, I hired a skiff to bring me out to visit Asa in her floating habitat.

"Have you been to Mars?" asked Jimmy, my guide. He was a man in his twenties, stocky, sunburnt, with gaps in his teeth that showed when he smiled.

"I have," I said.

"Is it warm?" he asked.

"Not quite warm enough to be outside the domes for long," I said, thinking about the last time I visited Watney City on Acidalia Planetia.

"I'd like to go when it's ready," he said.

"You won't miss home?" I asked.

He shrugged. "Home is where the jobs are."

It's well known that the constant bombardment of the Martian surface with comets pulled from the Oort Cloud and the increased radiation from the deployment of solar sails, both grand engineering efforts began centuries ago, had managed to raise the temperature of Mars enough to cause sublimation of much of the red planet's polar dry ice caps and restart the water cycle. The introduction of photosynthesizing plants is slowly turning the atmosphere into something resembling what we could breathe. It's early days yet, but it isn't impossible to imagine that a habitable Mars, long a dream of humanity, would be reality within two or three generations. Jimmy might go there only as a tourist, but his children may settle there.

As our skiff approached the hemisphere bobbling over the waves in the distance, I asked Jimmy what he thought of the world's most well-known hermit, who had recently returned to the Sea of Massachusetts, whence she had started her circumnavigation of the globe.

"She brings the tourists," he said, in a tone that strove to be neutral.

Asa's collected writings about her life drifting over the ruins of the world's ancient sunken cities has been a publishing phenomenon that defies explanation. She eschews the use of XP-capturing or even plain old videography, instead conveying her experiences through impressionistic essays composed in a florid manner that seems at once anachronistic and abiding. Some have called her book bold and original; others said it was affected.

Asa has done little to discourage her critics. *It was said by the Zen masters that the best place for hermits to find the peace they sought was in the crowd,* she wrote. And you could almost hear the disgusted groan of her detractors at this kind of ornate, elusive mysticism.

Many have accused her of encouraging "refugee-tourism" instead of looking for real solutions, and some claim that she is merely engaging in the timeless practice of intellectuals from privileged societies visiting those less fortunate and purporting to speak for her subjects by "discovering" romanticized pseudo-wisdom attributed to them.

"Asa Whale is simply trying to soothe the neuroses of the Developed World with a cup of panglossian chicken soup for the soul," declared Emma <CJK-UniHan-Glyph 432371>, the media critic for my own publication. "What would she have us do? Stop all terraforming efforts? Leave the hellish Earth as it stands? The world needs more engineers willing to solve problems and fewer wealthy philosophers who have run out of ways to spend money."

Be that as it may, the Federation of Maritime Provinces and States tourist czar, John <pylon>-<fog>-<cod>, claimed earlier this year that the number of tourists visiting the Sea of Massachusetts has grown fourfold since the publication of Asa's book (such rises in Singapore and Havana are even higher). No doubt the influx of tourist money is welcomed by the locals, however conflicted they may be about Asa's portrayal of them.

Before I could follow up on the complicated look in his eyes, Jimmy turned his face resolutely away to regard our destination, which was growing bigger by the minute.

Spherical in shape, the floating dwelling was about fifteen meters in diameter, consisting of a thin transparent outer hull to which most of the ship's navigation surfaces were affixed and a thicker metal-alloy inner pressure hull. Most of the sphere floated below the surface, making the transparent bridge-dome appear like the pupil of some sea monster's eye staring into the sky.

On top of the pupil stood a solitary figure, her back as straight as the gnomon of a sundial.

Jimmy nudged the skiff until it bumped gently against the side of the habitat, and I gingerly stepped from one craft to the other. Asa steadied me as her habitat dipped under my added weight; her hand felt dry, cool, and very strong.

I observed, somewhat inanely, that she looked exactly like her last public scan-gram, when she had proclaimed from the large central forum of Valentina Station that United Planets was not only going to terraform Mars, but had also successfully bought a controlling stake in Blue Cradle, the public-private partnership for restoring Earth to a fully habitable state.

"I don't get many visitors," she said, her voice tranquil. "There's not much point to putting on a new face every day."

I had been surprised when she replied to my request to stay with her for a few days with a simple "Yes." She had never so much as granted an interview to anyone since she started her life adrift.

"Why?" I had asked.

"Even a hermit can grow lonely," she had replied. And then, in another message that immediately followed the first, she added, "Sometimes."

Jimmy motored away on his skiff. Asa turned and gestured for me to descend through the transparent and open "pupil" into the most influential refugee bubble in the Solar System.

~*~

The stars are invisible from the metal cocoons floating in the heavy atmosphere of Venus; nor do we pay much attention to them from the pressurized domes on Mars. On Earth, the denizens of the climate-controlled cities in habitable zones are preoccupied with scintillating screens and XP implants, the glow of meandering conversation, brightening reputation accounts, and the fading trails left by falling credit scores. They do not look up.

One night, as I lay in the habitat drifting over the balmy subtropical Pacific, the stars spun over my face in their habitual course, a million diamantine points of crisp, mathematical light. I realized, with a startled understanding reminiscent of the clarity of childhood, that the face of the heavens was a collage.

Some of the photons striking my retinas had emerged from the crease in the rock to which Andromeda is chained when nomadic warriors from the last ice age still roamed Doggerland, which connected Britain to the European mainland; others had left that winking point at the wingtip of Cygnus when bloody Caesar fell at the feet of Pompey's statue; still more had departed the mouth of Aquarius's jar when the decades-long genocidal wars swept through Asia, and aerial drones from Japan and Australia strafed and sank the rafts of refugees fleeing their desertified or flooded homelands; yet others had sparked from the distant hoof of Pegasus when the last glaciers of Greenland and Antarctica disappeared, and Moscow and Ottawa launched the first rockets bound for Venus...

The seas rise and fall, and the surface of the planet is as inconstant as our faces: lands burst forth from the waters and return beneath them; well-armored lobsters scuttle over seafloors that but a geologic eyewink ago had been fought over by armies of wooly mammoths; yesterday's Doggerland may be tomorrow's Sea of Massachusetts. The only witnesses to constant change are the eternal stars, each a separate stream in the ocean of time.

A picture of the welkin is an album of time, as convoluted and intricate as the shell of the nautilus or the arms of the Milky Way.

~*~

The interior of the habitat was sparsely furnished. Everything—the molded bunks, the stainless steel table attached to the wall, the boxy navigation console—was functional, plain, stripped of the elaborate "signature" decorations that seem all the rage these days with personal nanites. Though the space inside was cramped with two people, it seemed larger than it was because Asa did not fill it with conversation.

We ate dinner—fish that Asa had caught herself roasted over an open fire, with the canopy open—and went to bed silently. I fell asleep quickly, my body rocked by the gentle motions of the sea and my face caressed by the bright, warm New England stars that she had devoted so many words to.

After a breakfast of instant coffee and dry biscuits, Asa asked me if I wanted to see Boston.

"Of course," I said. It was an ancient citadel of learning, a legendary metropolis where brave engineers had struggled against the rising sea for two centuries before its massive seawalls finally succumbed, leaving the city inundated overnight in one of the greatest disasters in the history of the Developed World.

While Asa sat in the back of the habitat to steer and to monitor the solar-powered water-jet drive, I knelt on the bottom of the sphere and greedily drank in the sights passing beneath the transparent floor.

As the sun rose, its light gradually revealed a sandy floor studded by massive ruins: monuments erected to long-forgotten victories of the American Empire pointed toward the distant surface like ancient rockets; towers of stone and vitrified concrete that had once housed hundreds of thousands loomed like underwater mountains, their innumerable windows and doors silent, empty caves from which shoals of colorful fish darted like tropical birds; between the buildings, forest of giant kelp swayed in canyons that had once been boulevards and avenues filled with steaming vehicles, the hepatocytes that had once brought life to this metropolis.

And most amazing of all were the rainbow-hued corals that covered every surface of this urban reef: dark crimson, light orange, pearly white, bright neon vermillion …

Before the Second Flood Wars, the sages of Europe and America had thought the corals doomed. Rising sea temperature and acidity; booming algae populations; heavy deposits of mercury, arsenic, lead, and other heavy metals; runaway coastal development as the developed nations built up the machinery of death against waves of refugees from the uninhabitable zones—everything seemed to spell doom for the fragile marine animals and their photosynthesizing symbiotes.

Would the ocean become bleached of color, a black-and-white photograph bearing silent witness to our folly?

But the corals survived and adapted. They migrated to higher latitudes north and south, gained tolerance for stressed environments, and unexpectedly, developed new symbiotic relationships with artificial nanoplate-secreting algae engineered by humans for ocean-mining. I do not think the beauty of the Sea of Massachusetts yields one inch to the fabled Great Barrier Reef or the legends of long-dead Caribbean.

"Such colors ..." I murmured.

"The most beautiful patch is in Harvard Yard," Asa said.

We approached the ruins of the famed academy in Cambridge from the south, over a kelp forest that used to be the Charles River. But the looming presence of a cruise ship on the surface blocked our way. Asa stopped the habitat, and I climbed up to gaze out the domed top. Tourists wearing GnuSkin flippers and artificial gills were leaping out of the ship like selkies returning home, their sleek skin temporarily bronzed to endure the scorching November sun.

"Widener Library is a popular tourist spot," said Asa, by way of explanation.

I climbed down, and Asa drove the habitat to dive under the cruise ship. The craft was able to submerge beneath the waves as a way for the refugees in coastal raft-cities to survive typhoons and hurricanes, as well as to avoid the deadly heat of the tropics.

Slowly, we descended toward the coral reef that had grown around the ruined hulk of what had once been the largest university library in the world. Around us, schools of brightly colored fish wove through shafts of sunlight, and tourists gracefully floated down like mermaids, streams of bubbles trailing behind their artificial gills.

Asa guided the habitat in a gentle circle around the kaleidoscopic sea floor in front of the underwater edifice, pointing out various features. The mound covered by the intricate crimson folds of a coral colony that pleated and swirled like the voluminous dress of classical flamenco dancers had once been a lecture hall named after Thoreau's mentor, Emerson; the tall, spear-like column whose surface was tiled by sharp, geometric patches of coral in carmine, cerulean, viridian, and saffron had once been the steeple of Harvard's Memorial Church; the tiny bump in the side of another long reef, a massive brain-shaped coral formation whose gyri and lobes evoked the wisdom of generations of robed scholars who had once strolled through this hallowed temple to knowledge, was in fact the site of the renowned "Statue of Three Lies"—an ancient monument to John Harvard that failed to depict or identify the benefactor with any accuracy.

Next to me, Asa quietly recited,

> *The maple wears a gayer scarf,*
> *The field a scarlet gown.*
> *Lest I should be old-fashioned,*
> *I'll put a trinket on.*

The classical verses of the Early Republican Era poet Dickinson evoked the vanished beauty of the autumns that had once graced these shores, long before the sea had risen and the winters driven away, seemed oddly appropriate.

"I can't imagine the foliage of the Republican Era could be any more glorious than this," I said.

"None of us would know," Asa said. "Do you know how the corals get their bright colors?"

I shook my head. I knew next to nothing about corals except that they were popular as jewelry on Venus.

"The pigmentation comes from the heavy metals and pollutants that might have once killed their less hardy ancestors," said Asa. "They're particularly bright here because this area was touched by the hand of mankind the longest. Beautiful as they are, these corals are incredibly fragile. A global cooling by more than a degree or two would kill them. They survived climate change once by a miracle. Can they do it again?"

I looked back toward the great reef that was Widener Library, and saw that tourists had landed on the wide platform in front of the library's entrance or against its sides in small groups. Young tour guides in bright crimson—the color of Harvard achieved either by skin pigmentation or costume—led each group in their day-excursion activities.

Asa wanted to leave—she found the presence of the tourists bothersome—but I explained that I wanted to see what they were interested in. After a moment of hesitation, she nodded and guided the craft closer.

One group, standing on what used to be the steps ascending to the entrance of Widener, stood in a circle and followed their guide, a young woman dressed in a crimson wetsuit, through a series of dance-like movements. They moved slowly, but it was unclear whether they were doing so because the choreography required it or because the water provided too much drag. From time to time, the tourists looked up at the blazing sun far above, blurred and made hazy by a hundred feet of intervening water.

"They think they're doing taiji," said Asa.

"It looks nothing like taiji," I said, unable to connect the languorous, clumsy movements with the quick, staccato motion I was familiar with from sessions in low-gravity gyms.

"It's believed that taiji once was a slow, measured art, quite different from its modern incarnation. But since so few recordings of the pre-Diaspora years are left, the cruise ships just make up whatever they want for the tourists.

"Why do taiji here?" I was utterly baffled.

"Harvard was supposed to have a large population of Chinese scholars before the wars. It was said that the children of many of China's wealthiest and most powerful inhabitants studied here. It didn't save them from the wars."

Asa steered the craft a bit farther away from Widener, and I saw more tourists strolling over the coral-carpeted Yard or longing about, holding what appeared to be paper books—props provided by the cruise company—and taking scans of each other. A few danced without music, dressed in costumes that were a mix of Early and Late Republican fashions, with an academic gown or two thrown in for good measure. In front of Emerson, two tour guides led two groups of tourists in a mimed version of some debate, with each side presenting their position through ghostly holograms that hovered over their heads like comic thought bubbles. Some tourists saw us but did not pay much attention—probably thinking that the drifting refugee bubble was a prop added by the cruise ship to provide atmosphere. If only they knew they were so close to the celebrity hermit...

I gathered that the tourists were re-enacting imagined scenes from the glory days of this university, when it had nurtured the great philosophers who delivered jeremiads against the development-crazed governments of the world as they heated the planet without cease, until the ice caps had collapsed.

"So many of the world's greatest conservationists and Naturalists had walked through this Yard," I said. In the popular imagination, the Yard is the equal of the Athenian Acropolis or the Roman Forum. I tried to re-envision the particolored reef below me as a grassy lawn covered by bright red and yellow leaves on a cool New England fall day as students and professors debated the fate of the planet.

"Despite my reputation for romanticism," said Asa, "I'm not so sure the Harvard of yesteryear is better than today. That university and others like it once also nurtured the generals and presidents who would eventually deny that mankind could change the climate and lead a people hungry for demagoguery into war against the poorer states in Asia and Africa."

Quietly, we continued to drift around the Yard, watching tourists climb in and out of the empty, barnacle-encrusted windows like hermit crabs darting through the sockets of a many-eyed skull. Some were mostly nude, trailing diaphanous fabrics from their bodies in a manner reminiscent of Classical American Early Republic dresses and suits; others wore wetsuits inspired by American Imperial styles, covered by faux body armor plates and gas mask helmets; still others went with refugee-chic, dragging fake survival breathing kits with artfully applied rust stains.

What were they looking for? Did they find it?

Nostalgia is a wound that we refuse time to heal, Asa once wrote.

~*~

After a few hours, satiated with their excursions, the tourists headed for the surface like shoals of fish fleeing some unseen predator, and in a way, they were.

The forecast was for a massive storm. The Sea of Massachusetts was rarely tranquil.

As the sea around us emptied of visitors and the massive cloud-island that was the cruise ship departed, Asa grew noticeably calmer. She assured me that we were safe, and brought the submersible craft to the lee of Memorial Church Reef. Here, below the turbulent surface, we would ride out the storm.

The sun set; the sea darkened; a million lights came to life around us. The coral reef at night was hardly a place of slumber. This was when the luminescent creatures of the night—the jellies, the shrimp, the glow-worms and lantern-fish—came out of hiding to enjoy their time in this underwater metropolis that never slept.

While the wind and the waves raged above us, we hardly felt a thing as we drifted in the abyss that was the sea, innumerable living stars around us.

~*~

We do not look.

We do not see.

We travel millions of miles to seek out fresh vistas without even once having glimpsed inside our skulls, a landscape surely as alien and as wondrous as anything the universe has to offer. There is more than enough to occupy our curiosity and restless need for novelty if we but turn our gaze to the ten square meters around us: the unique longitudinal patterns in each tile beneath our feet, the chemical symphony animating each bacterium on our skin, the mysteries of how we can contemplate ourselves contemplating ourselves.

The stars above are as distant—and as close—as the glowing coral-

worms outside my portholes. We only have to look to see Beauty steeped in every atom.

Only in solitude it is possible to live as self-contained as a star.

I am content to have this. To have now.

~*~

In the distance, against Widener's cliff-like bulk, there was an explosion of light, a nova bursting in the void.

The stars around it streaked away, leaving inky darkness behind, but the nova itself, an indistinct cloud of light, continued to twist and churn.

I woke Asa and pointed. Without speaking, she guided the habitat toward it. As we approached, the light resolved itself into a struggling figure. An octopus? No, a person.

"That must be a tourist stranded behind," said Asa. "If they go up to the surface now, they'll die in the storm."

Asa switched on the bright lights in front of the habitat to get the tourist's attention. The light revealed a disoriented young woman in a wetsuit studded with luminescent patches, shielding her eyes against the sudden glow of the habitat's harsh lights. Her artificial gill slits opened and closed rapidly, showing her confusion and terror.

"She can't tell which way is up," Asa muttered.

Asa waved at her through the porthole, gesturing for her to follow the habitat. There was no airlock in the tiny refuge, and we had to go up to the surface to get her in. The young woman nodded.

Up on the surface, the rain was torrential and the waves so choppy that it was impossible to remain standing. Asa and I clung to the narrow ridge around the entrance dome on our bellies and dragged the young woman onto the craft, which dipped even lower under the added weight. With a great deal of effort and shouting, we managed to get her inside, seal the dome, and dive back underwater.

Twenty minutes later, dry, gills removed, securely wrapped in a warm blanket with a hot mug of tea, Saram <Golden-Gate-Bridge>-<Kyoto> looked back gratefully at us.

"I got lost inside," she said. "The empty stacks went on and on, and they looked the same in every direction. At first, I followed a candy-cane fish through the floors, thinking that it was going to lead me outside, but it must have been going around in circles."

"Did you find what you were looking for?" asked Asa.

She was a student at Harvard Station, Saram explained—the institution of higher learning suspended in the upper atmosphere of Venus that had licensed the old name of the university lying in ruins under us. She had come to see this school of legend for herself, harboring romantic notions of trying to search through the stacks of the dead library in the hopes of finding a forgotten tome.

Asa looked outside the porthole at the looming presence of the empty library. "I doubt there's anything left there now after all these years."

"Maybe," Saram said. "But history doesn't die. The water will recede from here one day. I may live to see when Nature is finally restored to her rightful course."

Saram was probably a little too optimistic. United Planets' ion-drive ships had just succeeded in pushing six asteroids into near-Earth orbits earlier in the year, and the construction of the space mirrors had not even begun. Even the most optimistic engineering projections suggest that it will be decades, if not centuries, before the mirrors will reduce the amount of sunlight reaching Earth to begin the process of climate cooling and restoring the planet to its ancient state, a temperate Eden with polar ice caps and glaciers on top of mountain peaks. Mars might be fully terraformed before then.

"Is Doggerland any more natural than the Sea of Massachusetts?" Asa asked.

Saram's steady gaze did not waver. "An ice age is hardly comparable to what was made by the hands of mankind."

"Who are we to warm a planet for a dream and to cool it for nostalgia?"

"Mysticism is no balm for the suffering of the refugees enduring the consequences of our ancestors' errors."

"It is further error that I'm trying to prevent!" shouted Asa.

She forced herself to calm down. "If the water recedes, everything around you will be gone." She looked outside the porthole, where the reef's night-time denizens had returned to their luminescent activities. "As will the vibrant communities in Singapore, in Havana, in Inner Mongolia. We call them refugee shantytowns and disturbed habitats, but these places are also homes."

"*I* am from Singapore," said Saram. "I spent my life trying to get away from it and only succeeded by winning one of the coveted migration visas to Birmingham. Do not presume to speak for us or to tell me what it is we should want."

"But you have left," said Asa. "You no longer live there."

I thought of the lovely corals outside, colored by poison. I thought of the refugees around the world underground and afloat—still called that after centuries and generations. I thought of a cooling Earth, of the Developed World racing to reclaim their ancestral lands, of the wars to come and the slaughter hinted at when the deck of power is shuffled and redealt. Who should decide? Who pay the price?

As the three of us sat inside the submerged habitat, refugees enveloped by darting trails of light like meteors streaking across the empyrean, none of us could think of anything more to say.

~*~

I once regretted that I do not know the face I was born with.

We remake our faces as easily as our ancestors once sculpted clay, changing the features and contours of our shells, this microcosm of the soul, to match the moods and fashions of the macrocosm of society. Still unsatisfied with the limits of the flesh, we supplement the results with jewelry that deflect light and project shadows, smoothing over substance with ethereal holograms.

The Naturalists, in their eternal struggle against modernity, proclaim hypocrisy and demand us to stop, telling us that our lives are inauthentic, and we listen, enraptured, as they flash grainy images of our ancestors before us, their imperfections and fixed appearances a series of mute accusations. And we nod and vow to do better, to foreswear artifice, until we go back to our jobs, shake off the spell, and decide upon the new face to wear for the next customer.

But what would the Naturalists have us do? The faces that we were born with were already constructed—when we were only fertilized eggs, a million cellular scalpels had snipped and edited our genes to eliminate diseases, to filter out risky mutations, to build up intelligence and longevity, and before that, millions of years of conquest, of migration, of global cooling and warming, of choices made by our ancestors motivated by beauty or violence or avarice had already shaped us. Our faces at birth were as crafted as the masks worn by the ancient players in Dionysian Athens or Ashikaga's Kyoto, but also as natural as the glacier-sculpted Alps or sea-inundated Massachusetts.

We do not know who we are. But we dare not stop striving to find out.

~*~

About the Author

Ken Liu (http://kenliu.name) is an author and translator of speculative fiction, as well as a lawyer and programmer. A winner of the Nebula, Hugo, and World Fantasy awards, he has been published in **The Magazine of Fantasy & Science Fiction, Asimov's, Analog, Clarkesworld, Lightspeed**, and **Strange Horizons**, among other places.

Ken's debut novel, **THE GRACE OF KINGS** (2015), is the first volume in a silkpunk epic fantasy series, The Dandelion Dynasty. It won the Locus Best First Novel Award and was a Nebula finalist. He subsequently published the second volume in the series, **THE WALL OF STORMS** (2016) as well as a collection of short stories, **THE PAPER MENAGERIE AND OTHER STORIES** (2016)

In addition to his original fiction, Ken is also the translator of numerous literary and genre works from Chinese to English. His translation of **THE THREE-BODY PROBLEM**, by Liu Cixin, won the Hugo Award for Best Novel in 2015, the first translated novel ever to receive that honor. He also translated the third volume in Liu Cixin's series, **DEATH'S END** (2016) and edited the first English-language anthology of contemporary Chinese science fiction, **INVISIBLE PLAN**ETS (2016).

He lives with his family near Boston, Massachusetts.

~*~

A Note to Readers

~*~

So we've come to the end. This is where we thank the number of authors, editors, artists, and of course—YOU the reader—for making *OCEANS: The Anthology* possible. Without your support, themed collections such as this one would not be possible.

This is also the place where we say a special thank you to *The Future Chronicles* for inspiring this anthology as well as the first in the *Frontiers of Speculative Fiction, CLONES: The Anthology*. If you've enjoyed the stories curated in this collection, I highly recommend that you read any of the many *Future Chronicle* anthologies. You can find them at www.futurechronicles.net.

One last thing—

Please leave a review.

Let me share why that is so important.

The success of a book comes from readers.

Even with the best authors, stories, and editors, a book is nothing until it's read, and the only way our stories are able to be shared is if one reader shares with another. This is done through reviews.

And the book distribution system is designed to take these reviews into account. The more honest reviews, the more visibility a book garners. More visibility equals more readers.

And I'll be blunt—more readers mean more sales, and curating a collection like *OCEANS: The Anthology* relies on sales, to fund the book, and also to let the booksellers know this is a product they should display in their front digital window.

It's up to you and we need your help.

So even if you've only picked up this anthology to read one story—please leave a review.

If you enjoyed some of the stories and not all, that's okay, it's a collection—please leave a review. And if you read *OCEANS: The Anthology* and enjoyed the entire collection—definitely please leave a review.

Tell a friend, and then another, share a link on FB, or on Twitter. If we brought you entertainment—let the world know.

And always—thank you for reading.

For more information, visit danielarthursmith.com

~*~